With nothing but his skate___ ___rd and a few belongings
in a garbage bag, Sam goes to live with the strangers
his mum cut ties with seven years ago: Aunty Lorraine
and his cousins Shane and Minty.

Despite the suspicion and hostility facing him in
his new home, Sam reverts to his childhood habit
of following Minty around. Soon he is surfing with Minty
to cut through the static fuzz in his head, but the secrets
of the past refuse to stay hidden and not even the
ocean offers relief for long. What happened seven
years ago that caused such a rift? Why won't anyone
tell him who his father is? How can Sam feel any sense
of belonging when he doesn't know who he is?

And if things weren't complicated enough,
there's also this girl ...

'Zorn's writing is one of a kind. *One Would Think The Deep* is an extraordinary new work from a young adult genre star.'

University of Queensland Small Change

It seems that Claire Zorn can do no literary wrong ... *One Would Think The Deep* is deeply affecting and will be one of this year's must-read YA novels.'

Children's Books Daily

'*One Would Think The Deep* has a potent emotional heart, great characters and beautiful writing. Built around gorgeous evocations of surfing and the sea, it is driven by wonderfully evoked characters and an empathetic exploration of masculinity.'

State Library of New South Wales

'Zorn's greatest skill is her ability to create genuine, original characters, who feel fully developed and real ... It's an astonishing tour-de-force ... As a novel, it's brash, it's real, and it's alive. As an exploration of grief, it's harrowing and heart-breaking.'

Children's Books Daily

'Beautifully evoked against a 90s surfing background and culture, this exploration of a young male grappling with both loss and romantic attraction is heart-wrenching in its poignancy. Zorn creates a truly authentic teen voice in a work which is brilliantly realised.'

Queensland Literary Awards Judge's Comments

'... a slow burn, contemplative and emotionally nuanced, it is set apart by its almost reflective quality and temperate pace which provides plenty of space between the words on the page to consider how the scars of the past can shape the present, the importance of your heritage in determining who you are as a person as well as what it means to choose who you want to become and what paths you will take in life.'

allthewrittenworlds, amazon.com

'... a heavy story of secrets and the damage they can cause. Sam's pain is palpable, his issues enormous, and his future seemingly untenable.'

CBCA Reading Time

'... a story that surges with emotion, confrontation, and ultimately, hope. Each character is drawn with knife-edge sharpness. Each speaks with a clarity that never dulls. Every sense is heightened by the wrenching complexity of the lives of this very inconsequential, simple group of ordinary individuals. And it's not just Sam who is damaged and vulnerable. Each is noticeably flawed or at least weighed down by their own limitations to a point of exquisite confusion. I loved them all.'

Boomerang Books, Australia

Claire Zorn ... is an expert at navigating the complex relationships between teens and the adults that surround them ... *One Would Think The Deep* is perfectly placed in 1997, but the teenage voice resonates with contemporary authenticity.'

Books+Publishing

Winner, The Children's Book Council of Australia
Book of the Year: Older Readers 2017

Shortlisted for the 2017 Australian Prime Minister's
Literary Award for Young Adult Fiction

Shortlisted for the 2016 Queensland Literary Award –
Young Adult Literature.

Shortlisted for The 2017 Gold Inky Awards

ONE WOULD THINK THE DEEP

Also by Claire Zorn

The Protected
The Sky So Heavy

CLAIRE ZORN

ONE WOULD THINK THE DEEP

RAVEN

One Would Think The Deep
by Claire Zorn

First published 2016 by University of Queensland Press, Australia

This edition published in 2018 by Raven Books
An imprint of Ransom Publishing Ltd.
Unit 7, Brocklands Farm, West Meon, Hampshire GU32 1JN, UK
www.ransom.co.uk

Printed and bound in Great Britain by Clays Ltd, Elcograf S.p.A.

ISBN   978 178591 671 7

Cover design by Astred Hicks, Design Cherry
Cover photographs by Jeremy Bishop/Unsplash

Verse Job 3:8, 41:32, 41:7–11 excerpted from *The Holy Bible*,
New International Version®, NIV® Copyright © 1973, 1978, 1984, 2011
by Biblica, Inc.®
Used by permission. All rights reserved worldwide.

A CIP catalogue record of this book is available from the British Library.

For my fellas: Nathan, Elijah and Ayrton.

May those who curse days
curse that day,
Those who are ready
to rouse Leviathan …
Behind him he leaves a glistening wake;
One would think the deep
Had white hair.

— Job 3:8, 41:32

SUMMER 1997

1

Sam rang from the hospital. A social worker called Amanda gave him a dollar for the phone in the shop that sold teddy bears and balloons with declarations of love. Sam plugged his ear with a finger to drown out the chaos in the corridor behind him. He didn't know the voice of the guy who answered. He didn't know any of them anymore.

'Yeah?' said the voice. It took Sam a moment to respond.

'Hey. I'm looking for Lorraine Booner.'

'Yeah?'

'I'm her nephew, Sam Hudson. Rachel's son.'

'Yeah?'

'Yeah.'

'What d'you want?'

'I, um, I need to speak to Aunty Lorraine. Something … something's happened.'

There was a pause while Sam was evaluated.

'Hang on … MUM. PHONE.'

Sam waited. He watched his credit drop to eighty cents. Seventy.

'Yeah?' A new voice: female, scratched with nicotine.

'Hi Aunty Lorraine. It's Sam … Rachel's Sam.'

'Oh.' Pause. Sixty cents. 'What's wrong? What does she want?'

'Nothing. She …'

'Yeah?'

'She's …' Sam tried to control the waver in his voice, only making it worse. 'She's dead.'

'What?'

Sam took a breath and repeated the words.

'What happened?'

'Brain aneurysm.'

'I didn't know she was sick. How long she had that?'

'You don't … She wasn't sick. It was sudden, like a stroke.'

'God. When'd that happen?'

'Um.' Sam counted the days back in his head. Time had become fluid, no longer neatly partitioned into day and night.

'Two nights ago. Wednesday night.' He watched the credit drop to fifty cents.

'New Year's?'

'Yeah. She, um, she collapsed at home. Then she was in a coma … but then … I should have called you as soon as it happened … I didn't … I wasn't thinking straight.' He had to stop talking or he was going to lose it. He couldn't lose it. Not on his own.

Lorraine didn't say anything for some time. Sam waited. Forty cents. He heard her clear her throat. 'Right … Thanks for letting us know.' Her voice was weak. 'Will you let me know 'bout the funeral?'

'Yeah. Hey, um. I'm not eighteen yet and the social worker wants to know if there's family I can stay with. She … there's circumstances. Sometimes they let you live on your own when you're seventeen, but … I'm not … She thinks DOCS will want me to go into like a guardianship or something. She asked about family … I didn't know what to do …'

'Oh. What about Enid?'

'Enid?'

'Your nan.'

Sam paused. 'I don't know where she is.'

'Christ alive.' Lorraine seemed to be muttering to herself and Sam wasn't sure if he was expected to respond. He didn't. 'I thought your mum would have had contact with her.'

'No. I don't think so. She never said anything. There's no number in Mum's book. I found yours. The phone's running out of money.'

'You on your own?'

'Yeah.'

There was silence and Sam thought the call had been cut. Then: 'I'll come get you.'

'You don't have to come now. The social worker said they can get me care or a hotel room or something till we sort something out.'

'No. No bloody way. I'll come get you. Hang on. SHANE, THERE PETROL IN THE VAN?'

A muffled reply and then, 'Where are you?'

'The hospital. RPA, Royal Prince Alfred.'

'I'll come up. Give us a couple of hours. Where can I meet you?'

'Um. The cafe? Level two.'

'What d'you look like?'

'Um. I'm tall. Longish hair, it's dark. Haven't had a haircut in a while.' Sam didn't know why he was telling her this. 'Um, I'm wearing jeans. Black T-shirt.'

The phone went dead.

Sam felt the hurt shuddering through his chest. He wasn't expecting to feel it talking to Lorraine. He thought he was over all that. He took the phone from his ear and looked at it in his hand, his knuckles white with the grip – as if it was an object he didn't recognise. He could picture Lorraine, standing on the front porch of Nana and Pop's house, next to his mother, shandy in her hand, cigarette between her fingers. Eventually he set the receiver back on its cradle and rode the elevator up to intensive care where Amanda was waiting for him with her paperwork and her grim smile.

She'd been trying to teach him to slow dance. After three glasses of red wine she turned the music up. Jeff Buckley. It was his CD, but she loved it.

'Come on. Up,' she said.

'Mum. No.'

'Yeah, come on. It's my job to teach you important stuff and this is important.'

'No, it's not.'

'On your feet, Samuel. I'm not asking you, I'm telling you.'

He pushed his bowl away and stood up. He was a head taller than her.

'You can't be a gentleman if you don't know how to dance,' she said.

'No one actually dances anymore.'

'I'm teachin' you to dance.' His mum always dropped her 'g's when she'd had a couple of wines. She said it was the bogan in her coming out. She held out her hands and he took them. She had soft, small hands, delicate-looking like the rest of her. She was pale and slight, dark deep-set eyes like his own. She put his left hand on her hip, held his right at her shoulder.

'I can dance.'

'You bloody can't. You can stand with your arms folded or jump up and down on the spot like you're on a bloody pogo stick. Your generation is useless, Samuel. This is the basic foundation step: hold and sway. You need to keep loose. Drop your shoulders. Try not to look like you're in pain. Seriously, you're lovely. Lovely boys should know how to dance.'

Sam held her hand while she swayed from side to side.

'I'm not lovely.'

She looked him in the eye. 'Yes, you are.'

The fact that she still believed it made him feel sick.

'Now spin!' She pulled away, raised his left hand above her head and turned. Then her body dropped like a stone. He still had her hand. He caught her before she hit the floor and part of him thought she was kidding around but most of him knew she wasn't.

'Mum? Mum!'

She was a nurse. The first person you'd ask for help in a situation like this. Sam lowered himself, and her with him, to the floor. He knelt down, her torso on his lap, askew. Her head lolled back and to one side. Sam cradled her skull in his hand; her thick dark hair was still damp from her shower.

'Mum?'

Jeff Buckley's falsetto danced and Sam tried to move his mother onto the carpet so he could get to the cordless phone. He wouldn't have to use it. She would come around and then he'd have to explain to the ambulance guys that it was a false alarm. She would be embarrassed. 'I'm fine,' she would say. 'Just got a bit lightheaded.'

He waited. The song finished.

She didn't wake up.

Amanda gave him a bunch of forms and a business card.

'I'll tell all this to your aunt, but you need to get her to fill these in and then make an appointment with the Department of Community Services. I'll come down and wait with you till she gets here.'

'No. That's okay. You can go, I'll be cool.'

'I have to see that you're in someone's care before I can leave you,' she explained.

'She's gonna be a couple of hours.'

'It's fine. I can wait.'

*

Amanda bought him a sausage roll. They sat in the plastic chairs of Vibes Cafe. It was an ambitious name for a hospital cafeteria; the vibe was illness, fluorescent lights and disinfectant. Amanda had a novel in her bag. Sam figured she was used to the whole waiting-with-bereaved-relatives part of her job.

'If you want to talk, I'm right here,' she said. She gestured to his Discman on the table. 'I don't mind if you want to listen to music or whatever.'

He plugged his earphones into his ears and pressed play. Kurt Cobain screamed and it felt right. His whole being thrummed with fatigue and disbelief, and something else that was harder to define, some unseen restlessness, the urge to do something to change the situation, alter it, fix it.

Sam watched a woman in a tunic behind the bain-marie as she restocked the tomato sauce sachets. He felt the same way about her as he felt about all the hospital staff and Amanda. To them, this was another mundane, unremarkable day. Maybe they stitched up someone's head, or they filled out forms and took a fifteen-minute break every four hours. They restocked the tomato sauce. They mopped the floor. They were nice to the kid whose mum had just died. But to them he was no different to anyone else there: patient, friend or relative. He was a segment in their day. Amanda and the nurses talked gently to him because that was their job. They would finish their shift and go home, decide what to have for dinner, turn on the TV, feed the cat. Sam couldn't imagine ever thinking about dinner again. He had never felt envy the way he felt envy for these people who worked at the hospital.

*

Lorraine swiped the yellow parking fine off the windshield and dropped it in the gutter. The van was painted with a faded blue logo on the side: Booner Electrical. The letters, cursive and grandiose, curled at the edges. Inside, it smelled of cigarette smoke, pine-scented air freshener and a hostile, just-vacuumed smell. Sam hadn't expected her to be so familiar after seven years. She was completely different to his mother but you could find the thread of resemblance if you knew what to look for. Her dark hair was bleached yellow, but the roots were black and silver. It was a thick, undefined mass of waves and frizz, cut short to frame her face, long at the back. A lady-mullet. Mullét. She had the same small frame and high cheekbones as his mother, but she hadn't aged well.

'You wanna go home and get some stuff?' she asked. She kept glancing at him as she drove, like she was worried he might try to jump out of the moving vehicle.

'Alright.'

'Well, you better tell us where it is. It's been that long, I got no idea where I am.'

He guided her through the back of Camperdown, along the back streets of Newtown and into Enmore. Lorraine parked in a no-standing zone and followed him through the narrow door beside the 7-Eleven, up the manky stairs to the apartment above. It had been a feat getting his mum down those stairs on the gurney. The paramedic guys had jostled and twisted, tilted and grimaced. It was pointless in the end. Sam could have just tucked her into bed and let her die there.

Inside the flat, the bowls of dry spaghetti were still on the table, the glasses of wine half empty and stained.

'You haven't been here since?' asked Lorraine.

'No. Didn't want to leave her.'

Lorraine set her handbag down on the sideboard and started to clear the plates from the table. The cordless phone was lying on the floor, near the dining table, where he had sat with her and called the ambulance. 'Grab what you want. I won't be comin' back up here for a bit. Too far. So get everything you'll need. Where'd she keep all her documents and that? Birth certificates and bank stuff?'

'Bottom drawer in her room.'

Sam didn't want to go in there. He took a couple of garbage bags from the kitchen and went into his room. He stuffed them with random items of clothing. He wasn't thinking, just grabbing whatever. Everything felt other-worldly and off kilter. He had no template for this. Was he packing for a short stay or was he moving house? For a while he stood with a sweater in his hands, staring at it, trying to remember what the decision was that he should be making about it. It was too hard so he stuffed it into the bag. He grabbed his tape deck. He also emptied two shoeboxes and filled them with CDs. Back in the lounge he popped the lid of the boom box, placed the Jeff Buckley in its case and added it to a shoebox. His eye was caught by the bookshelf, the bright spine of the book his mum had bought him when he was eight, *The Illustrated Encyclopedia of Meteorology*. It was authoritative and reassuring in its cloth-bound hardcover, with little ribbons to mark various pages, so big he struggled to carry it when he was young. He would lie on the lounge room floor on his stomach and pore through the pages of an evening while his mum played records.

He looked at weather charts and the grainy photographs of towns flattened by cyclones. As a kid, from the cosy comfort of his lounge room, he was fascinated by the drama of natural disasters. The novelty of catastrophe.

Sam opened the little cabinet under the television. It was full of VHS tapes: shows taped off the TV. They were stacked on two flat boxes. One was a Monopoly box, the other a big biscuit tin. His mum had said that some parents taught their kids chess, but she thought Monopoly was more useful. The box, tattered and held together with yellowing sticky tape, was like a black star, a wormhole pulling him back in time. He used to play with the little silver pieces before he was old enough to know how to play the game. There was a sense that they were special and he knew that he had to be careful playing with them and always make sure they went back in the box. In the biscuit tin she kept mementos from his childhood: cards he'd made her, little notes where she'd jotted down funny things he said, school photos. The tin had always been around, she let him look through it, but it was hers. Seeing it gave him the distinct feeling of his past being distilled into one small but potent collection. A childhood sense of fun and carelessness, coupled with an uneasy wariness about the world.

Down beneath the ocean waves, deep under the sea,
Swim some little fishes: one two three.
They swish their little tails, they turn and dance and splash.
Swimming bright and colourful,
'till away they dash.

His mother used to sing it to him. It was her go-to song whenever he was upset in the night. He'd never told her how much it disturbed him: he would imagine himself out in the dark ocean, under the waves, no company except the little fish who swim away as soon as they are found. He knew the fish would swim away and there was nothing he could do to stop them because the song was always sung to the very end and the end was always the same.

The song was the first indicator that there were things going on in his head that no one else understood. Even his mum.

Lorraine was in his mum's room. He could hear her opening and closing drawers, riffling through. She was going through his mum's things but he couldn't make himself go in there. She came out holding a Grace Brothers bag. Whatever she'd filled it with was heavy. Sam wondered about a will. It seemed crass to think about it so soon, so he didn't ask if she'd come across it. He didn't care what Lorraine would have thought if he'd asked. He cared that he'd even had the thought.

'That all you need?' Lorraine eyed the garbage bags.

'Yeah. I'll just grab my skateboard.'

'You gonna bring those?' She was looking at the book and the biscuit tin.

'Yeah.'

'Here.' She held out her hand and took the memories from him.

2

Sam pretended to sleep for most of the drive. After an hour and a half, Lorraine pulled the car up onto the grassy kerb and got out of the van. There was no guttering, just a bleed of bitumen and ochre into grass. It was balmy out, not humid. A salty breeze licked at Sam's arms. It took him a moment to recognise the faint rumbling in the distance as the sound of waves crashing on the beach. The house was ghostly pale fibro. No garden. A leaning letterbox in the corner of a square of patchy grass. Lorraine pulled her handbag onto her shoulder and smacked toward the front door in her gold thongs.

The house was a mess. Sam was allocated the spare room: a patched-on annex with dimensions barely wider than a hallway, no window and furnished only with a small shelving unit crammed with videos and cassette tapes. A camp bed was made up with a pair of mismatched flannel sheets. Overkill for January, but he didn't remember Lorraine as the sort of mum to have a a variety of clean sheets folded in the linen cupboard.

'Thanks, Aunty Lorraine.'

She wouldn't look him in the eye. 'No trouble anyway. Ruby stays here a lot, Minty's friend. Sometimes uses this room. Just don't go callin' her his girlfriend. She'll have your balls. I'm gonna have a drink. You want one?'

'Thanks.'

He followed her into the kitchen. She switched on the light and a flood of small brown bugs scattered across the benchtops into shadows. Lorraine didn't acknowledge them. She opened the fridge and passed a can of cola to Sam, then cracked one for herself. The liquid was thick and molasses-sweet in his throat. Lorraine jerked her head toward the lounge. He followed.

'Were you with her when it happened?' Her eyes were lined with blue eyeliner. She was like an old, really tired version of Madonna.

Sam nodded. 'I just … I thought she'd fainted. But she didn't—' He couldn't breathe. The giddy sensation came over him, as if he was on a ride that he was desperate to stop.

'You still at school?'

He took a deep breath. 'Supposed to be going into year twelve next year. I mean this year.'

'You always were a bright one.' She almost sounded sad about it.

'I've seen Minty in the paper,' he said.

'He won the Pro Junior.'

'Yeah. That was it.'

'First big comp. Five thousand dollars prize money. If he puts his head down and works on it he'll be on the WQS – World Qualifying Series. He's gonna make the Pro tour, you watch 'im … Youse were peas in a pod when you were little.'

'I remember.'

'He'll be home soon. Needs his sleep for training. Not in school anymore. He's that bloody talented he doesn't have to be.' She cleared her throat. 'I haven't seen your mum for seven years, you know.'

'I know.'

Lorraine took a pack of cigarettes from her pocket and shucked one out. She put it between her lips and flicked a pink lighter. On her foot was a tattoo in swirling, cursive script: 'Glen'. It ran along the top of her foot, diagonally an inch above the toes. So you could see it when she wore thongs. Sam remembered it from childhood. His mum had a tattoo, too. She was embarrassed about it, said she was too young to know the definition of tacky. It was a little star on the inside of her wrist, with the letters S-H-I-N-E. Sometimes she would laugh and say she felt like changing the 'n' to a 't'. Sam didn't think she meant she was shite, just the tattoo. But he could never be exactly sure.

Sitting beside her for hours in the hospital, he had held her hand and stared at the little star on her wrist. Any time he had to leave her side he had tucked her hand under the blanket, the same way she had done for him as a child. In case she got cold.

Headlights swept through the front window. A car door slammed and there was the slap of feet up the front steps. The screen door whined and in walked a guy with white-blond dreadlocks past his shoulders and tattoos curled up the bronzed skin of his forearms. He was shorter than Sam, but strong looking, broad-shouldered. He stopped dead and stared at Sam.

'Look who's here, Mint,' Lorraine sighed. 'Your cousin, Sammy.'

To watch Minty smile was to watch a whole person transform in an instant. His mobile eyebrows shot up and his whole face widened into a grin. His eager expression seemed written into every part of his body; he couldn't be still, couldn't contain himself. Sam remembered Minty so clearly and despite the tatts, despite the hair, he was the same as he'd always been. He was tightly wound energy, labrador enthusiasm – a glint in his eye like he'd let you in on some genius plot to hitchhike to the Amazon or build a nuclear bomb in the garage. Shane wasn't with him though and Sam was relieved.

'No way! Sam! How's it goin'?'

Sam stood and offered his hand. Minty took it and pulled him in, slapping him on the back, hugging him tightly. The gesture caused a lump in Sam's throat. He squeezed his eyes shut to try and flush it away.

'What you doin' here?'

Lorraine pursed her lips. 'Aunty Rachel died.'

'Whoa. What?'

'Brain stroke,' said Lorraine looking away. 'Sam's gonna stay here.'

'Oh brah. Sorry about that.'

'You'll have to let Ruby know,' said Lorraine. 'That he's here. She'll just have to make do at home.'

15

'No worries. Sam, it's good to see you, brah. I mean, it's heavy about Aunty Rachel. But it's been a long time.'

'Yeah, it has.'

Lorraine picked up the empty cans and took them into the kitchen. 'Youse should get to bed.'

Sam didn't sleep. He hadn't for more than an hour at a time since his mum went into hospital. When he closed his eyes he heard the hiss of the ventilator and the beeping of the machine, as if he was still in the hospital room. The smell of antiseptic was trapped in his nostrils.

Sam lay on his back and stared up at the ceiling. The only thing he wanted to do was phone his mum, tell her what had happened. She was always his first port of call for anything big. Almost anything. The camp bed squeaked sharply every time he moved, as if reminding him over and over that he was in a space that wasn't his own. He was watching a daddy-long-legs busy itself with a bug in the corner of the ceiling when a loud whisper came from the doorway.

'Sam! You awake?'

He looked over and saw Minty beaming at him. 'What time is it?'

'Dunno. Sun's comin' up. Goin' for a surf. Come with me. Got a board you can use.'

'I don't have any boardies.' He didn't even own any, let alone pack them.

'No worries.' Minty tossed the black skin of a wetsuit onto the bed. 'Should be a goer.'

Sam got up and stretched. Putting on the wetsuit, he felt like a monkey trying to get into a leotard. He left it rolled down at the waist like Minty. Sam's skin was fluoro white in comparison to Minty's tan.

They walked barefoot along the bitumen. The air was humid and sticky with salt, tempered by the occasional cool breath of sea breeze. Seagulls and plovers congregated in the middle of the road, their squawks piercing the silence. Sam's pale feet were sensitive and prickly to the gravel, soft like a child's. The street was flat and wide: no guttering or lines marked. The houses were mostly little fibro places like Lorraine's and there was the odd cluster of housing commission flats – the same ones they built in the city.

He couldn't remember the last time he walked outside barefoot. It was probably a holiday. Port Macquarie with his mum. They never went to the city beaches; none of his friends did either. Weekends were usually spent skating with Luke, his best mate – the crappy half-pipe near the train yards during the day or in a shopping centre car park at night.

His mum was fine with him being out late on weekends as long as she knew exactly what he was doing and where he was. Her only rules were: don't hurt yourself and don't hurt anyone else. Her definition of 'hurt' included damage or theft of other people's property. As far as trespassing was concerned, property laws were flexible; she would get pissed off if security guards turfed them out of a car park, saying they were using the space in a 'creative' way that wasn't hurting or disturbing anyone. You could justify almost anything to her if the word creative was used.

He would have to call Luke and tell him where he was.

Minty had given Sam a longboard the size of a boat. It wasn't the easiest thing to carry. Minty carried his own board like it was part of his body.

'You still skate?' Sam asked.

'Not as much since I got the car. Used to skate when the swell was flat, but now I can always drive to find a wave,' he shrugged, looked over at Sam, caught his eye. 'You alright? Must be cut up about your mum. Unbelievable.'

Sam felt his throat tighten. He shook his head. Minty nodded. It was still easy between them, after all this time. Sam had thought it would be awkward and stunted, but it wasn't.

They weren't even at the end of the street before the wide metallic strip of ocean rose on the horizon. The van ripped past them, horn squealing. Sam jumped. Minty raised his arm in a wave and the van skidded to a halt a few metres up. Minty jogged over.

Sam caught up. The driver was a big guy: shaved head, long goatee. Sam caught a flicker of recognition in his eyes. His memory of Shane was more a feeling of hostility and mild fear. Shane looked him up and down and Sam remembered clearly his talent for opportunistic cruelty. The dread that would come over him as a kid whenever Shane would show up. He'd smashed up Sam's skateboard one year just to prove that he was bigger and he could. Now, thinking back, it seemed odd more than anything else: a fifteen-year-old kid smashing up a ten-year-old's skateboard. Sam hadn't said a word about it to his mum, but there had been a row between Lorraine and Rachel afterwards. It was one of the last times he'd seen them.

Sam wondered if he could take Shane on now, or if he'd still be as intimidated and useless as he was when he was little.

'Shane, you remember Sammy?'

Shane assessed Sam and must have decided he still didn't think much of him because he didn't smile. Instead, he shifted his gaze to the road in front of him. 'Piss weak swell this mornin'. Gotta job on anyway. You surf, Sam?'

'No. First time.'

'Shiiiiiit, Sam!' Minty laughed. 'You didn't say. You'll be good, brah. It's little this mornin'.'

Shane eyed the longboard. Sam lifted his chin, kept his gaze steady.

'Alright. See ya,' said Shane.

Minty waved and the Booner Electrical van sped off, gravel spitting behind him.

'Why didn't you say you don't surf?'

'Didn't ask.'

'Can you swim?'

'I can swim.'

'Like dog paddle?'

'Shut up, Mint. I can swim. Just don't ask me to save anyone.'

'I'll bring ya some floaties next time ... It's cool if you don't wanna, ay. Like, I can teach you a bit, but whatever. Do what you want.'

It was a reassurance, not a challenge.

'I'll come out.'

They continued up the street to the gravel car park that fronted the point: a narrow finger of grass with a steep drop on either side down to the rocks. Looking at it, there didn't seem to be any way down.

'We surf the point most of the time. It's a good spot. People come down from Sydney and that. When it's crankin' it goes off, you can get a three-, four-metre swell. No shit.'

Sam nodded as if it meant something to him.

'Could take you in off the sand bar, ease you in, like. But's tiny today, anyway. Piece of piss. Just don't smash your head on a rock, yeah? Low tide soon. Watch out for that.'

Minty walked to the edge of the point as if he was about to step off into thin air. Sam followed him and realised there was a thin track worn into the grass down the side of the drop. Minty tackled the track at a jog, with the precision of someone who could find the way with eyes closed. Sam struggled down with the longboard, losing his footing several times, grabbing handfuls of saltbush to stop his slide. At the bottom, glassy, ankle-deep water rolled across the flat rocks riven with urchin-lined channels. Sam picked his way across the rocks. Minty called back to him over his shoulder.

'Few metres, then you wanna push off. Wait till a wave comes in, jump on it and paddle like crazy, sucks you back out. Or you'll get pushed up on the rock, ay.'

'Yeah … Right.'

'Easy as.'

'Sure.'

Minty held his board to his chest and vaulted out, meeting the water in one swift, natural movement. He moved his arms in high arcs, kicked and nosed his board over the waves.

Sam was less elegant. The water rushed over his feet, bubbling up his ankles. He jumped out, slapping the board into the water and landing askew. He was pushed sideways by whitewater. He paddled his arms like a madman trying to straighten up before the water had a chance to dump him back onto the rock. A head of whitewater roared toward him and he tried to dive under it like he had seen Minty do. There was no time for a deep breath. Salt up his nose, in his eyes, in his ears, but he was still on the board. His heart pounded in his ears and he felt the hot shot of adrenaline at the base of his skull. In that moment he forgot everything. Minty sat on his board a few metres away and laughed. Sam struggled and spat salt water, then he paddled and kicked until he was out behind the breakers, next to Minty.

'You can bodysurf, yeah?' asked Minty.

Sam shook his head. 'Don't go to the beach.'

Minty laughed and slapped the water. 'For real?'

'Never been out like this.' Sam stopped talking when what looked like a large wave, glittering in the early sunlight, began to build in front of them. Minty glanced across to him.

21

'Over!' he yelled, and Sam paddled and kicked the board over the crest, scooting down the other side.

'If it looks like it's gonna break, go under it. You have to push the board under. Most of these you just paddle over. Or you could, you know, catch one.'

Sam flicked him the finger. Other surfers came in and eyed him but, when they saw he was with Minty, they left him alone.

'When you sit out here, out the back, waitin' for a wave, this is the line-up. You don't take a wave from a local, you don't drop in on someone already on a wave. There's a priority order, ay. You'll get it eventually.'

'Where are you in the order?'

Minty grinned. 'I'm at the top, brah. 'Cept for a few older dudes, grey bellies. They been here longer so they get first pick if they're in.'

Sam bobbed on his stomach. The light shimmered in prisms through the water and Minty paddled out a little further into the line-up. Sam rolled over the waves. He watched as Minty turned and paddled to catch one. He sprang up and coasted along. Watching from the back, Sam could only see Minty's head and torso. Minty leaned casually into the wave, shoulders loose; he turned back and forth, seeming to generate his own speed. The wave collapsed and Sam expected Minty to go under. But he was still upright, riding out the whitewater like it was a crappy amusement park ride. All the other waves were the same. Minty bailed gracefully off the side when he got bored. You didn't need to know anything about surfing to know Minty was good. After a while, he paddled over to Sam.

'Wanna go back and get pissed?'

Sam laughed, then saw that Minty wasn't joking.

'Yeah. Yeah, I do.'

Minty paddled north, around toward the beach. They moved further and further out beyond the breakers, practically out in the open ocean. The water rolled gently: glossy and sapphire blue. The sky was luminous. It was like being on another planet, a peaceful shimmering world of water and colour. Minty turned back to Sam with a grin.

'Take you in the easy way so you won't stack on the rocks.'

'Thanks.'

Sam followed Minty in, paddling behind him. His arms ached and he felt the muscles pulled taut across his shoulders. Minty coached him onto a wave and Sam rode it in like a ten-year-old on a boogie board. He couldn't help but smile, although, in an instant, the joy of the ride threw a sharp glaring light on the ache in his chest.

The beach was edged with a long concrete concourse: an ocean pool, surf club, kiosk and a line of showers. Minty pulled his wetsuit to his waist and rinsed under the shower, so Sam did the same. Already, there was a group of girls sprawled by the pool, openly staring at Minty and giggling. In the water, a handful of dedicated swimmers slapped up and down the lanes: three men and a girl in black Speedos. Her skin was pale and milky; a dark swash of hair rippled along her spine as her body rocked side to side with each elegant stroke of freestyle. Sam stood under the shower and watched her while Minty talked about the surf.

Back at the house, Minty hosed off the boards and leaned them against the back wall. He tossed Sam a towel off the line and they dried off. Inside, the house was chaos like there had been some freak disaster and everyone had fled, mid-activity. The rubbish bin in the kitchen overflowed onto the peeling lino; on the bench were open packets of food, newspapers, catalogues, crumbs, a chopping board and knife with half a block of cheese and some slices of tomato. A sock. Minty didn't comment on it, instead making a beeline through the detritus to his bedroom.

Everything in Minty's room was organised, a military tidiness that you wouldn't expect from a guy who mustn't have shampooed his hair in years. The floor was clear, the bed neatly made. It had a temple-like quality, a functional shrine to all things surfing. Minty kept his boards in a custom-made rack against the wall; his various wetsuits – a dozen or so – hung on a wheeled clothes rack. They were grouped, long legs and sleeves up one end, short up the other. A collection of rashies hung between them. The west wall was carefully papered with posters from surf magazines. In the centre, an A2-sized poster of a *Surfer* magazine cover showed a wave the size of a building with a tiny figure on a board on the lip; he looked like he was just about to fall down the face and be crushed by the mountain of water.

'Jay Moriarity,' Minty said. 'Youngest dude to ever surf Mavericks. You know Mavericks?'

Sam shook his head.

'Big break in California. Like real big, Waimea big. Moriarity was sixteen there. Brah, I'm gonna get there one day. There or Hawaii.'

'You wanna do that?'

'That's where it's at. I mean, it's cool to muck around and do tricks and stuff.' He shrugged, pointing at the poster. 'But that there, that's the real deal, brah. That's the ocean. That's as heavy as it gets. That's what I'm gonna do. You know, the guy who first discovered the break there, he was surfing it for years on his own, no crowds, no one watching, just him and the water. That's what it's about. Gotta win this comp in June – Cronulla Open, twenty-five grand prize money. If I win … anything could happen. I could take off if I wanted. Hit Mavericks, hit Waimea.'

He crouched down and reached under the bed, rummaged around and pulled out a bottle of whisky. He handed it to Sam and came up with another.

Sam stared at the picture of the boy about to be tipped off the edge of the world: the crushing weight of water about to pummel him. He knew that moment exactly, the disbelief that what was about to happen could even be possible. The intake of breath before the flood.

3

Sam sat on a fold-out chair next to Minty on the front lawn. Minty leaned back, hands clasped behind his head. A breeze had picked up, a south-easterly. A mottled front of heavy cloud gathered around the top of the escarpment in the east. Sam watched it, wondering what it would do.

'So you been up in Sydney?'

'Yeah. Were you living down here when I last saw you?'

Minty scrunched his eyes closed, thinking. 'When was that? We musta been ten or somethin', ay? Nah, we came down here after Dad went to prison.'

'He's in prison?'

'Yeah. He went down for assault and then they got 'im for armed robbery.'

'Whoa. What?'

'Yeah, him and a few other guys were doin' all the petrol stations round Yagoona and Bankstown. Mum had no farkin' idea, ay. She knew he was up to somethin', but she was scared of him.'

'Who'd he assault?'

Minty scratched his scalp, sliding further down in the chair. 'Mum, mostly.'

The picture Sam had in his head of his uncle didn't fit. Sam saw a lot of him as a little kid, much less after he and Minty were around eight. When Glen was around, Sam was captivated. Other than Pop, Uncle Glen was the only grown man in Sam's life. He was funny and Sam remembered being chased through Pop's flowerbeds, held upside down by the ankles and tickled until he was out of breath from the laughter. He sat beside Minty now and tried to take in what he was being told.

'I had no idea.'

'Yeah. He was always dodge, ay. Like, he'd disappear for weeks and if we asked Mum where he was she'd go crook at us. I mean, he didn't work much, so he musta been getting money from somewhere, ay. We were little, but. Didn't know any different. Looking back on it now, though,' Minty pulled his head back and widened his eyes. 'It's like, shiiiit, ay. Then there's all the crap between Mum and Aunty Rachel. What happened there? You know?'

Sam shook his head. 'I asked about it and Mum told me not to. Figured they had a fight or something. You seen Nana?'

Minty scratched his scalp again and his dreadlocks moved as one mass. 'Nah. Mum's heard from her though. Who knows. Weird, ay?'

'I just remember that she was around and then she wasn't,' Sam said. 'Same with you guys. It was like everyone disappeared.' Sam couldn't say anything else. It was too much. He took a slug of alcohol, hoping it would burn away the lump in his throat. He didn't look Minty in the face, but the silence before his response, and the change in his voice indicated a shared grief over the woman who had helped raise them.

'Nana was overseas. Travelling or some shit. She's back now, up north somewhere.'

They sat in silence, gazing out at the empty street. Somewhere a dog barked. A metal gate scraped on bitumen.

'You start surfing when you moved?' Sam asked eventually.

'Yeah. It's like I was shit at everything else until I got in the water. Changed my life, brah, changed my life. You'll get it, ay. You can skate, so you'll get it. Same thing, just on water.'

'Yeah, right.'

'When you get it, like, you won't be able to stop. You'll get hooked. It's like flying. No. That's not it. It's like you're part of the world and the world's moving.'

'The world is moving, Mint.'

'Yeah. It's like you're moving the world.'

'That's deep, man.'

'I know.' Minty belched loudly. 'I farkin' know ... No, you know what surfing's like? It's like having amazing sex with this girl that you really love. Like not smutty stuff. Romantic.'

'I wouldn't repeat that to anyone else, Mint.'

'It's like flying and having sex at the same time.'

'Like in a plane?'

'No. I'm serious. Like flying like a bird and having sex.'

'Birds don't fly when they have sex, I don't reckon.'

'They should. I would if I was a bird.'

'Who taught you to surf?'

'Shane took me out there for the first time. I was eleven, I think. He would have been, what? Fourteen? We never went near the beach before that. Mum never took us or nothin'. There's a whole heap of people who live here and work in the mines and the steelworks, who never go near the water. I could hardly even swim. Shane started going down the beach all the time, and I just followed him around. We got some of them little styrofoam boogie boards, you know? Dunno where from, probably nicked 'em. Then we started to try and stand up. Too funny. We nicked some cash from Mum and bought boards at a garage sale, fibreglass ones. Mine was way too big when I was starting out. Grew into it, though. Shane learned then took me out the back and taught me.'

It was difficult to imagine Shane being sensitive enough to teach anyone anything.

'He pushed me, ay. I was pissing myself when I started out. He'd make me go right out the back. I could barely swim. He'd push me under the water and hold me there, longer and longer each time.'

'Sounds fun.'

Minty shrugged. 'He wanted me to be able to handle myself out there, I guess. I kept going in with him. I wanted to learn. After a bit we started to enter in comps.'

'How'd you go?'

Minty shrugged. 'I won most of 'em.' He said it without ceremony, like it was banal. 'Shane went okay, but he shifted focus to me, ay. Says I'm the one who could make it. But, you know, it's different competing, ay. You gotta stay psyched.'

Minty shifted in his chair and Sam sensed he was telling him more than he would admit to anyone else. 'Dunno, it's intense, all the judges and that. I try to just have fun. But I kinda freak out sometimes. Shane's so into it all. If you make it, like go on the World Tour, that's it, that's your job. It's all I know, ay.'

The van pulled onto the grass in front of the house. Shane got out and loped across the grass. He stopped in front of the picnic chairs and pulled a face like he smelled something rank.

'What's this?' he grunted.

'Havin' a drink, brah. Join?'

'No piss during the week. You know that.' He shifted his glare toward Sam. 'He's training. Don't get him on the piss.'

Sam held up both palms in surrender. 'I didn't—'

Shane leaned down and took the bottle from Minty's hand, passed it to Sam. 'Then let him get pissed. You gotta stay clean.' Shane left them and went into the house.

Minty leaned further back in his chair and stretched his legs out in the sun.

'He's mellowed, old Shane.'

'Doesn't seem heaps mellow. That his van?'

'Yeah. Was Dad's. First time it's actually been used for legal work in about ten years.'

4

In the afternoon Sam slept, passed out on the camp bed in a glorious way. He dribbled on the pillowslip and didn't register the rest of the day going by. He was woken by the thrashing pulse of Metallica from the other side of the fibro wall. 'Enter Sandman'. The irony was not lost on him. He got to his feet and staggered, bleary-eyed, out into the kitchen. His mum would have been making dinner now, or he would be, if she wasn't home from work. It probably would have been stir-fry, that was her usual. The kitchen was empty. And still looked like a crime scene. Sam had the urge to howl, to bawl, to clutch onto the bench and sink onto the lino. He didn't. Instead, he grabbed his skateboard and took off.

Sam remembered Minty as the quiet kid with the white-blond bowl-cut who used to piss in Pop Hudson's garden at the house in Punchbowl. Pop would wrench his pants down and smack his bare bum whenever he caught him.

Minty would always look stunned, like he had no idea he was doing anything wrong.

As kids they would ride their skateboards up and down their grandparents' long driveway, all the way up beside the little house to the garage at the back of the block. Pop would haul planks of plywood out of the garage and prop them up on bricks for Minty and Sam to use as jumps. He would stand on the lawn and watch them, pipe hooked out the side of his mouth, arms folded across his white singlet. Whenever they landed a jump he would say, '*Fan*-tastic.' If they fell he would give a curt nod and declare, 'You're right. Up you get.' Minty always wanted the jumps higher. Sam always followed Minty.

The back lawn at Nana and Pop's was a neatly kept carpet divided by great circular garden beds that teemed with carnations, roses, chrysanthemums, daffodils, jonquils. A narrow concrete path led from one bed to another, with an off-shoot path running up to the outside toilet. Pop tried to teach them the names of the flowers but Minty could never remember any of them. Sam was better and Pop would grin and tell him he was sharp like his mum. Minty didn't seem to mind; he would just laugh.

Sam and Minty would catch skinks in the garden beds, holding them between thumb and forefinger as they wriggled. Sam was fascinated by the delicate pulse of their heartbeats drumming. If Shane caught a lizard he would crush its head into the concrete with his thumb so the brains would ooze out. The memory made Sam think of his own mother's brain and how it had self-destructed, like one of those secret messages in the *Get Smart* reruns they used to watch together.

Sam's mum and Lorraine would sit on the front veranda eating scones and drinking shandies with Nana while he and Minty dashed up and down the concrete, the steady whir of the wheels like a train on tracks. He couldn't remember the last time he saw Aunty Lorraine, Minty or Shane. His mum told him they had moved south for a fresh start but Sam didn't know why it couldn't involve him and his mum. She had said it was a long drive but Archer Point really wasn't that far away.

He did remember the call the night Nana went missing. Pop had come home from the shops and found the door unlocked, the house empty, none of Nana's possessions missing but her handbag.

Sam never went around to the house in Punchbowl after that. His mum would go, but never take Sam. He didn't see Minty again. Six months later Pop died of a heart attack while he was transplanting bulbs from the greenhouse to the flower-bed. Sam wasn't allowed to go to the funeral. His mum said she wanted Sam to remember Pop the way he'd last seen him. Sam wasn't supposed to know the details, but he overheard that his pop had lain on the grass all afternoon and overnight until a neighbour saw him over the fence the next morning. Sam would always picture Pop lying alone on the cool grass in his white singlet, clouds of dew on his glasses. He hated the snapshot but once it was in his mind he couldn't get it out. He knew he wasn't supposed to know and he worried about upsetting his mum, so he never told her about it.

Now he had a new snapshot: his mum in his arms, head tilted back, mouth slack. Heavy and gone.

*

Sam thought about Pop as he glided down the empty streets on his skateboard, beneath a flat blue sky, faded and bleached out at the edges. He wanted to believe his mum was with Pop again, maybe in a garden, but he couldn't make the thought stick. He could only see her head lolling against his arm as he punched triple zero into the phone. Sam stepped off his board, leaving it to roll down the street without him. He leaned over the gutter and vomited. He wiped his mouth, then jogged off after the board.

He didn't know what day it was. Saturday? The disorientated feeling hadn't left him. It didn't help that he hadn't told anyone from home what had happened. Were his mates wondering where he was? Luke would have tried to reach him at home. Sam knew he should phone him. He planned to. But he couldn't imagine describing what had happened. For the moment it was easier to stay here in this strange parallel universe and stop the two worlds from overlapping. He pushed off and glided down the hill.

The town was built on the flat between the mountain ranges and the sea. It was one of a string of towns that led south to Wollongong: a grid of weatherboard miners' cottages – tiny windows, bare squares of lawn – and a queue of sad-looking shops. The highway and a train line divided the leafy escarpment from the coastline, with houses on either side. The shopping strip was on the escarpment side, Lorraine's house on the flat, 500 metres from the beach. Most of the houses were clearly built in a time when the coastline was viewed as an inconvenience more than anything else, the saline air a force that eroded door hinges and caused house frames to swell and contract. The older houses were built back from the beach, closer to the shops and the shelter of the escarpment, tight boxy places with little windows to keep the heat in and the harsh light out. Blow the ocean and its views. When he had gone to the beach with Minty he had seen how the headland loomed over the curved, open mouth of the coast. The town didn't loom, it cowered. New houses were being erected on the coastline – weekenders for Sydney people. Outdoor showers, sliding doors and big windows. Decks. But back toward the town more cottages than not had mobility ramps with sturdy rails to the front doors, unfurled like tongues panting in the heat.

A long strip of battered shops lined the gentle undulation of the main road. Being evening, they were mostly shut. The charcoal chicken shop wasn't; it glowed as Sam rolled past. The Jewel supermarket was also open, stray trolleys dribbling out onto the street. Streetlights flickered on, the odd car drove past, but mostly it was just Sam and his board. He rode down the main road and saw that there was nothing to see. He turned back toward Lorraine's, following the streets and hardly remembering where it was he'd come from. A battered street sign pointed toward the beach and he followed it. It was almost dark as he slipped into the car park on the headland next to the surf club. There was a handful of cars and out on the water he could see the slippery shadows of surfers. Beyond the southern point, the towers of the steelworks pumped soot into the orange sky. The swell was big, the waves looked good but he wouldn't really know. He spotted the white of Minty's hair, right out the back, straddling his board, straight-backed like he was in church. Most of the others were straggling in now. A wave rolled toward Minty; he slipped onto his stomach and worked at the water with his arms as the wave built behind him, the board caught and he was up, weaving his way across the face of the wave into the shallow. He was a flash of white teeth and whiter hair. Minty stepped casually off the side into the water and swooped the board up under his arm.

Minty walked, dripping, up to the car park. He saw Sam waiting in the glare of the streetlight and grinned, surprised as if he was caught by the novelty of having Sam around, as if he didn't believe he was really there in the first place.

'Nice out there. Shark feedin' time, but. What you doing?'

Sam shrugged. 'Just looking around. Couldn't remember how to get back to the house.'

'Ha. Surprised you can remember anything. You were out of it, brah. Figures. Wanna get some food? Bloody starving.'

'Sure.'

In the chicken shop, Minty stood in his wetsuit, feet planted wide, eyeing the menu board above the counter. He gnawed his bottom lip as if the future of humanity depended on his order.

'Burgers are good. Fish is shit from here. Savs are good,' he said.

'What are you getting?'

'Dunno. Burger.' He rolled a twenty-dollar note over and over in the palm of his fist, jiggling his right leg. A girl came out from the back of the shop. Minty swallowed visibly and

Sam noticed his ears pinken. She was dark-skinned, tall, lean and long limbed. An auburn pixie cut. Big eyes rimmed in kohl eyeliner, nose stud.

'Sup, Mint?' she smirked.

'Hey, Ruby.'

Her treacle-brown eyes fell on Sam and the smirk grew. 'Who's this?'

'Sam. My cousin. He's … bereaved.'

'Bereaved? That's a big word, Mint. What happened?'

Sam looked away and Minty filled in the silence for him.

'Nothin'. Just … he's stayin with us for a bit.'

'In the spare room?'

'Yeah.'

Ruby scowled. 'Not good timing.'

'Get your own family then.'

She tilted her head to the side and fixed Minty with a glare, then dismissed him and turned her attention to Sam. 'How's it going?'

'Alright.'

'Ruby.'

'Hi.'

'Hi yourself.' She pushed her jaw out. 'Well?'

'I'll have a burger,' said Sam.

'Get out. Really?' she deadpanned, scribbling on the pad.

'Yeah, I'll get a burger too,' said Minty.

'Wow, really pushing the boundaries.'

'And two bucks' worth of chips.'

'Ten-forty.'

'And two chocolate Mooves.'

'Fourteen-forty.'

He handed her the twenty. Ruby worked the cash register, took out the change and put it in her back pocket rather than giving it to Minty. She tore a number from the bottom of the pad and handed it to Sam with a wink. Then she turned and sashayed out the back of the shop.

Minty exhaled.

'She took your change.'

'She takes everything, brah.' He rolled his neck back, flexing his shoulders.

'How do you know her?'

Minty gave him a funny look, like he didn't know how to answer. 'Rube's ... she's ... we're mates, you know? She stays with us a bit. She's alright. I mean, she's a nightmare but she's alright.'

'Sure.'

Minty went out onto the footpath and slumped in a white plastic chair. Sam took two chocolate Mooves out of the fridge and followed him. He sat down and put his feet on his board, rolled it back and forth.

Minty grinned. 'So, you gonna be around long?'

'I don't even know. Don't know how it goes, legally or whatever. DOCS'll be in on it a bit, I reckon.'

'They don't know what the fark they're doin.' Minty hocked a glob of spit onto the footpath.

Sam opened his mouth to ask what he meant but Ruby came out holding a wad of butcher's paper and two styrofoam boxes. She dumped them on the table and sat down between Minty and Sam. Tiny shorts, black Doc Martens.

'Table service?' noted Minty.

She picked up Minty's chocolate Moove and took a long slug. Then leaned back in the chair and put her feet on the table, legs outstretched, ankles crossed.

'In tomorrow?' Minty asked.

She shook her head and unwrapped the chips.

'Help yourself.'

Ruby turned to Sam. 'What's your story?'

'Don't start on him,' said Minty.

'I'm just asking a question. Being friendly.'

Minty snorted.

'What's tomorrow?' Sam asked.

'Gonna be crankin' tomorrow.'

'It's 'cause of El Niño,' Sam said.

Ruby looked at him and crinkled her nose. 'What the—'

'El Niño. It's a weather thing. They've found that the western half of the Pacific Ocean's way warmer than it should be. Gonna cause havoc later in the year. Like typhoon havoc. Already there's changes in the swell 'cause of storms.'

Minty grinned, bobbing his head with enthusiam. 'Sick.'

'Not so much if you live in the Cook Islands. People are probably gonna die. But sick for you, sure.'

'I'm surfin' El Niño, baby.'

'I'm working,' said Ruby.

'What? Here?'

'Bakery.'

'Piss off.'

'It's called a job, Minty.'

'So? Come first thing. Six.'

'Start at six.'

'You've changed.'

'What's that supposed to mean?'

Minty shrugged.

'Five years, Mint. Five years I'll be gone, I'll be in New York or London or some shit, and you'll still be here, getting pissed, screwing around, chasing the Bombie.'

'No break in London.' Minty frowned. 'Wait. They got beaches there? Fuckin' pebbly ones, ay.'

'Next time you're wondering why I won't do you, Minty,' she popped a chip in her mouth, 'that's your answer right there.'

Sam felt all wrong and out of place in the space between them. He wanted Minty to make a wisecrack and break the tension but Minty just folded his arms and looked away. Ruby was either oblivious or didn't give a shit about the awkwardness of the moment. She leaned across the table and picked up Sam's Discman. She put an earphone in and pressed play, made a sour face and ripped the earphone out.

'Skater punk shit.'

'Hardly. Beastie Boys.'

'Whatever.'

'Ruby only listens to Led Zeppelin,' Minty said, tuning back in. 'Nothin' else.'

'Nothin' else worth listening to.'

A couple of tradies wandered into the chicken shop. Ruby uncrossed her legs and stood up.

'See ya,' said Minty.

'Later, dickhead. Say hi to El whatsi for me.'

Minty watched her saunter past him and into the shop.

'She seems nice,' said Sam.

'She's a nightmare.'

'I can tell.'

'Wanna come tomorrow?'

'Surf? Yeah, I do.'

Minty laughed. 'You'll probably die.'

'Good.'

'Didn't know you were such a nerd, brah. You hide it well.'

'Thanks.'

That night Sam waited until he was sure everyone was asleep, then he got out of bed and crept across the lounge, into Lorraine's room. She was snoring, lit by the streetlight through thin curtains. At the foot of the bed was the Grace Brothers bag she had carried from his apartment two nights before. He took it back to his room, tipped it out and picked through the contents: passports, bank stuff, Centrelink letters, Medicare, insurance papers for a car sold ages ago. Anything that looked important he took, including the chequebook, a letter from a solicitor, the Centrelink stuff and her keycard and licence from her wallet. He still had her little address book where every name and number she needed to know were carefully printed in her neat cursive handwriting. He'd taken it from her bedside drawer on that last night, as the paramedics had strapped his mother to the gurney. The Booners' old Bankstown address was struck out in firm sharp biro lines. There was no Archer Point address noted down. Only the phone number. Sam had felt the address book in his back pocket while he sat with her in the hospital. He'd resisted calling that number until the very last moment when he knew for certain she wasn't coming back and he had no choice. He'd known that phone call would pull him, as if through a black hole, into the past. Now he traced her handwriting with his finger, feeling the faint bumps in the paper like braille. He put the address book and all the important stuff in a plastic bag and stowed it in the gap under the shelf in the corner of the room. Then he returned the Grace Brothers bag to its place in Lorraine's room. She would notice things missing. He would deal with that when it happened.

5

They left before first light. Sam had been awake until three, then slept heavily and now was hopeless and bumbling in the dark. Minty was chirpy, eyes too bright for 5 am. He was zipped into his wetsuit and ready to go before Sam had even woken up properly. Shane was out the front waiting. He looked Sam up and down but said nothing.

Minty whistled to himself while he walked. Like Pop used to. He tried to explain how catching a wave was about anticipating the movement of the swell, becoming part of it, coaxing it to allow you to join. Speed and timing were everything. He talked about it the way a horseman might talk about breaking a horse. 'You can skate, brah. It's the same. But better,' he said.

'It's nothing like fuckin' skateboarding,' Shane grunted.

When they arrived at the headland, Minty and Shane dropped their boards on the grass and joined the handful of surfers standing, arms folded, gazing out at the ocean. There was a solemn unwavering reverence among the group.

The sky had brightened a little, ready to welcome the sun, but the water was a heaving, dark mass: roaring, rumbling, swelling in peaks and engulfing the rocks in spluttering foam. Flumes of spray rose from the tops of the waves, white veils caught in the whipping wind.

'You still in?' Minty asked.

Sam nodded.

Minty took the board under his arm and jogged down the goat track just as the sun crowned the horizon, throwing light into the sky, rippling orange and candy pink over the water. Sam copied him. He could imagine how it would feel to be scared of the water. If he flicked his mind back to before his mum died he knew he would have been wary. Now he felt nothing. He ran across the rock into the whitewater, knees high. He pushed out, landed stomach down on the board. A monster wall of water rolled in and he put his head down, slipping under like a seal.

Minty was hanging back, waiting for him. A wave built and Minty shouted at him to take it. 'Go hard, brah. Paddle!'

Sam did as he was told. He felt the moment that he united with the wave, like when the wheels of a plane leave the tarmac. It surged behind him. Minty was shouting instructions but Sam couldn't hear him. He tried to spring onto his feet the way Minty did but as soon as he shifted his weight onto his arms and tried to move his legs up, the nose of the board dipped into the water and the next thing he knew he was being flipped down the front of the wave. Water surged up his nose, through his throat, scouring his insides. It took what felt like an age to find the sky and air. He came up spluttering, just in time to see Minty slide past him, languidly drawing patterns on the wave. When he was done he dropped into the water and then turned back toward Sam, motioning to him to come in to the beach.

It wasn't until Sam was sloshing through the shallows toward the beach, lugging the board under his arm, that he realised he hadn't had anything at all in his head when he was in the water. The snapshots that crowded his mind and blocked out the light had all dissolved and, in those moments when he was trying to catch the wave, he had felt a lightness that he hadn't felt since his mum passed out in his arms. As soon as he made the realisation, the snapshots shoved their way back in, like a reel of film being changed.

Minty spent the next half hour with him, board on the sand, instructing him on how to 'pop up'. He drilled him again and again, his zeal unrelenting, until – arms and chest aching – Sam finally got the hang of the movement. Minty then took him into the breakers, where the water was waist high and Sam lay on the board while Minty pushed him onto wave after wave and Sam tried to stand up.

After another hour in the water Sam's muscles felt as though they had melted. He caught a wave in to shore, finally standing up for three seconds, his personal best. Minty whistled as he followed him onto the sand. Sam dropped the board, yanked his arms from the wetsuit and sat down, waiting for more oxygen to find its way to his head.

'Going back to the point,' Minty said and Sam nodded.

He watched the surfers in the water. Most wrestled with the waves. Minty danced with them. It was absurd, his elegance, the calligraphy lines of the board across the glassy faces of the waves. He decorated them in flicks and swirls. His board sliced the water, speeding, hurtling, yet there was nothing quick or urgent about his movements. His left shoulder and arm were relaxed by his side, palm waving occasionally in the air, his torso tilted into the face, right arm trailing behind, smooth. Balletic.

Sam's gaze followed the curve of the beach around to the southern point. A figure was running along the sand, a girl in Speedos sprinting toward him. She came to a stop about ten metres away. Her body was a smooth, compact hourglass shape. She wasn't skinny, but toned and athletic. He tried not to openly stare at the curve of her thighs and bum. She turned to face the horizon, her hands clasped behind her head. She had caramel-coloured hair, a mass of curls pulled back into a messy knot. A stray curl clung to the nape of her neck. He pretended he was watching the waves until she turned and sprinted away again, toes flicking sand behind her. He watched her until she was a blurry dot in the distance then he picked up the board and headed for the house.

When he left the headland and turned onto Minty's street a darkness passed through Sam, a pulling pain in his chest that felt like the black hole had opened up inside him and everything was being sucked in.

Swimming bright and colourful,
'till away they dash.

6

Sam spent the afternoon hours curled on the camp bed, earphones in, Jeff Buckley on repeat. Jeff sang about the clouds pulling him into the sky and taking him away. The delicate notes and then the soaring wail, it sounded like flying, like being above everything only to crash down to reality again, over and over. They had laughed at him if he cried at school. Seven years old and wanting his mum so much his lip trembled. He, like any boy, learned early, earlier than he could even understand, not to show it. Not to show the raw feeling. But Jeff laid everything bare. It seemed you were allowed to if you could sing on a stage with a microphone and a guitar.

Sam couldn't play guitar and he couldn't sing.

At some point he made his legs work and went to the phone in the kitchen. His fingers knew the pattern of Luke's number; he'd been calling it since he was ten. The phone rang and rang until it was answered. The familiar sound of his friend's voice carved the hole deeper in his chest.

'Sam! Dude, where you been? I been calling you. New Year's was a joke. There was like, no beer left after ten. You didn't miss anything. How 'bout you?' Luke laughed. 'You watch the fireworks on TV?'

'No.'

'Where are you anyway? We're goin' to the half-pipe tonight. I got new trucks, dude—'

'My mum died,' Sam blurted out the words.

'What?'

'My mum died. On New Year's. She had a massive bleed on her brain. Burst aneurysm.' He said the words exactly like the doctor had, like he was telling Luke what he'd had for lunch. There was a silence. 'She's dead.'

Luke's voice was quiet. 'You serious?'

'Yep. I'm at my aunt's near Wollongong.'

'Shit. Are you okay? What? Are you coming back?'

'Don't know. Look, I gotta go.'

'Tell me when the funeral is.'

'Sure thing. I gotta go.'

'Sam—'

'Later.'

He hung up on Luke, went out the front of the house and picked up his skateboard.

Sam stopped when he came to a bus stop on the main strip. A sign told him the city shuttle would be by in ten minutes. He waited. When it came, the bus was scattered with pensioners and mouthy locals who looked like they'd just come from the methadone clinic. He didn't know what to expect of Wollongong. Fifteen minutes later he found it was six blocks' worth of office buildings, a library, town hall, a couple of bowling clubs, an RSL and an RTA. He rode the pavements, gliding between business people, women with strollers and tradies on smoko. Along the main strip of shops he came across a newsagent. He flicked the board up and went in. The shopkeeper eyed Sam as he scanned the garish magazine covers: shiny, lipsticked models pouted on fashion magazines, *New Idea* had exclusive news about Princess Di, *Dolly* offered dating advice and a Backstreet Boys poster. Sam found the music section and picked up a copy of *Rolling Stone*, a picture of Jeff Buckley on the cover. He flicked through the pages.

'You can buy it, you know,' said the shopkeeper.

Sam looked up and smiled. 'No thanks.'

He left the shop, magazine in his hand and stepped onto his skateboard. The shopkeeper ran out after him, yelling. But Sam was already down the hill and across the intersection. Mum wouldn't have liked it. She would have told him that the owner of the newsagent was just a guy trying to make a living, putting his kids through school, dreaming of a holiday on the Gold Coast. He deserved the money for the magazine.

But she was gone.

She had left him alone among the shattered remains of her family. She had left him without any answers as to why she'd cut them off all those years ago.

He had nowhere to direct the anger, the fear, the rage. He was angry at her for dying. So he spat it back at the shopkeeper and the universe in general. She was a good person. She tried to do good things and live in a way that was fair and decent. She taught him the definition of the word 'integrity' before he even started school. And the universe decided she didn't deserve a place in it anymore. So screw the universe. And screw the shopkeeper.

Sam was stepping off the bus, about to head back to Minty's when a girl's voice yelled out to him. He looked up and saw Ruby sitting on the squat garden wall of a house just down from the bus stop.

'Hey,' he said.

'Got a smoke?' Ruby asked.

'No.'

'Well, that's useless. What're you doing?'

'Went into town to have a look around.'

'Ah, see it's obvious you're a benny because you just called Wollongong "town". To people round here, that's "The City".'

'It's not a city.'

'No shit.'

'What's a benny?'

'Only a benny would ask that. Minty said you were bereaved. What, your dog die or something?'

'No. My mum.'

'Bloody hell. When?'

'Wednesday. No. Friday.'

'So you're staying with Mint?'

'Yeah.'

Ruby didn't say anything else, staring at Sam, squinting in the light.

'What're you doing?' he asked her.

'Finished work. Was gonna bum a ride home, then go for a surf.' She craned her neck, looking up the road past the shops. 'But no one's come by. My board's back at my place. Hey, you gotta key to the Booners'?'

Sam felt in his back pocket for the spare key Lorraine had given him.

'I can see your undies, skater boy,' Ruby said with a smirk. 'Like, I get that you guys wear your pants all like, low and shit. But that's farkin' ridiculous.'

'Whatever.'

'You gotta swap those denims for boardies if you wanna fit in here, bud. And pull 'em up for God's sake.'

'Who are you? My grandmother?'

'I'm the coolest girl in town. You gotta pay attention. Mint in?'

He figured she must have meant in the surf. 'I think so. Was before. He's pretty good, hey?'

She shrugged. 'I'm better.'

Sam laughed and she glared at him, dead serious. 'I am. But I gotta work. And I don't wanna compete. I'm comin' with you back to the Booners', grab one of Mint's boards. Go from there.' She started walking and glanced back over her shoulder to Sam. 'Come on, slowpoke.'

Sam followed her, thinking about how 'slowpoke' was a word used by mums, not long-legged girls in combat boots.

At the house Sam unlocked the door and Ruby went ahead of him to Minty's room. Sam shadowed her, unsure if he should have let her in. She ran her fingertips along the rack of Minty's boards, making her selection.

'He gonna be cool with you using that?'

She turned to face him with a look like he was the dumbest guy she'd ever met and didn't bother with a reply. She took a board and leaned it against the wall, looking it up and down.

'Where's he get them all from, anyway?'

She pointed to a large Rip Curl decal. 'Sponsorship.'

'He's got sponsorship? How much?'

'No cash. Just gear. He's got a shaper further down south. Rip Curl pays for 'em to do his boards.' She motioned to the wetsuits. 'Hit him up with all these. It's made him piss weak, but. You get him in the water without his wettie and he won't stop whingeing about dick shrink.'

Sam laughed. 'You've known him a long time?' he asked.

'Yeah. He's a dickhead, but he's my best mate, you know? Everyone loves Minty.' She took the board under her arm. 'But he loves me the most,' she said with a sly smile. 'You comin' down?'

'Nah. Tell Mint I'm just gonna hang here.'

She nodded and watched him with an intensity that made him blush. 'You alright? Not gonna top yourself or nuthin'?'

'Not yet.'

'That's the spirit.'

Dinner was a barbecue chook and a tub of coleslaw in front of *Home and Away*. Minty and Shane slumped, quiet and glassy-eyed, on the couch. Lorraine gave them each a kiss on the top of the head and a can of no-name cola. From what Sam had gathered he knew that Lorraine had a job in the kitchen of a retirement home. She wore a pale blue smock for a uniform and now she perched on the arm of the couch holding a drumstick with her purple-lacquered fingernails, like talons.

'Has Minty been looking after you, love?'

Minty grunted.

'Gonna have to sort a funeral,' she said.

Sam nodded.

'Never thought I'd be the one picking her casket,' she mumbled. 'Shows you never know, s'pose. Called the hospital today 'bout a death certificate. Need it to access her accounts, you know.'

'She's got a lawyer, I'm gonna call him,' Sam said.

Shane took his eyes off the television, wiped grease from his mouth with the back of his hand. 'That's Mum's job.'

'You let me sort it, love,' Lorraine said.

'I've got his number. I'll call him.'

Shane straightened, pushed his shoulders back. 'Mum'll sort it.'

'Leave it, Shane.' Lorraine looked back to Sam. 'We'll sort it. Don't worry, love.'

Minty sat in his boxers, chewing his food methodically, caught up in *Home and Away*. 'Get some good ones today, Michael?' Lorraine asked him.

Minty nodded, absorbed in the television.

'Thatta boy.'

'Gotta call the social worker, too,' said Sam. 'Work out where I'm gonna go, like, after the funeral.'

Lorraine swallowed a mouthful of chicken. 'We'll see.'

Shane put down his plate, shook his head and got to his feet. He gave Lorraine a warning look and muttered something as he stepped past her. She ignored him. 'I talked to 'em on the phone. They don't want you on your own yet.'

Sam knew why. The memory of the police station was crisp, even though he'd left it untouched. He felt his pulse quicken when he thought of it. He could see the image of his mum's eyes when she'd come to pick him up. Not angry, just hurt. He looked at the chicken cooling on his plate. He could just take his mum's keycard and get a train back to Sydney. Where though? Luke's place? Minty took his attention from *Home and Away* and looked over at Sam with a glowing grin, the grin that greeted a jump on Pop's driveway. You could see the pictures forming behind his eyes.

'It'll be sweet, brah. You're good on the board, ay. You're a natural, it's in your blood. Nuthin' else to it. You gonna love it here.'

She wasn't even in the ground yet – the person who loved him most in the world. Where was she? Was she in a fridge? A big stainless steel thing with a label on her toe like you see in cop shows? Only in death do you wear a label on your toe. There was something degrading about it, like a labelled cut of meat in the fridge at Coles. He shifted the plate from his lap to the empty sofa seat beside him. He stood up.

'What's wrong, love?'

He lurched past the coffee table, knocking Shane's can of drink over on his way to the front door.

'What's up?'

But he was gone, out the front door. Shane was sitting on the front step; he stood as Sam came out the door and stepped in front of him.

'Oi. You're gone, right. After the funeral, you're gone. She doesn't know what she's sayin'. She's cut up about Aunty Rachel. But you're gone.'

Sam didn't say anything. He was as tall as Shane. Not as broad, but as tall. He knew how to use his size and he was quick. Always quicker than expected. 'At what point does an opponent become a victim?' his mum had demanded. 'Because to the law there's no difference.' He tried to shut down the thought as soon as it edged in. He took his skateboard from where it leaned against the wall and pushed past, heading in a direct line across the patchy sword grass to the bitumen.

He had to take the line down the middle of the road, the edges were gravelly shit. He pushed faster and faster. His frustration built because he couldn't get the speed he needed to shut it all down in his head. To numb it. The southerly that had lashed the coast in the afternoon had died leaving a tranquil stillness. The sky wasn't yet dark, the sun in the middle of its graceful exit from the stage. It was like a big 'fuck you' right in Sam's face. A beautiful evening in a world that could inflict enough pain to make him wish he wasn't here at all. The breeze caught behind him and he sailed along the silent street. He reached the headland and took the road down to the beach. Further down, there was a figure walking toward him. He took his eyes off her but his line of sight caught her again: swimsuit with a towel around the waist. Not a bikini. Speedos. Barefoot. The running girl. He sped closer toward her, looked away, didn't see the stick in the middle of the road. The wheels caught and he was flying. The slowing of time that always comes with a fall let him see himself surge upwards and take flight, swooping below the overhead wires and into the pink clouds and away from it all. Instead, he hit the ground, left elbow copping the fall. Body rolling. He must have been caning it. He let a roar out of his throat realising, too late, that he was being observed. He sat up slowly in the middle of the road in time to watch his board rolling down the hill. And then the girl, turning and running after it, one hand holding up the towel around her waist. The board rolled off to the side, came to a stop in the dirt. She leaned over and picked it up. Sam examined his elbow, the skin ripped and gashed, little black stones stuck in the goo. He squeezed his eyes shut like a little kid trying to be invisible.

'Are you okay?'

'Yeah.' He opened his eyes and only looked at her face once. She was pretty. Of course. The humiliation of it flooded him.

'You sure? Because, it looked like you fell pretty hard. I live just—'

'I'm fine,' he stood and took the board from her, dropped it and pushed away down the hill. He didn't look back. The sting of the gash sliced up his forearm. Further down the road, out of sight, he checked the graze again. Bright blood trickled from his elbow to his wrist. His mum would have laughed. She always did: 'You'll lose a limb one day.' He would shrug her away but she would insist on coating the wound with Savlon and taping him back together. She would have stitched this one up herself, the tip of her tongue sticking out in concentration.

He wiped the blood with his T-shirt.

A shout came from behind him. 'Sammy!' Minty caught him. Puffing after the run, shirtless. His Homer Simpson boxers two sizes too big. 'Sam?'

Sam stopped, flipped the board up. 'Sorry.'

'Nah, s'alright. You right?'

Mars was high and twinkling in the sky. Or was it Jupiter? He couldn't remember.

'What happened to your arm? You stack?'

'Yeah.'

They walked to the main road. Minty in his boxers, blood dribbling down Sam's arm and dripping from his pinky. He took off his shirt and wrapped it around the gash. A car sped past and someone yelled Minty's name out the window. Minty waved.

'Where we going, Mint? Not the chicken shop.'

'Nah. Not the chicken shop.'

They came to the supermarket and Minty wandered inside, squinting in the white lights. There was one checkout open, manned by a pale, lanky guy with long, greasy hair and glasses. He looked like a teenage J Mascis with a skin problem.

'Mintaaaay.'

'Jono, brah. Wassup?'

'Working.'

'Yeah?'

'Yeah. Till ten-thirty.'

Minty took a Snickers from the stand and ripped it open. 'This is my cousin, Sam. Living with us for a bit.'

'Hey.'

'Hey.'

'Jono's at school still, aren't ya, Jono.'

'Yeah. Archer Point High. It's a fine institution.'

'Not bad there, ay Jono?'

'Decent enough. Not everyone can be a pro surfer.'

Minty grinned. 'You comin' to Rickard's?' Minty asked. 'Party before school starts,' he explained to Sam. 'Tradition. At Rickard's Reserve.'

'You're not going to school,' Sam said.

'Not the point, brah. Big freakin' party. Goes off every time. Gonna bring the tunes?' he asked Jono.

Jono shrugged. 'Sure.'

'Jono knows heaps about music,' Minty said. 'Jono, you should see how many CDs this dude has, boxes of them.'

'Oh yeah? What you into?'

'Everything,' Sam said. 'Except teeny-bopper Hansen shit.'

'Sam's from Sydney,' Minty said.

'I'm jealous. Like, you've got the Enmore and the Horden. They all do underage gigs. Nothin' like that down here.'

'Ease up, Jono. I'm tryin' ta sell Archer Point to him. Tell him how awesome it is here.'

'Oh yeah. It's awesome,' Jono deadpanned.

An obese man with a noisy trolley pulled in to the checkout behind Sam and Minty. He coughed loudly.

'Sea change, Sammy,' said Minty. 'It's a good place, innit, Jono?'

'Oi, you working here?' said the man.

'Yeah, he's working, brah,' said Minty, chewing the Snickers. 'But we're holdin' the joint up.' He picked up another Snickers. 'I'm takin' this, brah,' he said to Jono. 'You can't stop me.'

'Have mercy,' said Jono.

'We won't hurt you, but we'll be back.' Minty tossed the Snickers into the man's trolley. 'There ya go, buddy. Have a good one. Don't eat it all at once.'

Sam and Minty left the supermarket. 'You gotta stick around, brah, you'll love it. Just like old times.'

'Maybe.'

7

'Do you wanna come with me?'

Lorraine was leaning against the doorframe. Pink lipstick, her hair pulled back into a blue toothed clip, clamped like the jaws of a determined creature on the back of her head. She was definitely dolled up. For what? The funeral home?

''Cause if you wanna come, you're gonna have to get up. Shane's lendin' us the van, but gotta get it back by ten-thirty. He's gotta job on.'

Sam looked up at the ceiling. The daddy-long-legs had caught one of the brown kitchen bugs and had it tightly wrapped up for later. It was moving very slowly, delicate legs picking across fine web.

Lorraine pushed away from the doorframe and approached his bed. She peered down at him. 'You should probably come. If you want. I just … I think you should come. If you can.'

Sam didn't say anything.

Lorraine pressed her lips into a grim smile.

'I know it's not what you want to do, plan her funeral, I mean. But, you gotta do it. We gotta do it. Trust me, love, you can't pretend it hasn't happened. Doesn't work.'

'Give me a minute.'

'I'll wait in the van.'

Sam figured this information was supposed to tell him she wasn't going to wait around for him and he'd better get a move on. Sam got up and felt around in the pile of clothes by his bed for a clean shirt. There wasn't one. He padded down the hall to Minty's room. He knocked but there was no answer so he pushed the door open. The bed was made with hotel precision. The dresser top was clear of clutter bar one black and white photo of Minty, much younger, running toward the sea with a board under his arm. Sam slid open a drawer and found Minty's T-shirts, each folded and stacked. He selected one and pulled it over his head. A horn sounded from out the front of the house. Sam left, pulling the door behind him.

He found Lorraine riffling through the glovebox, cigarette hanging from her lips. She pulled out a pair of sunglasses that Sam could only guess were Shane's – huge mirrored wraparound Oakleys – and put them on.

'Christ,' she muttered. 'Bloody bright enough.' Lorraine shoved the van into reverse and swung out onto the road, narrowly missing the letterbox. 'You right?' she glanced at him. 'You'll be right. We get in there, we pick a box, set a date, hand over a shitload of cash and, hey presto, we got ourselves a funeral. Not ourselves, like, Rachel.' She cleared her throat and turned on the stereo. A John Farnham tape whirred into life.

'How you goin'?' asked Lorraine.

'Alright.'

'Hmm. Well, I don't know anything about you anymore.'
She cleared her throat and wound down the window. 'Are
you a good kid? You used to be a good kid. I got no time for
trouble, right? I'm done with that. You want to mess around
and get into trouble you can go sleep under someone else's
roof.' She shot him a look.

Sam didn't say anything. It was a clean slate, a new leaf, a
new dawn, all of those clichés. He had to look at it like that
or he'd disintegrate right there in the passenger seat.

'Minty likes having you around, anyway. I mean, Minty
likes most people but he's always taken to you.' The van
rumbled and lurched and Lorraine seemed to have to put all
her weight behind the stick just to change gears.

'His room's heaps neat. Don't remember him being like
that.'

'He copes better with it like that.'

'Copes?'

Lorraine sniffed loudly. 'We had to start over again, down
here.' She didn't offer anything else. They rode in silence for
a bit, Lorraine humming along to the music every now and
then. Sam rolled the window down and let the wind whip his
hair around his face. His memory flashed a snapshot at him:
the last time he'd seen Lorraine, barefoot on the driveway of
Nana and Pop's hissing words at his mother.

'Lorraine?'

'Yeah?'

'Where's Nana?'

She gave him a quick sideways glance, leaned forward
a little, forearms draped on the wheel. 'Aww. Your mum

should have gone through this with you,' she said, almost to herself.

'She didn't.'

'Yeah, I'm getting the picture.'

'So?'

'Look. It's complicated, love. God knows. Your nan … it was all such a mess. We all did things we shouldn't have. Your nan, I was angry at her for a load of reasons. We all say things we shouldn't. She had to take off. She calls it a breakdown. Says she couldn't cope with it anymore. The stress. Something had to give. So …'

Sam couldn't frame it in his head so that it made any sense. Pop made scones, Nana made the jam from fruit Pop grew in their garden. Nana had a full set of Golden Books, kept in numerical order, on the shelf for the grandkids. Sam had shown her how to play *Space Invaders* and *Wimbledon Tennis* on the Atari. Nana was good at it. She kept framed photos of her three grandkids crowded on the top of her dresser. She had been there with his mum when Sam was born. Why did she leave?

'Did you know she had left? Or did you think something had happened to her?'

'Yeah. Nah. Your pop kept goin' on about how something nasty had happened to her.' Lorraine sighed. 'He told people that. But nothing bad happened to her, he knew that.'

'Mum didn't tell me anything. Only that we wouldn't see you guys anymore.' Sam changed tack. 'Do you talk to Nana, like now? Do you know where she is? She needs to know about Mum.'

Lorraine eased the van around a corner. He couldn't see her eyes through the sunglasses.

'Yeah, I've tried to call her. Got a number. But haven't spoken to her yet, keep getting the answering machine.'

'She doesn't know?'

'Well, I wanna tell her myself, don't I. I'm not leaving it as a bloody message.'

'Where does she live?'

Lorraine pressed her mouth into a firm line and didn't reply.

'Where does she live?'

'Up north.'

'Where?'

'I'm not telling you. Don't want you skiving off up there with some idea about her in your head.'

'I'm not going to.'

She pulled the car into a small car park out the front of a benign-looking beige brick building and killed the engine. She turned to him, pushing the sunglasses onto the top of her head. 'I don't believe you. She doesn't …' Lorraine sighed. 'I don't want her getting into your head.'

Sam didn't reply. He looked up at the big sign above the building. *Bob Crapp Funerals*.

'You're kidding?' Sam said.

'What?'

'Not here. Bob Crapp? No. I'm not getting it from here.'

'Everyone goes to him.'

'No. Not here.'

'I've got an appointment.'

'Why are we having it down here anyway? We should have

it in Sydney. She's not from here. Everyone she cared about is in Sydney ...' Sam caught himself too late. 'Sorry.'

Lorraine looked away and took a piece of gum from her bag, popped it in her mouth.

'I'm not going in.'

'Yes, you are.'

'No, I'm not.' He opened the door of the van, got out and took his skateboard from where it was stowed at his feet.

Lorraine was out of the door, striding around to him, her jaw set in determination.

'You're not pissing off! Got it? I'll mow you down with the bloody van if I have to.' She had him by the arm. He tried to shake her off but she was stronger than she looked.

'Let me go!'

She pursed her lips and narrowed her eyes, honing in. 'No. You wanna fight me, kid? Go ahead. I've danced with bigger blokes than you.'

Sam tried to control the breath as it caught in his chest, the hot blood thud that coursed down his neck. He squeezed his eyes shut to try and stop it. It was a feeling that had come and gone for so long that he'd grown accustomed to it and he didn't question it anymore. He felt like one of those racehorses you see on the television before a race, jittery, all his senses amplified like he needed to fight something he didn't understand. Or bolt.

'You can't run away like a little boy. She's gone, love.' Her voice was softer now. 'She's not coming back. You gotta accept it or you'll lose your bottle. This is what you gotta do, go in there, we'll have the funeral then you can get on with it.'

*

Just after his family had fractured apart he'd stood in front of his mother full of hurt and anger and confusion, hands in fists, his scrawny little body desperate to lash out. He'd wanted to see Minty and Lorraine, or Nana, and she refused him, telling him there were things that had happened in his family that he was too small to understand. It was complicated, she'd said. The same words Lorraine used. It had only made him angrier. The implication being that he wasn't old enough. It had magnified that horrible feeling of inadequacy that only a boy who is his mother's one remaining protector can understand. He'd screamed at his mum that he hated her and she'd burst into tears covering her face, defeated and deflated by this child who didn't understand. Now, he didn't know what it was he was supposed to be getting on with. There was nothing left.

'I don't want to go in there,' he forced the words from behind his teeth.

'Okay.' She let go of his arm. Looked around. 'Okay.'

Sam held his board and breathed, looking at the sky.

'You haven't changed, Samuel Hudson. You always wanted to run away when you were upset.'

Fight or flight. At some point it had switched, but Lorraine didn't know that.

8

They didn't go with Bob Crapp in the end. Lorraine found another company in the Yellow Pages and three days later the funeral was held in the middle of an industrial estate, next to a plumbing supplies place in an anonymous outer Sydney suburb. A venue chosen not for any sentimental value, but rather because it wasn't too far a drive for anyone who might want to come. No one got an unfair advantage. The official funeral stuff was to be done by a guy in a grey suit who had never met Sam's mum. His tie was too short and he used the words 'Okay now' as a prefix to everything he said. He showed Sam and Lorraine the 'ceremony room' where the funerals, or as he called it, 'the action', took place. It was a large generic room with industrial carpet, bright lights and a little podium with a velvet curtain around it for the casket.

At the funeral Sam sat next to Minty, sweating in his hired polyester suit, and felt himself teetering on the line between numb detachment and complete emotional breakdown. There was nothing in-between. He wouldn't be able to grieve in a polite, composed way so he chose not to allow the grief in at all. While all the talking happened around him, he sat and breathed, focusing all his attention on one of the white flowers on the coffin. A cabbage rose; Pop would have been proud of him for knowing. He honed in on the very edge of a petal curling and discolouring ever so slightly.

Sam and the petal got through until the velvet curtains scrolled across the coffin and it whirred away to the silent unspoken place where coffins go after the ceremony. They had opted for cremation although Sam wasn't sure exactly when the cremating took place. Was it while the trays of party pies were being passed around?

He stood up and the first face he saw was Luke's. He looked like he was wearing school pants and his dad's shirt and tie. Luke said words to him about Sydney and asked when Sam was coming back. He kept laughing nervously. Minty said words to Luke and then some of his mum's friends came over with their words, hugging him and sniffling. He bore it for as long as possible before he excused himself and ducked through the clusters of people. He pushed through the door and walked out into the glaring heat of the sun. There was no green to soak it up, just asphalt, concrete, glass and metal. The horizon seemed to warp in the heat. Across the road was a pool supply place and a shop selling dirt bike parts. Sam watched people going about their mundane business – buying chlorine, dropping off a wheel for repair – with envy. He longed to be doing something boring and unremarkable. He didn't want to have to affix any significance to this date. He heard the door squeak behind him and turned, thinking it would be Lorraine coming out for a smoke. It wasn't. It was an old woman in a hot-pink suit, an odd choice for such an occasion, Sam thought. Her hair was dyed an unnatural shade of red and it gleamed in the sunlight as she rummaged around in her little handbag for something; a hanky. She blew her nose loudly and looked over at Sam in that awkward moment when she was folding the last of her snot into the fabric. As soon as he saw her eyes he recognised her, despite the fact she was about twenty kilos lighter than she had been the last time he saw her. The weight loss only accentuated her resemblance to his mother.

'Samuel.'

'Nana?'

She regarded him for a moment with watery eyes and fiddled with the stacks of rings on her fingers.

'How are ...' it came out in a croak and she had to clear her throat and start again. 'How are you, love?'

'I'm okay.'

'What are you doing out here?'

It didn't seem to be the most pressing question after seven years of unexplained absence.

'Just ...' Sam shrugged. 'Don't wanna be inside. I didn't know you were going to be here. I mean, Aunty Lorraine didn't say.'

'It's been a long time. You're all grown up.' There was a tired sadness to her voice. 'Didn't expect it would be your mum's funeral I'd be going to. She always looked after herself.' She said it as if a lapse in judgement had killed his mum, rather than a blood clot. 'No, I thought there was a chance I could be going to Lorraine's funeral, Glen'd eventually kill her.'

Sam wondered if she was drunk.

'Or worse, one of the boys. But no. Goes to show you never can tell.'

The only thing he'd ever seen her drink was a shandy or a sherry at Christmas. Where did she go beforehand to get herself loaded? A pub? A car park with a brown paper bag?

'I just wish it had been in a church. Sorry, love.' She laughed. 'Listen to me. You've had enough of a shock. I wanted to see you kids, you know. But Rachel and Lorraine wouldn't have it.'

The thought that he knew her well and at the same time barely at all surfaced. She was a stranger whose otherness to him was punctuated by lemonade in a glass in her kitchen and the occasional Golden Book story.

'Can I give you a hug?' she asked.

'Um, okay.'

She stood in front of him and put her hands on his shoulders. 'Come here.' She said it with casual affection, perhaps in an effort to mask the awkwardness of the moment. She pulled him toward her and hugged him with her tiny frame. He didn't know what to do with his arms so he just patted her stiffly on the back. He could smell the alcohol on her breath – and something else: talcum powder that took him back to the bathroom at the house in Punchbowl, the tiny hexagonal tiles in blues and greens, a fluffy shagpile mat contoured to fit around the base of the toilet and a toilet roll dolly, the roll hidden by her skirt, as if the toilet roll was the most offensive thing that had to be hidden. Nana pulled back, looked up at him with his mother's eyes. He couldn't hide it from her; it was like his skin was stripped from him. There was nowhere to go.

'Oh, sweetheart.'

He pulled away from her, shaking his head. He went to the kerb and sat down in the gutter, pulling his arms free from his jacket. She followed him, stepping down onto the asphalt of the road in her white court shoes.

'I'd sit next to you, love. But I'd never be able to get back up … Oh bugger it.' She slipped her knobbly feet out of the heels and, with one hand on his shoulder to steady herself, sat on the kerb next to him.

'Everyone can probably see me knickers. Half their luck.'

They watched cars drive by, a metre from their toes, and guys going in and out of the bike shop. A storm front – plumes of gunmetal grey clouds – was looming in the south. It rolled in along the edge of the piercing blue, bubbling, brewing. They watched the sky, side by side on the gutter's edge. A motorbike pulled in to the car park opposite.

'Oh, I used to love riding on one of them. My brother had one before the war. Arthur, his name was. You always looked like him. Handsome devil, he was. He used to take me out on the bike on a Sunday. All of this was farmland back then, long deserted roads. We'd tear along, no helmet or nothing. God, I loved it. He taught me to ride the thing in a paddock up from our house. My parents didn't know, of course, they would have died. My mum didn't think women should ride bicycles, let alone motorbikes. She was worried about the wind going up yer privates.' Nana burst out laughing. 'She was a silly chook, that woman. Then the war started and

Arthur went off, and that was that. We never saw him again. Never rode another motorbike.'

'Pop never had one?'

'God, no. No, he thought anyone on a motorbike was a criminal. He liked to follow the rules, did your grandfather. Never went over the speed limit, never crossed against the bloody lights. You ever gone really fast, love? My word, you go sixty miles an hour on a motorbike and you know you're alive. That's the old system, don't know what it would be these days. I used to wear a pair of Arthur's overalls, and my mum's gumboots to ride. Not the most glamorous get-up, but nobody would recognise me either. I'd tie a scarf around my hair and we'd be off. Zoooooom! Lightning.'

The guy with the motorbike came out of the shop and got on the bike.

'Reckon he'd give me a ride?' Nana chuckled. 'Ooooh, what I'd give. That'd be a good way to go, I think. Ride a motorbike off a pier or some such. Never mind this wasting away with age, I don't care for it, I tell you. No, a blaze of glory would be the way to go.'

'Pop died in the garden, on his own.'

She twisted the rings on her fingers and didn't say anything.

'It wasn't fair.' He expected her to get up and walk away but she didn't. She just gave a loud sniff. 'We thought you'd been kidnapped or something.'

'Who'd kidnap an old woman? Haha. No one's got any use for me. You were too young, love, to understand what was going on. Those boys,' she flicked her head back toward the funeral home, 'they knew too well. There's only so much you can do. It was going to kill me, the worry. I had a heart attack, you know? Didn't make any difference to her. She wouldn't leave him. He was gonna kill someone in that house. You know, Shane, he'd fight back, Lorraine too. But little Michael.' He heard her swallow. 'I had him one night and there were bruises all over his back. "That's The Belt, Nana," he said to me. Sweet little thing, both of you were. I said to him, "Why'd you get the belt, love?" He said he'd wet the bed. My God. I just …'

There were tears in her eyes. 'I said to her, "We'll take you and the boys away. We'll go. We'll do anything." But she wouldn't do it. Said he'd follow her and kill them all. I talked to the police, that was the end of that, she wouldn't speak to me, wouldn't let me see the boys. The stress of it. I was going to die of it and I didn't want to. I wasn't ready.'

'Uncle Glen? He's in prison.'

'I know. Thank heavens.'

Footsteps sounded behind them and Sam turned to see Minty. He looked down at them, scratching his scalp, his dreadlocks fastened behind his head with an elastic band.

'Nana?'

'Hello, love, gimme your hand.' She held up her hand daintily and Minty helped her to her feet. 'Look at you! My word. You've been riding that surfboard, haven't you? Saw you in the papers. You don't know how proud you've made me.'

Minty watched her with a sceptical frown, the most serious expression Sam had seen on him. A worry line bunched the centre of his eyebrows. 'Mum see you?'

'I don't think so. I was up the back.'

'You been talking to Sammy?'

'Yes, love.'

Minty looked at Sam. 'You know she was gonna be here?'

'No.'

'You want something to eat, Nana? There's food in there.'

'No, love. Think it's best for me to lie low.' She took out the hanky and blew her nose again. Sam felt the cavity in his chest expanding, pushing him out and sucking him in all at once. 'Is Shane here?'

'He's inside,' Minty said. 'Didn't wanna come, but Mum said he had to.'

Nana nodded and didn't ask any more about him, but Sam sensed her measuring things.

'I want to go home,' Sam said. He shoved his hands deep in his pockets to stop the trembling. 'Can we go?' he asked Minty.

Minty shrugged. 'I got the car so ...'

Nana opened her handbag and fished around for something, pulling out a small piece of tightly folded paper. 'That's my address and phone number. I'm in Port Macquarie. I'm always happy to have you. Will you give me a call?'

'Alright.'

'God love yer.' She pulled his head down to her height and kissed him on the forehead – the way she'd always done when she'd tucked him into bed. Sam was taken back to all the nights he'd spent at her house when his mum was working night shift. Minty was often there. He and Sam, side by side, in the big mahogany bed, Nana reading them stories from her illustrated bible. The ocean always played a part: tales of storms, floods and waters parting or people being swallowed by giant fish. 'Are there any stories about monsters, Nana?' Sam asked her once. She had thought for a moment and then found the passages about the Leviathan. The Leviathan was usually left out of children's bible stories. She explained to the wide-eyed boys that it was a fearsome underwater creature that showed how God could create things that were vicious as well as things that were beautiful.

'Like a shark?' Minty had asked.

'No, no. Big. Huge.'

'Like a whale?'

'I'll read it to you,' she said. *'Can you fill his hide with harpoons or his head with fishing spears?*

If you lay a hand on him, you will remember the struggle and never do it again.

Any hope of subduing him is false; the mere sight of him is overpowering.

No one is fierce enough to rouse him.

Who then is able to stand against me?'

'Is it the Loch Ness Monster?' asked Minty.

'I don't think so. There's more, earlier.' She licked the tip of her index finger and turned the delicate pages back. *'Behind him he leaves a glistening wake; one would think the deep had white hair.'*

The sky began to splutter fat drops of rain as they pulled out of the car park. Minty was the most relaxed driver Sam had ever seen. He drove leaning forward, forearms draped over the steering wheel like he was captaining a yacht on a Sunday afternoon. When he turned the wheel he moved his whole torso with it, swaying gently around the corners, his movements slow. He turned his head to look at Sam, that same worry line between his eyebrows.

'Alright, Sammy?'

Sam shrugged and looked out the window, watched the clouds swallow up the sun. 'Weird to see Nana.'

'Yeah. How 'bout that, ay? Shit. You never heard from her, all this time?'

'No. I mean, Mum stopped talking about it after Pop … She said she used to ride motorbikes.'

Minty laughed. 'Na! No shit? Good on 'er.'

The wind picked up, sending leaves and twigs swirling in the sky. Sam looked up to where he could see the nose of Minty's board in its bag, strapped to the roof.

'You got plans, Mint?'

Minty laughed. 'You just wait, Sammy.'

'What?'

Minty took the turn-off to the highway, but he didn't head south, he turned north.

'What're you doing? I wanna go home.'

'Na-ah. You get a storm come up from down south, north-easterly wind and it's perfect. You never seen anything like it.'

It felt like they were in the middle of nowhere: flat paddocks filled with shipping containers and roads with numbers instead of names. Then the shipping containers gave way to saltbush and scrub, the tar turned to dirt. A faded wooden sign with white writing told them they were entering national park.

'Where are we?'

'Big break, man. You wait. I been biding my time, today is the day.'

The scrub gave way to juts of granite, like platters stacked on the cliff. The road ran to an end. Minty stopped the car just as a mighty clap of thunder sent a jolt through them and sheet lightning illuminated the sky, the whole world it felt like. A photographer's flash in a dark room, like the world had never been properly lit before then.

'Come on.' Minty opened the door.

'You're kidding.'

But he wasn't kidding, he was out of the car, pulling his suit off. He reached through to the back and pulled out a wetsuit, rapping on the roof of the car. 'It's on, Sammy! You gotta come be my witness, brah!' He pulled the board off the roof, tucked it under his arm and skipped off across the rock.

Sam got out of the car. The rain spat icy bullets over his shoulders. He tilted his head back and looked up at the wide expanse of sky. Droplets of rain kissed his cheeks and forehead, rolling into his eyes. The clouds were like a watercolour painting, textured with billowing light and shadow. A flash of lightning tipped white light over the grey and a clap of thunder sounded, so loud he felt it quake through the rock beneath his feet. He ran in the direction Minty had gone and found a track through the scrub. The saltbush and spinifex swayed and warped in the wind and Sam felt like he was chasing a white rabbit down a hole. His squeaky vinyl shoes gnawed his heels. When he felt he'd been running for an age, the track ended at a lookout. Minty was nowhere to be found.

The ocean opened up in front of Sam. Waves bigger than he had ever seen, like cliff faces, sucking water off the rocks and rearing up before rolling back in again. The sound was like a hurricane or a bushfire, a merciless roar, the water devouring everything in its path. The sky seemed to become water, the horizon line gone altogether. Blinking the rain out of his eyes, Sam scanned the dark rolling water. He could just make out two figures. He peered over the edge to see Minty jumping off the rocks and into the churning black water.

'Minty!' he screamed. Sam's voice was lost in the bellowing, shattering noise of the ocean. Minty was going to die. The Leviathan was going to take him. He was going to die out there and Sam was going to have to watch it. Again. A colossal wall of water rose up in front of Minty and Sam felt his stomach drop. But Minty dived under, disappearing beneath the wave. He was lost. Sam searched the water and finally spotted Minty's white head. He paddled and dived with his board, clawing his way further and further out to where the sets were building. The rain sliced through the humid air, prickling icy droplets against Sam's cheeks and neck. His tie fluttered like a banner over his shoulder.

'Who the hell is that?'

Sam turned and saw two guys standing behind him. They were older, twenties maybe. Big guys with tatts and thick necks. 'You know who that is?'

'Minty Booner.'

'That's little Booner? He's gonna die.'

'Should have a jet ski in with him,' said the other one. 'He's gonna get hammered.'

The three of them watched as Minty manoeuvred the board onto the crest of a wave. Sam held his breath and watched in disbelief as Minty got to his feet. One of the guys gave a low whistle. Minty, a tiny speck compared to the colossus of water, drifted down the face of the wave with his trademark casual stance, crouched low, shoulder into the water, the fingertips of his right hand trailing along behind him, skimming the wall, like a kid playing with a fountain. Sam watched as the wave changed, forming a step midway down the face. Minty jumped the board off like he was skating. He landed crouched low, gripping the side of the board and rode into the barrel. The other guys whooped. The wave collapsed and Sam saw Minty's feet in the air as he bailed into the whitewater. Long moments passed and when Sam was sure he had drowned, Minty's head popped up.

'Ha. Now he's gotta get back in,' laughed one of the guys. 'He's gonna have to get in at the bay.'

Minty scrambled, kicking and pulling at the water. He dived under as another wave broke, rolling over him. Slowly he edged his way south, out of the channel where the waves were breaking. He disappeared around the headland as the sky opened up and the rain began to pummel down, soaking Sam through to the skin.

9

In the car, Minty went over and over the wave, buzzing with the details. His energy seemed to fill the whole car. He fizzed. Sam had never heard him say so much all at once. The storm passed as quickly as it arrived and Minty wound down the window and turned up the radio.

'I thought you were going to die.'

'I know! Same! How heavy was it! Shit. But I knew, brah, I knew as soon as I got that wave, I knew it was gonna be epic. Woah. Unbelievable.'

They were flying along, ten kilometres over the speed limit, the little Datsun rattling its bones like it might disintegrate at any moment. Minty didn't seem to care.

'Dude, Ruby's not gonna believe me! She's gonna spew that she missed it. Ha. Did you see that?!'

'Cop, Mint.'

Minty slammed on the brakes as they approached a crest, the nose of a highway patrol car just visible between the bushes on the median strip.

'Thanks, brah.' Minty waved to the cop.

'Way to finish a funeral,' Sam said.

'Oath.'

They drove and Minty sang along to the radio. It was another half hour before he calmed down.

Minty called Ruby and the three of them sat on the front step with a beer each. The porch light was on and bugs flicked against the light, clicking and falling, rising again. Midges, moths. Sam and Minty leaned back with their elbows propped against the top step and stared up at the sky – a twinkling ocean: vast and deep and unknowable, humans forever paddling at the edges. Ruby sat on the step below, leaning on Minty's leg as he revelled in the retelling of the wave. Sam knew Minty had taken a day that was one of the most horrible in Sam's existence and reshaped it entirely.

'You shoulda seen Sam's face at the turn-off! He was all like, "No way!"'

'Man, I couldn't believe it. Thought we were heading back home for a cup of tea. Then I see Mint's got his board on the roof and I'm like, who brings a surfboard to a funeral?!'

'Yeah, brah! Fully. And those guys, at the lookout, they think they farkin' own the place, brah. Ha. You see 'em?!'

'They were like, "Little Minty, he's gonna die!" And I'm like, yeah, he's gonna die! Shit!'

'You take a photo?' Ruby asked Sam.

'Didn't exactly have a camera on me.'

Ruby sipped her beer, tilting her head back to look up at him. 'How do I know you're tellin' the truth, Michael?'

She pointed the neck of her beer bottle first at Minty then at Sam. 'You two having me on?'

'Nah, Rube! I swear, ay. You're just jealous. It was all in the timing. Like Sam said: El Nini.'

'El Niño,' Sam corrected him. 'You surfed there before?'

'Nah. First time. I've been waiting so long. I felt I was ready, you know. I felt it in myself.'

'Why didn't you bring Shane?' Sam asked.

Minty didn't answer. He took a slug of beer and shook his head.

'Shane'd never let him do that,' Ruby said.

'For real?'

Minty stretched his neck side to side like it was the source of his discomfort. 'Doesn't want me gettin' injured.'

'Minty's his meal ticket.'

'Ay, Rube. Ease up.'

Ruby let out a laugh, but it wasn't in humour. 'As if he's not gonna ride on your wins.'

'That's not what it's about.'

'Why doesn't he compete?' Sam asked.

'He did a bit. But …'

'He's not good enough,' supplied Ruby. 'He knows if anyone's got a shot, it's not him. So he's all like making videotapes of Minty and training him like a bloody racehorse or something.'

The pained expression hadn't left Minty. He rolled the bottle neck between his fingers and stared straight ahead.

'So … you've gotta comp in June?' Sam asked Minty.

'Yeah.'

'Amped?'

Minty shrugged his shoulders. 'Yeah. Dunno. I wanna win, but ...' He let out a long sigh. 'There's bigger waves, brah. You know, it's all different when there's judges and shit. It's just about the waves for me. And there's better waves than Archer Point. I wanna hit Pipeline or Waimea. I mean, there's places here, in Oz like – Margaret River, Shippy's. But man, Hawaii: it's like Mecca. It's my spiritual home.'

'You've never even been there,' said Ruby.

'Yeah, but I feel it in me heart, ay? It's the origins, isn't it? There's somethin' about it. You know, they're all doin' tow-ins though – getting towed onto waves by a jet ski – dunno about that, ay. Bit like riding a mechanical bull or, I don't know, shaggin' a blow-up doll. There's no connection. It's gonna shift, I reckon, go back to pure paddle in. It has to. Otherwise it's like getting choppered into the top of Everest and saying you climbed it. You do need a jet ski, sure, to pull you out if you get pummelled. Which I guess is a lot. You can be underwater for like four, five minutes.'

'You still gotta ride the thing, though,' said Ruby. 'Not like a jet ski does that for you.'

'Yeah, but, it's the feel of it, you know. You should work for a wave, it's instinct, like eating a moose you hunted yourself instead of buying it in the supermarket.'

'You can buy moose?' asked Sam.

'Yeah. Canada. Saw it on the telly. You know what I'm saying, brah.'

'So, you're bored here.'

'Yes!' He nodded, pointing a finger at Sam. 'Yes! Bored

as. I mean, I could play the game, do the comps. But who gives a shit? If you're just out there to do tricks or whatever, you're not risking anything. It's cool but, that wave, that wave today – that's a farkin' rush, brah. Once you've had that, that's all you want. I just wanna get the biggest farkin' wave I can paddle into. I want Waimea.'

'Not here.'

'You are so … what's the word? You are so … sharp, brah. You got it figured.'

'So win the comps, get the money and go,' said Ruby.

Minty narrowed his eyes and nodded slowly, like he was on the edge of some sort of enlightenment. 'That's it, Rube. That's what I gotta do.'

'That's what you gotta do. Shane's a dickhead, but—'

'Ay, ay, ease up.'

'Yeah, but he's always on at you about getting your head straight for a comp. Not letting the nerves get to you. He's got a point. Make the choice. Go for it, don't be all over the place. Put your head down, win the cash and go to Hawaii.'

'I gotta watch the videos Shane makes.'

'Yeah. Do that. Like every night.'

'I'll make you a tape,' said Sam. 'To listen to on headphones at comps. Might help with—'

'Might stop you dropping your guts every time,' said Ruby.

'We'll see,' said Minty.

'How long you staying anyway, weather boy?' Ruby asked Sam.

'Don't know.'

'Don't you have a dad?'

85

'No. I'm the immaculate conception.'

'Piss off, you know what I mean.'

'You just want the camp bed back, Rube,' said Minty.

'Nah. Yeah, a bit. Whatever. Where's your dad?'

'Dunno. Dunno who he even is.'

'You ever ask your mum?'

'She said he wasn't worth knowing.'

'I know what that's like.'

'Ruby's adopted,' Minty said and she slapped the back of his leg. 'What?'

She gave him a look of exasperation. 'It's my life, dickhead. That's my information to give.'

'Like you're not givin' him the third degree!'

She ignored him and turned to Sam. 'It's a messed-up thing not knowing who you are.'

'I know who I am.'

'Oh? Lucky you.'

The van swung into the driveway and parked behind Minty's Datsun. Lorraine got out of the passenger side, pulling the strap of her handbag over her shoulder. She strode toward them, her stride visibly off kilter.

'Whattya doin' back here?' she squawked. 'I was lookin' for you everywhere!'

'We drove back,' said Minty, stating the obvious in his wide-eyed way.

'Your mum's funeral!' she said to Sam. 'Your mum's bloody funeral and you take off!'

She was right. It had been his own mother's funeral that day. It took one sentence from his aunt to pull down the facade he and Minty had constructed.

'Leave him, Mum,' Minty said.

'I'll do as I please. This is my house.' She pointed a shaking finger at Sam. 'My house, my rules, yeah? And my rule is you stay for a decent time … after your … After your own mum's funeral.'

'Sorry, Aunty Lorraine.' Sam felt everything in him tighten. He had been loose and okay, now he was wound tight again and the trembling in his hands was back.

'Oh yeah. Sorry are you? Geez, I've got a right mind to hand you over to your nan right now.'

Shane got out of the van and loped across the grass. His suit pants were too short, mismatched socks peeping out from his black Volleys. He stood back, folded his arms and made sure Sam knew his eyes were on him. Sam could feel the beer and the way it made him hate Shane and his stupid polyester trousers. He was still a yob who thought he was a big man.

'Wanna beer?' Minty asked.

'Oi!' squeaked Lorraine. 'I'm trying to have a word here!'

'Go to bed, Mum,' said Shane.

'I'll be talking to youse in the morning. You can count on it.' She went up the steps and inside, leaving the four of them sitting in the porch light with the midges.

Shane watched as the front door closed behind his mother. 'You too, Mint.'

Minty was confused.

'I wanna talk to Sam.'

Ruby stood up and and set her bottle down on the porch beside Minty. 'This is when I call it a night.' She gave Sam a grim smile and wandered off across the grass.

'I need to talk to Sam, Mint. Go.'

Mint took a swig of his drink and scoffed at his brother.

'Suit yourself.' Shane walked up to where Sam sat on the step, leaned down, stopping inches away from his face. 'Tomorrow. You're gone.'

'Oi, Shane!' Minty protested.

Shane turned to Minty, his expression hard. 'Shut up, Mint. You don't know what you're talking 'bout. Stay out of it.'

As if he was in charge, as if he had some authority over Sam and Minty. His mum would have told Sam to remove himself from the situation, to not let his anger control him and take control of it instead. She was gone.

'Fuck off,' Sam spat.

'What'd you say?'

'I said, "fuck off".' Sam stood, jutted his chin up and pushed Shane in the chest.

'Oh come *on*,' said Minty. 'Leave it. Sam, brah …'

Sam pushed him again and Shane grabbed his arm. 'Don't touch me, little boy.'

Sam threw the first punch, his knuckles connecting clumsily with Shane's shoulder. It had been five weeks since the last fight. His desperation to forget it only served to embed it in his mind so he was endlessly calculating how far it was behind him. Shane growled and pushed him away but Sam was determined, driving in, head down. It was on and the feeling inside was nothing but relief, a shattering, unfurling release. He had to work for it, but finally Shane swung back at him. For those blessed minutes his mind, his memory, was blank. The black hole shrank away to nothing. Nothing but stillness. They both ended up on the ground at one time or another. Sam got leaves and grass up his nose, in his mouth. He tasted the coppery flavour of blood on his teeth. He pummelled Shane and welcomed every returning blow. Minty shook his head and swore to himself. Eventually they both ran out of breath, though Shane was the first to hold a palm up. 'Enough.' Blood trickled from his nose.

'Come on!' Sam screamed.

'Enough.'

'Come on!'

'I'm done.' He dropped his hands to his knees, doubled over to get his breath. 'You're out tomorrow, you little shit.'

Sam shrugged, wiped blood from his eyebrow. 'We'll see.'

'You're screwed up,' Shane said.

'You don't say?'

'I'm gonna have a shower.'

Minty sipped his beer and watched Sam.

'For real, brah? Didn't know that was your thing.' He held out another beer in Sam's direction.

'Nah, I need some water.'

She'd never tried to shut down his feelings. She'd always given them space and acknowledged that they were valid. Sometimes it was helpful, sometimes it was infuriating and he'd shouted at her that if she understood she wouldn't be so calm about it, she'd be shouting too. His mum bought him a Walkman when he was eleven and couldn't sleep. Whenever he was wound up she would hand him his headphones. *Listen. Breathe.* Would she give him the same advice now? When the pain of it felt like it was shredding his skin? Would she smile in her quiet, calm way and tell him music would help?

The pain only brought shame with it. Nearly a man and crying for his mum.

In the morning the light was switched on and there were hands on his shoulders, shaking him out of his sleep.

'You. Wake up.' Lorraine's breath smelled of instant coffee and cigarette smoke.

'What?'

'Kitchen. Now.' She turned and left Sam rubbing the sleep out of his eyes. He pulled himself out of the bed, every one of his ribs making itself known. He found a T-shirt and stumbled into the kitchen. Lorraine stood, feet apart, hands on her hips, waiting for him.

'That don't happen here. Got it? Not in my house.' She jabbed her finger in the direction of the lounge room. Shane sat on the couch, watching cartoons on the television with a box of frozen fish fingers pressed to the side of his head. 'Come here, Shane.'

He gave a loud sigh and stood.

'I don't need that crap in my house anymore. You wanna fight, you find somewhere else to live. You think it's funny?'

'No,' said Sam. She kept her eyes on him and pulled up her T-shirt to show her pillowy belly. A scar ran up her side: a silvery, puckered ridge.

'You know what happened here? Glen kicked me so hard he shattered three of my ribs. Needed surgery to fish out all the bits of bone from me innards. That sound fun to you?'

'No.'

'He thought kicking the shit out of me and his kids was a good way to sort his stress out. Buggered if I'm going to let you think the same.'

'I don't.'

'Shut it. God knows I don't owe your mum much, but I owe her that.' Her eyes welled up. She turned to her eldest and pointed a polished fingernail at him. 'You? *You* should bloody know better.'

Shane gave a loud sniff and didn't apologise for anything as far as Sam could tell.

'She would be ashamed, Samuel, and you know it. That does not happen in my house. Got that?'

'Yeah.'

'I can't hear you.'

'Yes.'

'Good. Now get out of my sight.' She folded her arms and looked up at the ceiling. 'God bloody help me.'

She had let him put on shorts at least. And get his Discman. He left, head down, earphones in and rode his skateboard down the centre line of the street to the car park and the point overlooking the break. The sun was a bastard. He flicked the board up and walked barefoot across the grass until he could get a clear view of the line-up. There was Minty, lying on his board, focused on the waves. Sam's stomach was rumbling and his mouth was gritty. He walked back to the road and pushed off toward the main street. It was early. The bakery was open and nothing else. Sam felt in his pockets for loose coins. Nothing.

He felt the days lined up in front of him, each one waiting to be endured before the next. Any cognitive thought he had about his mum's funeral had been replaced by a dark static in his head which dissolved all meaning. Minty cared about nothing except the water. Sam didn't even have that.

He went to the Jewel car park and skated for a while. If he listened to Green Day loudly while he skated maybe he could pretend that he wasn't on his own, that his mates from Sydney were with him and his mum was at home. It didn't work. He didn't hear Jono come up behind him and he swore when he turned around to see him standing there. Jono was with two younger kids, each holding a skateboard.

'Sorry, man! Didn't mean to creep up on you. How's it going?'

'Yeah. Alright.'

'Whoa. What happened to your face?'

'Nothing. Fight. It's okay.'

Jono looked sceptical. 'Nothing. Sure. Hey, these are my brothers, Paul and Adam.' He kicked one of them in the leg. 'Say hello!'

They mumbled a greeting. Sam felt the gaping void beside him where he wished a sibling was. There was Minty. But they weren't brothers. Brothers were different.

'You cool if we hang here for a bit? Mum wants them out of the house. They're little psychos.'

Jono beamed at Sam as if he really were asking permission to hang out with him. Sam shrugged.

The reality was that Jono was a terrible skater. He went full throttle but stacked constantly. His little brothers were better than he was. It didn't seem to bother him. He jumped up each time and carried on. One of the brothers fell off and threw his skateboard; it flew up in the air and landed with a clatter.

'No. If you're going to be a little brat, you gotta go home,' Jono said to him. 'That's my board, man. You can't do that.'

'Whatever.'

Jono pointed to the ramp out of the car park. 'You can go, buddy.'

The kid pouted and Jono gave him a warning look. They skated for an hour before Jono told them it was time to go.

'Hey, Sam, wanna come over? We got *GoldenEye* on Nintendo. You played it before?'

Lorraine would not want him in the house. 'Yeah, okay. Thanks.'

10

The black feeling shadowed Sam as he walked with Jono up the street. As they rounded a corner and headed up the hill he looked up and noticed two girls walking ahead of them. He didn't have to see her face to recognise her; he knew her shape. She was wearing cargo pants, snug on her hips, striped singlet, hair in two little knots behind her ears.

'Stassi! Gretchen!' Jono called and they turned around. The other girl was tall and broad shouldered. She grinned at Jono and did a funny robot movement with her arms.

'Hey Jon-o, how's it go-ing,' she said in a robot voice. She cracked up and glanced at Sam. 'You know how everyone always asks the same questions? Cyborg-style?' His failure to smile didn't deter her; she dismissed him with a wave of her hand and turned back to Jono. 'Who's Mr Serious?'

Sam was ultra aware of Speedo Girl who was standing a metre away from him. He didn't know whether she was Stassi or Gretchen. He couldn't look at her. This fact was one small glimmer, a tiny indicator that he had not lost all human feeling.

'This is Sam. He's Minty Booner's cousin,' Jono said.

'*Ohhh* too cool then,' the tall one said. 'Figures. Doesn't like robots.'

'He's alright.'

'Stassi.' She thrust her hand out. 'Pleased to meet you.'

He smiled grimly and shook Stassi's hand. Gretchen. Her name was Gretchen. Stassi watched him and laughed. 'Oh yeah. You're a cool one. We're nerds, so feel free to ignore us. How old are you? You look, like thirty-two or something.'

'Stass, don't be weird,' said Gretchen.

'I'm just asking. Hey, Jono, you see *The X-Files* last night?'

Jono's brothers were kicking a can back and forth in the gutter. He jerked his head up the hill and told them to go home. They rolled their eyes and obeyed. 'Yeah! How good was it!'

Sam didn't watch *The X-Files*. From the look on her face, neither did Gretchen. In his old life, Sam was good with girls: smooth, charming, he'd even made a few laugh. But he was only good with girls he was moderately attracted to. He wasn't moderately attracted to Gretchen. He thought she was really cute when he'd seen her before, but now that she was in close proximity, the dial was in the red. He didn't have to talk to her to know that. But the static had closed in. He remembered the ever expanding black hole within him, sucking in all life, all meaning. Did he even care about the cute girl with curly hair and dimples and a slither of bare skin between the bottom of her tank top and the waistband of her pants?

'So … you live around here, Sam?'

95

He looked at her but he couldn't smile, he just stared. She had a nose piercing. He hadn't seen that before. It looked so good it was ridiculous. He still hadn't smiled. She kept her smile but it changed from friendly to confused and then went away altogether. Her cheeks flushed rosy pink, showing up the caramel freckles across her nose.

'Living with Minty for a bit.'

'Oh. Cool.'

Silence.

'You?'

'Yeah! Yeah, I live here. Over near the beach. Didn't I ... haven't I met you?'

Now he was blushing.

'You're the guy that practically ripped your arm off and then got up and powered on.' She craned her neck forward and peered at his elbow. 'They reattached it? Did a good job. You can hardly tell. Did you need a blood transfusion?'

'No. Luckily ... how's it going?' he asked. Not great but not creepy.

'Okay. Good. I mean, it's holidays, so it's hard not to be good in holidays, I guess. Unless you're having a really bad holiday. That's possible. You?'

'I'm having a bad holiday.'

She nodded but didn't ask. He liked that about her. 'I'm not really an *X-Files* fan.' She glanced at Jono and Stassi and scrunched up her nose.

'Me neither.' He should make a joke.

'I just don't care about sci-fi,' she said. 'You can't say that to sci-fi people though, they think it means you are fundamentally flawed as a person. It's like a religion that I'm not deep enough to want to understand. I'm a sci-fi heathen. I mean, I'm friends with Stassi and Jono, so obviously they have come to accept that I don't like sci-fi …' she caught herself and trailed off.

'That's generous of them.' Almost a joke. Jono and Stassi had stopped talking. Stassi narrowed her eyes at Sam.

'Don't even think about it, punk,' she said.

Did she have no filter at all between her brain and her mouth?

'What?' It came out more aggressive than he intended.

'Whoa! Sorry. Did I, like, ruin your vibe or something?' She said 'like, ruin your vibe' in a mock-stoner voice. Girls this nerdy were usually shy. Shyness wasn't a factor Stassi had to deal with.

'Sam's cool, Stass,' said Jono. 'Don't worry.'

'Oh, we know he's *cool*. He's Minty Booner's cousin, aren't you, Cool Sam?'

'I'm mates with Minty, too,' Jono protested.

'You're mates in that you've known him since primary school and he comes over whenever he wants to play Nintendo.'

Gretchen didn't say anything; she looked at the pavement.

Stassi rolled her eyes. 'Okay, okay. I'll shut up, whatever. See you, Jono.' She glared at Sam, held up two fingers, pointed them at her eyes then back at Sam. 'I'm watching you.' She spoke in a Russian accent. Gretchen laughed and pulled her away by the arm.

'What's her problem?' Sam asked.

'Well, she's Stassi, so she's got that to contend with.'

*

Jono's house was up on the escarpment, a two-storey brick place nestled in a cul-de-sac among tall eucalypts. It was the kind of house people lived in on television. They had to step over piles of shoes all over the front porch. Sam followed Jono's lead and took his off, adding them to the long line by the front door. The entrance hall was decorated in the country cottage style his mum had always hated, with apricot walls and fussy printed friezes lining the skirting boards. A formal family portrait that looked like a class photo hung on the wall.

'I've got nine younger brothers,' Jono said. 'Mum and Dad are like, extreme Roman Catholics. Lucky the Pope isn't into terrorism, 'cause Mum would totally blow herself up for Jesus Christ.'

'Sure.'

Jono led him into the kitchen where three boys of varying sizes were fighting over a Hacky Sack. They were shouting and one of them grabbed the other by the neck. Jono behaved as if it were nothing out of the ordinary, handed Sam a packet of chips and went down some narrow stairs into the underground rumpus room. It was windowless but cooler than upstairs.

'We've got Foxtel. There's like, ten channels. Channel V's the best. They show sick stuff, hey.'

Jono talked a lot, but he wasn't tedious; he was someone who knew a freakish amount of information about obscure topics without being irritating. They played *GoldenEye* while above them the ceiling rattled with the thumping of feet. There was shouting and squealing and laughter. It was the kind of place that felt as if at any given time there was someone, somewhere, in a headlock. Sam liked being among the mayhem. There was something calming about it.

'You listen to the radio last night? They played Pearl Jam's Berlin gig from last year.' Jono spoke in a rush like he was afraid he was going to run out of time before Sam decided he was boring and left.

'Not really into Pearl Jam.'

Jono stopped playing for a moment and gawked at Sam. 'No way? Really? Shame. Don't know if I can respect you anymore. Give it time. I reckon I can convert you. You hear *No Code*? Most underrated album ever. I'll lend it to you. It's not what you expect, in a good way. What about Alice in Chains? *Dirt*?'

'It's okay.'

'C'mon, man! It's good stuff.'

'Most grungy music, I dunno, it's so dramatic, you know? "Oh, life is so hard in Seattle with my record deal and my groupies." Takes itself really seriously.'

He wanted to ask Jono if Gretchen had a boyfriend. That was wrong, wasn't it? If you had been at your mum's funeral the day before?

'Man, I wish I lived in Seattle,' Jono said 'Imagine just walking down the street, going to a club and seeing Mudhoney or someone. Soundgarden playing at your local. Here it's some Abba cover band. Sad.'

'I don't know Mudhoney's stuff.'

'What?! They are seminal. Seminal. Really important to the evolution of the Seattle scene. The Melvins?'

Sam shrugged. 'I miss Nirvana.'

'Nirvana is grunge! You said you didn't like that stuff!'

'Yeah, but they're different.'

'Ohhhh, you're one of *those* guys. Hendrix too, yeah? Jim Morrison? The thing about Nirvana is, Kurt Cobain, he hasn't made any mistakes. Wasn't around long enough.'

'Shooting himself in the head wasn't a mistake?'

'Ha, good one. I mean musically. He went straight into the canon of musician saints. It's so easy to idolise him, put his face on a T-shirt, he can do no wrong. Like Lennon. The dead can do no wrong. We automatically idolise them. Rose-coloured-glasses and all that.'

Jono obviously didn't know Sam had been at his mum's funeral the day before. Sam couldn't speak. He reloaded his gun and kicked a door down.

'Are you going into year twelve? Archer Point High?' Jono asked.

The plan was physics, chemistry, three-unit maths. A science undergrad, then further studies in meteorology. The plan belonged to someone else, the person who had a home and a mother. It now seemed laughable.

'Don't know. Can't really be stuffed with school anymore. Not much point.'

'I wanna do journalism. Gonna be a music journalist. Gotta get the HSC for that.'

'So you know Gretchen from school?'

'Yeah, man. She's super cool. I mean, I've known Stassi forever, Gretchen only came last year. Oh hey, you gotta do something for me. Get Minty to come to this gig in a few months, Shihad and Tumbleweed at the Archer Point Tavern. It's not all ages, though. I need Minty to get me in.'

'Minty can get you in?'

'That guy can do anything round here. He's the golden ticket. And he's got like, no fear. This one time, he rode a skateboard down the roof of someone's house into the swimming pool. No joke. I saw it. You always have a good time with Minty. I mean, he's mental but he's not boring.'

When Sam was growing up, his family gathered for dinner at Nana Hudson's every Saturday night. After, Sam and Minty would watch *Hey Hey It's Saturday* while the adults talked. Often, when murmurs of home time began, Minty would close his eyes and pretend to be asleep. Sam would copy him and they would listen as Nana told their mothers not to wake them, that they could stay over. They would be carried into the spare room and Minty was always genuinely asleep by the time Nana had tucked them in to the big bed. He would sleep deeper than Sam ever did. As if he couldn't sleep anywhere else and he had to catch up. There was usually a damp patch under Minty in the morning, though Sam always pretended not to notice.

Minty had clung to Sam when they were little kids. Always needing to be with him, never wanting to leave and concocting endless adventurous plans to keep Sam hooked. Sam didn't really get it – Minty had a mum of his own, and a brother. And a *dad* – one of those powerful mythical creatures that eluded Sam.

*

Minty was in the garage when Sam got home. He had it set up with weights and a session plan in Shane's sloppy handwriting was tacked to the wall. Minty sat up from the bench press, eyebrows raised. 'Sammy! Where you been, brah? Hidin' from Mum, ay? Good idea.'

'Skated for a bit. Went up to Jono's.'

'Sweet. He's a good guy, ay.'

'No surf?'

'Nah, flat as, all up and down.'

'El Niño's gonna deliver in the winter.'

'I'm amped, brah. Bring it. Patience, that's the name of the game. Shane doesn't mind 'cause it gets me in here. He's always at me about workin' out. Nah, he's got a point, ay. Everyone underestimates strength, fitness. It's important, though.' Minty stood up and motioned for Sam to give the bench a go. He adjusted the weights and lowered the bar down for Sam to hold it above his chest. Sam was bone and sinew, not much else. Minty laughed at him as he tried to push the weight up.

'If you're fit you can paddle harder, kick harder, match the wave's speed. If your core's strong, you can do more with a wave, like. And when you go under you last longer on your breath, less likely to drown. Not an issue so much in tame swell, but once you hit the big waves, you can be underwater for up to four, five minutes before you get up.'

'I don't catch big waves.'

'What I'm saying is, if you've got confidence in your body, in what it can do, then you won't freak out in the water.'

'I don't freak out in the water.'

Minty grinned. 'Everyone freaks out sometimes. Unless you're a psychopath without normal human feelings. Are you a psychopath without normal human feelings?'

'I didn't cry much at Mum's funeral.'

'Brah, that wasn't a funeral. That was like an infomercial or some shit.'

Minty was strong now, it was undeniable. He had built armour for himself.

11

The week before school was supposed to start, Minty drove Sam and Lorraine up to Sydney to pack up Sam's home. They took everything out of the back of the van so there'd be room for stuff. Sam was grateful to have Minty there because he broke the tension between Sam and Lorraine. She'd been colder with Sam since the fight with Shane; it was barely perceptible but she didn't make eye contact with him and she pressed her lips into a grimace whenever he spoke to her. Sam wondered how long she would stay dirty with him. If the silence between her and his mum was anything to go by, it was likely to be a long time. Minty was, of course, oblivious to the tension and drove in his usual relaxed state, singing along to the radio and chatting to Lorraine. Sam sat on the floor in the back and focused on the road rolling away out the back window. The plan was for Minty to drop him off at the half-pipe where he would meet Luke. They would go skate at the old haunts. Minty said it would be therapeutic. Minty and Lorraine would drive the van back south and Sam would get the last train back. It would get him home just in time for Lorraine's curfew.

*

It seemed disrespectful to his mother to pack up the apartment. The finality of it was horrible, like his life was an unaddressed package shoved in a postbox. Sam went into the 7-Eleven below the flat to get some empty cardboard boxes. The door buzzed as he walked in. It was so brightly lit inside that Sam pulled down his sunglasses from the top of his head. Music played loudly, Cliff Richard was 'Wired for Sound'. Ricky, the manager, brightened when he saw Sam.

'Sam! Good to see you. Where have you been? Holiday? I haven't seen you since Christmas.'

Sam paused and took a deep breath. Ricky watched him expectantly.

'Mum's sick, we have to move. Do you have some boxes?'

'Oh no! What's wrong? Moving? Where?'

'Not sure yet. Do you have anything we can use to pack things in?'

Ricky was the kind of guy who smiled no matter what the conversation was about.

'Yes! Yes! Here, I'll get them for you.'

He went into the storeroom and came out with a stack of flattened cardboard. Sam took them and smiled.

'Thanks. See you.'

'You come and say goodbye! And your mum! Tell her to come say goodbye!'

'Yeah, I'll come back before we go.'

Sam left knowing he wouldn't.

*

Up in the apartment they went from room to room putting things in boxes. Sam was emptying his shelves when Lorraine came in.

'Look, love, you can bring three boxes, but that's all I got room for.'

Sam looked down at the stuff at his feet: books, clothes, CDs, posters. He opened his mouth to plead his case but she had gone back into his mum's room. She came back a few moments later with an armful of his mum's textbooks.

'These yours?'

'No. Mum's. She was at uni. Just started medicine.'

Lorraine looked down at the stack of books and took a deep breath. 'I can't take 'em with us.'

'They're expensive books.'

'I know, but ... We don't need 'em, love.'

Sam gave a small nod and returned to trying to sort his own things.

Lorraine went around with Post-it notes and labelled all the furniture 'keep', 'sell' or 'dump' – the formica table they had found on the side of the road, the set of bentwood dining chairs his mum had bought at a garage sale, the tattered couch covered in a rug she had knitted. *I can knit a square or a rectangle, anything other than that and I'm stuffed.* Lorraine moved through the apartment silently sticking on notes. Sam tried to remember the very last night he had spent there, the last twenty-four hours of his life as it once was with his mum. As soon as he remembered that soft, safe feeling he wished he couldn't.

Lorraine brought his mum's jewellery box out to the kitchen table and emptied it out, picking through the shiny bits and pieces.

'That's not yours,' said Sam. He intended it to sound forceful, but he could only manage a whisper and it sounded like a plea. He breathed deeply and tried to ignore the pain in his chest, the feeling that he was plummeting from a great height, the ground rushing toward him.

Lorraine watched him, hand on her hip, like she was deciding how to respond.

'It's not nice, love. I know. It's a shame, but that's the way it is. I'm next of kin.' She opened her handbag on the table, rooted around inside and pulled out a folded piece of paper. She unfolded it and held it in front of him. The paragraph was highlighted. Lorraine turned the page and pointed her hot-pink fingernail at his mother's signature.

'She should have talked to you about it. God knows I wish she'd talked to *me* about it. But she had no health issues, she had no reason to think she'd go anytime soon. You can have what you want, but I don't know where you're going to put it all.'

She would have given him a hug if he'd wanted it. But he didn't.

'Keep the dining chairs. They're worth something.'

'They're old.'

'Mum said they were good quality.'

'I'll see if we can fit them in the back of the van.'

*

They carried boxes down and loaded up the van, along with three of the bentwood chairs. Lorraine stacked the rest of Sam's and his mum's possessions on the kerb, including the textbooks. Sam couldn't look at the pile. He put his sunglasses on and got in the van. Minty put the van in gear and looked over his shoulder to Sam.

'Where to, brah?'

'Down by the rail yard. I'll show you.'

Luke and the rest of them were already there. Like time travellers visiting Sam from a past life. They were sorry, all of them. They told him and slapped his back. They kept it brief. The half-pipe was the same. Sam knew every groove, every chip, every spray-painted mark. It was a thumbprint linking him back to the scene; it made his time in the water with Minty feel like a flimsy alibi. For the first couple of hours he felt different on the board to the way he used to. There were days in the past when the sensation had been like he was on tracks almost, like he was floating above the surface yet glued to it, like he could do no wrong. Now he felt out of rhythm and like every eye was on him even though it wasn't.

The talk eluded him as well. Every exchange was a thread of conversation woven over the past month. Sam couldn't pick any of it up. He didn't know the cues, he didn't get the punchlines. When the talk did swerve into familiar territory – and someone made a crack about Sam's suspension from school – he resented it.

It had felt like the worst thing in the world, the principal phoning his mum and telling her he wasn't welcome back there for the rest of term. On the outside he had taken the piss – extended holiday! As if he was spending the time having a laugh instead of waiting in an empty house watching daytime television and counting down the hours until his mates were free from class. As if he wasn't stressing about the effect it might have on his HSC, on his plans, on the grand dreams he had for himself. But he'd never been able to cop discipline like other kids. He always felt like he'd let everyone down. One sharp warning from his kindy teacher and he would be fighting back tears.

His mum'd always told him he needed to get perspective and learn that little problems were just that, not worth stressing over, not worth the angst.

He had perspective now. She'd given it to him.

After dark he rode his board to the train station. Luke and he said 'see ya' to each other and Sam thought about it on the train south. *See you.*

He wouldn't. He knew he probably never would again. He would rip the band-aid clean off.

12

The sky was bigger here than in Sydney. It was a show-off. This morning it rippled with grey and muted light, a majestic, sweeping expanse of cloud above. In the month since he'd arrived in Archer Point, Sam had been in the surf almost every time Minty was. He was the one doing the shadowing these days. Although, when Shane had driven Minty to a comp down south last week, Minty had asked Sam to stay behind. It made him too nervous, he said, if anyone other than Shane was there. When Sam had asked him afterwards how he'd done, Minty muttered that he'd come third and didn't want to say any more about it.

Minty urged him to use the weights and Sam felt his physicality changing. He doubted it was enough for anyone else to notice, but he felt different in himself. His feet were toughening up to the bitumen and he was easier with the board in and out of the water. He was more at home out the back in the line-up, behind the break with who knows what swimming around beneath the board.

The break off the point wasn't crowded. There were usually

only about ten of them in the water – more on the weekend. Minty said that in Sydney, at the good breaks, it was that crowded that you couldn't get a wave because there was no room. Out here you had to be committed enough to paddle all the way out and around the headland, or have the balls to jump in over the rocks. Minty said it kept most holiday surfers away. The locals all knew each other. Ruby was the only girl and she was more aggressive than any of them; she would verbally abuse anyone who remotely got in her way or looked like they were perhaps thinking of dropping in. There was always talk out the back, ribbing, sledging. Sam sat back and watched. The flawless grace of Minty on the water never dulled and Sam remained struck by the transformative ability of a piece of fibreglass to take an inarticulate, hulking lump of a guy and turn him into a vision of fluid beauty.

Sam fell into a pattern without making a conscious decision. Out of the water he was messed up, he had turned every good thing he had to shit. In the water he was Minty Booner's cousin and he would take on any wave that rose up against him. Recklessness or measured risk – the hazy space in-between was solace.

The more Sam went out in the water the more he felt the divide between the surf and the land. The ocean was like a parallel dimension, with its own laws of gravity, its own time; it felt like nothing that mattered on land mattered in the water and vice versa. Every time Sam caught a wave he felt the phenomenon of time slowing; nothing else in his mind, nothing, not even the snapshot of his mum lying unconscious in his arms, head lolling back. Or Pop Hudson dead on the grass. There was nothing at all except him and the velocity of the water. That same clear feeling he used to get during a fight. Something cleansed. Maybe, he thought, that was why Minty's heart wasn't completely into competing. What he did in the water during a competition could impact the direction his life took. The two dimensions overlapped.

Like when they were small and Minty would beg not to go home and whisper to Nana that he wanted to stay at her house forever.

Sam was learning that there was nothing, nothing at all, like walking up the beach – salt water trickling down his back, breath heaving in and out, limbs aching – and stopping to turn and look back at where he'd been. There was nothing like watching the horizon, his skin cool from the water, sun warming his face and shoulders.

That morning Sam had already got two waves, scrambling to his feet to ride both of them before they closed out. The next came and Minty shouted at him to take it. He paddled in, feeling the sensation of the wave lifting him up. He was up quicker this time and had enough presence of mind in the short moments to push his weight on the back foot so he was driving the board forward. The wave built and built behind him and the next thing he knew he was two storeys in the air with the simultaneous realisation that he was both slamming the biggest wave he'd ever had and about to be crushed beneath it. He imagined that the feeling as it dumped him was like standing on a mountainside during an avalanche. He thudded downwards and the water folded him into its fist, knocking all the breath from his lungs, pushing him under until his chin caught on the sandy bed below. A couple of metres to the south and it would have been the craggy rock of the reef, a broken jaw or worse. The whitewater surged in front his eyes and in the lengthening seconds he was reminded of the time Shane held him under the water in a spa at the Bankstown Leisure Centre. He came up, salt scorching his throat and nasal passages. The air thudded in violent gasps into his lungs. The next wave came and he had just enough presence of mind to take a deep breath and dive under it. When he came back up he clambered back onto the board like it was a life raft. Somehow he made it to shore. On the sand, he doubled over, hands on his knees, hauling the air into his lungs. Eventually he picked up his board and headed toward the concourse. He needed to get water into him, the drinkable kind.

The beach was crowded with people sucking the most from the day. They milled over the white-hot concrete: ice-creams, dogs, bikes, roller-blades, skateboards, naked tantruming toddlers, stray grease-blotted sheets of butcher's paper and shrivelled wedges of lemon, tomato sauce squeezies. The ocean pool was chockers with people, bombing in the recreation lane, slapping sloppy freestyle up and down the fast lane. There was a girl in a black one-piece doing elegant, honed strokes. It was Gretchen, he was sure of it. Kicking steadily she overtook the sloppers: stroke, stroke, stroke, breathe, repeat. Her ponytail trailed along the line of her spine, water sliding over the curve of her neat bum as it swayed side to side through the water. A tumble turn at the end and she was under, surging dolphin kicks then up and back into the rhythm of the stroke, metronome steadiness. He unzipped the wetsuit and pulled his arms free, rolled it to his waist as he watched her. Her hand slapped the end of the lane, no more than four metres from where he stood. He pretended to be watching the surf, but in his peripheral vision he saw her pull black goggles from her head and drop them onto the pool deck. Fingertips gripping the concrete stucco, she arched her back, head bowed, stretching the length of her spine. Palms down on the concrete, she sprang out of the water, turning to sit on the edge. With her legs dangling in the water she reached around behind her back and stretched out her shoulders. Sam crossed his arms in the hope it would make him look more toned rather than skinny. He watched the water and she stood up, pulled her Speedos at the bum, slicked the water from her hair and walked off toward the bench seats where her towel was.

There were change rooms near the seats. And bubblers. She vanished into a change room and Sam gathered himself and wandered over. It was quieter over there in the shade. He took a long slug of cool water from the bubbler, straightened and began the walk back toward the point, right at the moment Gretchen came out of the change room, directly in front of him. He was too slow to avert his eyes as she looked up. She was in cut-off shorts and a faded 'Zero' T-shirt, earphones in, a canvas bag over her shoulder. He stopped dead in the most awkward way possible.

'Oh,' she said, taking the moment to process that she knew him and should probably acknowledge the fact. She pulled an earbud from one ear. 'It's you. I mean, shit. Sorry. Hi.' She didn't look or sound like the kind of girl who said the word 'shit' a whole lot. It was adorable.

'Hi.' *Don't rush off because you're piss weak.* 'How's it going?'

'Good. Just went for a swim. Obviously. I wasn't just lurking around in the change rooms. Haha!' She seemed stunned at herself, looking around, anywhere but at him. In the silence that followed he could hear the tinny sound of the music pulsing from her earphones. Billy Corgan singing that he'd tear his heart out. 'Um, you?'

'Yeah. Surf. Got dumped. By a wave. Like, surfing.'

'Oh no!'

'It's okay.' He could put his hand on her waist, ease her against the wall and kiss her. If he was a character in a movie that is what he would do. But he was fumbling and hopeless in front of her, heart thudding in his chest like a twelve-year-old in front of a swimsuit model. Why? She wasn't in-your-face hot like other girls. There was something more understated about her – the round, perfect peal of a bell struck in a dark room.

'Oh. Sure. Well …'

He didn't move. He should move. He was staring at her. She had sherbert-pink lips, a slight gap in-between her two front teeth.

'See you round,' he said.

'Yep. Sure. Okay. Yep. Bye!'

'Bye.' He turned. 'Wait. You going to the party?'

'Tonight?'

'Yeah.'

'That's not really my kind of thing.'

'You should come.'

'I don't really hang out with those people.'

'But you're friends with Jono?'

'Hmm, yeah, but Jono's like Switzerland. He's neutral territory. Everyone else there is all like, you know, the surfer crew. I'm not really—'

'You should come.'

'Maybe.'

'Maybe then.'

A slow smile. 'Well, see you.'

13

Sam had the piece of paper Nana had given him. If Lorraine was grumpy or there was nothing in the cupboard for breakfast, or he had a bad night on the camp bed, he thought about calling her.

He wasn't expecting Nana to be waiting for him in the car park on the point. It was late afternoon, the air so warm that his hair was dry by the time he had walked up the hill from the beach. She was standing on the gravel, leaning on the door of her car, surrounded by utes and bombs and guys talking about the waves. She looked more comfortable than he would imagine most ladies in their sixties would. She was wearing gym gear, like she'd just come from aerobics class, her thin arms bare and bronzed. She wore a gold chain with a little love heart pendant, which she held between her thumb and forefinger and ran back and forth on the chain. It was the kind of fidgeting that she would have scolded them for as kids.

'Samuel?'

'What are you doing here?'

'I came to talk to you. Thought you might be in the surf with Minty.'

'What do you want?'

She looked like she was going to tell him off for being rude, but thought better of it.

'Can I buy you a milkshake?' She resembled his mother more now than the nana he remembered.

'Did you come all the way from Port Macquarie?'

'Can I buy you a milkshake? Caramel? You used to love a caramel milkshake.'

'Yeah. I remember. You and Pop used to take me to the milkbar for one, before you pissed off and Pop died alone in his effing garden.' He would have never spoken to her like that before; maybe Lorraine was rubbing off on him. He wanted to swear, but that was as far as he could go.

'That's fair. I understand, love. But I really think we need to have a talk.'

Sam took a deep breath. 'Five minutes. Don't want a milkshake.'

'Right. Well, ah … Do you want to sit down?' She indicated in the direction of a picnic table on the grass.

'Whatever.'

He followed her and they sat on opposite sides of the table. She twisted the rings on her fingers as she spoke.

'Is Lorraine looking after you?'

Sam shrugged. The silence sat awkwardly between them.

'Darlin', I had my reasons. You know that.'

'Everyone thought you were dead.'

'No one thought I was dead.'

'How would you know?'

'I told you. It was Lorraine, mostly. She wouldn't leave that man and it was doing me in, the worry. I couldn't be around it anymore. And, more than that. I couldn't, I couldn't … Your pop wasn't an easy man to live with. You wouldn't understand, love.'

'It's not Pop's fault. You left.'

She seemed to be collecting her thoughts. She reached out to touch his hand and he moved it away.

'I wasn't … I was depressed. But people of my generation, we don't get depressed, we just get on with it. I didn't want to get on with it. I didn't plan it. I was home one afternoon and he was in the garden as bloody usual. "Let's go to the club for tea," he yelled through the door. "Iron my slacks, would you?" He didn't even say please. That was it.' She shook her head. 'Lorraine had ignored my calls all day. It was enough. I picked up my handbag and walked out the door.'

''Cause you didn't want to go to the club for dinner?'

'It was more than that, love.'

Sam looked out across the water to where the last remaining handful of surfers, Ruby and Minty included, bobbed like seals.

'But you used to … make jam and read the bible.'

'I still make jam and read the bible. I've also been to Budapest and Florence and Morocco.'

'Where did you get the money from?'

'Always had access to the accounts. Just because I never used them before doesn't mean I didn't know how to. The thing you have to understand about your grandfather is that his reputation meant more to him than anything else. *Anything.'*

Sam sat and stared ahead.

'He would never tell the bank that he didn't want his wife using the account because she'd done a bolt. He cared more about what a stranger in a bank thought of him than his own family. And I think that he did have decency. He wouldn't leave me out there with nothing.'

Sam felt the build of tension in his chest like the rise of a wave in front of him. 'What the fuck do you know about decency?' He was on his feet. He wanted to grab the edge of the table and flip it over. 'You left us all! You left Mum! Pop died and she didn't have anyone, no one.' He stabbed his finger at his chest. 'Except me, I was the only one left for her and I was ten. Don't talk to me about fucking decency! Now she's dead. She's DEAD. I have a dead mum. I was all alone with her in the hospital. I was holding her hand when she died. Where the hell were you?!'

'Samuel.'

He picked up Minty's board and slammed the nose down onto the ground over and over, the coursing flood of hurt streaming through his veins, bursting through his sinew and muscle. He saw his grandmother stand up and steady herself against the table, flinching at him and his rage. He saw his cousin's broken surfboard in his hands. The cousin who was the only person he belonged to in the whole world. Tears began their descent down his cheeks and he was furious at them too. He tossed the broken board on the ground and walked away from it all.

*

Sam lay on his back on the camp bed and stared up at the ceiling waiting for the static fuzz to dissipate. Jeff sang about not wanting to step on the cracks for fear of hurting his mother, about being sucked into a nightmare and pulled under. Then all restraint was lost and the guitar sounded more like a chainsaw, the screaming crescendo of sound unleashed before stopping with the same brutal suddenness as it started. It was too much. Sam stopped the Discman, pulled his headphones off and flicked the radio on. He listened to song after song until time warped and stretched and stopped meaning anything at all.

Sam replayed the conversation with Nana, making alterations in his imagination until the futility of it slapped him like a rebuke. He tried to push it from his mind and focus on the radio. They were like family, the presenters – their voices so familiar and reassuring that Sam could almost pretend that his world hadn't dissolved around him and left him in freefall. The news rolled around and, as a force of habit, Sam flicked the dial over to the AM station to catch the weather report. He listened intently to the information about high pressure fronts and wind direction, currents and tidal times. There was a time when he was younger and would make notes of it all in a little weather journal, later performing the weather report to his amused mother as she cooked their dinner in the kitchen. The memory cut into him with a sudden, gasping savageness.

The tape deck had been a Christmas present from Nana and Pop Hudson that last Christmas before Nana disappeared and Pop died. It must have been 1989 or 1990. It was grey with a red stripe across the front, under the dials. It was a double one, so you could copy tapes. They gave him three tapes for Christmas, the first ones he'd ever owned. Two he had requested: AC/DC and Guns N' Roses. The third was one Nana and Pop had chosen: Kenny Rogers.

Pop had looked at the tapes after Sam unwrapped them, holding them up and peering over his glasses. 'Don't they make records anymore?'

'You can still get records, Pop. But tapes are better.'

'Is that right?'

'Yeah.'

He pulled the pamphlet out and unfolded it. 'They look like a bunch of women with their hair all long. Why are you listening to this rubbish?'

Nana looked over his shoulder. 'It's the fashion, Frank. You wouldn't understand.'

'Well, they need a haircut.'

'They broke the mould when they made you, Frank.'

Sam thought she meant it with affection.

Lorraine, Minty and Shane had been there. Minty's dad wasn't. Sam scanned his memories for signs of the violence that had been hidden just below the surface of the Booners. He thought of the time Shane had snapped his skateboard. He hadn't read anything into it other than Shane was a tool.

Sam did remember his mum having tense phone conversations with Lorraine, where the phrase, 'You have to get them out of there' was repeated. Sam always thought she was talking about the school his cousins went to.

Minty pushed his head through the curtain. 'Waddya do to my board?' His tone was serious, but there was a glint in his eye.

'Shit, man. Sorry about that.'

'S'cool. It was ancient. I'll give you another one, but you can't do it again.'

'Sure. Sorry.'

'Goin' up to Rickard's. Party time, brah. School starts Monday.'

14

A bonfire plumed on the sand. Someone's hatchback was parked on the grass at the edge of the reserve, doors open, music booming – Chili Peppers, 'Suck My Kiss'. There were eskys and bare chests and the guttural hoot of laughter that comes after beers. Sam scanned the faces. There were lots he recognised. No Gretchen. Minty and his mates greeted each other by slapping their palms and grasping each other's wrists in a complex well-practised manoeuvre that made anyone watching feel like an absolute outsider – it was a combination lock of a gesture, either you knew it or you didn't and Sam didn't. But he was Minty's cousin.

'Wassup,' said Minty. 'Pumpin' this arvo.'

'Yeah. Epic …'

And it went on, the retelling of various waves and wipeouts, laughter and back slapping as the waves became bigger and bigger and each wipeout more spectacular. Sam was growing accustomed to it. He knew when to laugh (whenever Minty did) and when to keep quiet (most of the time). Minty talked and grinned and nursed his longneck. Girls wandered over, bikini tops, tiny skirts. They fawned over Minty. One skinny girl with bleached hair and too much black eyeliner whispered in Minty's ear and he rubbed a palm under the tie at the back of her bikini. Sam looked up the beach toward the other clusters of people. Ruby was sitting on her own, arms slung over her knees. She took swigs from a bottle of beer that dangled by its neck from her fingertips, and kept glancing up the beach toward Minty. A southerly whipped up the sand, turning the balmy twilight chilly. Why was he disappointed that Gretchen wasn't there? Why did he even like her? *Did* he like her? He ran through all the reasons he shouldn't care that she wasn't there – he barely knew her, and she was pretty but she really wasn't incredible to look at. She was kind of plain, like a caramel milkshake on a warm summer afternoon, creamy and smooth and delicious. With hair like a fairytale and pale eyes.

It wasn't working.

Gretchen would be with someone better than him. Maybe the kind of guy he might have been able to become if everything hadn't fallen apart. There was talk of school among those who were going back and Sam knew he wasn't going to be one of them. Pulling himself out of the hole he was in required reserves he didn't have and wasn't sure he would ever have again. No, Gretchen would end up with someone stronger than him. Someone who knew who they were. A good guy. 'A lovely boy.' A guy who opened doors and knew his manners and was intelligent and smart and knew how to slow dance and didn't snap when somone said the wrong words. A guy who had a job and did some fancy double-major degree like biomedical engineering and human rights law with a sub-major in owning an Audi. A guy who wasn't scared of the world.

And himself.

Someone lit up a coconut and it was tossed back and forth among hoots of laughter and shrieks from the bikini girls. Sam drifted away from the war stories and headed over to Ruby. He dropped his bum in the sand beside her.

'How's it goin'?'

She tilted her head back and puffed smoke rings. They hovered like abandoned halos before disappearing in the wind. 'Alright. You?'

'Alright.'

'Let me guess, they're talking about what hot shit they are and how amaaaaazing the swell was this arvo.'

'You got it.'

She scoffed and took another swig of beer. 'It wasn't amazing. It was okay. Any food over there?' Ruby asked.

'Nah.'

'There's supposed to be pizza. And what the hell is this shit they're listening to?'

'Um, it's the Chili Peppers.'

'I'm tellin' ya, no good music since 1978.'

'Really?'

'Really.'

'No offence, but you're totally wrong. There is some seriously good music—'

'You think this is good music?'

'No, yeah, but there's other stuff too. Good stuff. Have you heard Jeff Buckley? Man, that guy is incredible.'

'Yeah, I heard him.'

'And?'

Ruby took a swig of beer. 'And Robert Plant is the only singer worth listening to.'

'Ruby, no way.'

'Way.'

Near the fire Minty was entangled with the bleached-hair girl who appeared to be taking the Chili Peppers' recommendation. Ruby glowered at them.

'Maddie Clark, Minty? I mean really. She is such a little slut. He is so predictable. Sorry, I know he's your cousin, but for fuck's sake.'

'Do you care?'

'I don't care 'cept for the fact that he is an absolute, total cliché. I mean, what's Minty gonna be doing in ten years, you reckon? He's gonna be here, bloated and broke, surfing when he's not unconscious. Oh, and he'll do it better than anyone else, but he'll be a wash-up.'

'He's competing, but. He won the Pro Junior. He could go anywhere.'

'You seen the guys he's up against? They got coaches and physios and … Kelly Slater's got a bloody nutritionist. What's Minty got? Shane with his camcorder telling him not to eat Twisties for breakfast.'

'Sounds like you don't want him to make it.'

Ruby looked like she might punch Sam in the face.

'I want him to make it. But at the moment he's too scared of what everybody thinks. He wants to be the good guy, the guy everyone loves. Everything went his way at the Pro Junior. Conditions were good, he got the right waves, he was in a good headspace 'cause me and him … whatever. It all went the right way for him. It's not gonna be like that every time. If he wants to win, to be consistent, he needs to focus and stop being Mr Nice Guy to everyone he meets.'

'Why don't you compete? Couldn't you make some cash?'

'Not as much as if I had a dick. I did for a bit, a coupla years ago. It's boring, all the shit that goes along with it. I don't wanna spend my life with people who can't talk about anything other than how big their balls are.'

'So you don't think the conversation's good enough?'

'You know what I mean. It's tedious. I'm gonna get the HSC. Do uni. Move. You want something, you gotta get it for yourself. Sit around and expect to get handed it all on a silver platter,' she shook her head, 'you're in for a rude shock. I reckon you have a choice: you can listen to the radio and think Jeff fuckin' Buckley is singin' about you or you can listen and know that he's not and he never will be and the chances of anyone ever singing about you are tiny and the chances of *your* song being played on the radio are smaller still.'

'Um, I don't follow.'

'I'm saying you have to be realistic. I'm realistic.'

'I don't think Jeff Buckley is singing about me.'

'You're not a girl.'

'Good observation.'

She took a swig of the beer and pointed her index finger at Sam. 'No, even worse! You think he's singing *for* you. You think you're him. That's pathetic.'

'Um, okay. Thanks for that.'

'No, I get into uni in Sydney and I'm outta here. This town's a terminal illness, I'm tellin' you.'

'Have you always lived here?'

'Since I was two. That's when I was adopted. Don't remember anything before that.'

'So, you don't know anything about your parents?'

Ruby held out her forearm, wrist up, in front of Sam. 'What's that tell you?'

'Um. You have arms?'

'No, dickhead.' She pointed at her skin. 'I ain't vanilla, that's for sure.'

'Oh. Right. Do you know where your parents are from?'

'My *mum,* like, my adopted mum, told me she thinks they're like Indian or Bangladeshi or somethin' but my birth certificate says my mother was born in Toomelah, Boggabilla.'

'Boggabilla?'

'Kinda near Moree. How many Indians you reckon live in Boggabilla?'

'Um.'

'None. Toomelah's an Indigenous community.'

'You're Aboriginal?'

Ruby let out a heavy sigh. 'Maybe. There's this woman lives around here, old Aboriginal woman, she hassles me all the time. Reckons I need to know who my family is.'

'You talked to Minty about this?'

'Minty? Minty reckons it's irrelevant. Says it doesn't matter who your parents are, what they've done, it's got nothin' to do with you and you make yourself up, like. He bloody wishes.'

Sam watched two figures nearing the beach: Gretchen and Stassi. They didn't belong, you could see it in the way they held themselves. They were wearing shoes for a start. Gretchen was in a little floral dress that clung to her waist and flared at her hips. And a pair of Chuck Taylor's.

Ruby was watching Minty eating Maddie Clark's face. 'Stuff this. I'm gonna find some food.' She got to her feet and dropped the bottle in the sand.

'See ya,' said Sam, but she didn't seem to hear him.

Jono had met up with Gretchen and Stassi. He waved to Sam and watched Ruby walking away.

'How's it going, Sam?'

'Alright. Hi,' Sam said in the vague direction of Gretchen.

Minty had pulled away from Maddie and wandered over. Stassi and Gretchen looked at him and then each other. Stassi rolled her eyes and shook her head.

'Jono! What's happening?'

'Not much.'

'I'm going over here,' said Stassi and turned away from the group. Gretchen hesitated a moment before following her. Jono and Minty were talking about a guy Sam didn't know. Someone had lit up another coconut. More people arrived; Sam didn't know any of them. Gretchen and Stassi stood awkwardly. They were looking around like they were planning their evacuation route. Sam sipped the beer and flicked through a mental Rolodex of possible conversation subjects. He came up with nothing. Gretchen looked over at him and he felt his neck burn; he looked away like he hadn't noticed her. It was easier. Then Gretchen and Stassi turned and started walking away. Other than running after her there was nothing he could do.

When most of the others had drifted away and Minty's closest mates were the only ones left, they gathered around the fire on the sand. Ruby had returned, though she sat with a disgruntled expression and looked away every time Minty glanced in her direction. Like she was only there to demonstrate to Minty how little she thought of him.

'Gonna be blown out tomorrow. Grovelly as,' said Shane. 'Might get in an hour at dawn patrol, but it'll go to shit quick. Same all the way up and down.'

Sam cleared his throat. 'You wanna go further south. Nari Bay.'

The group fell silent. No one ever contradicted anything Shane said; he was treated like an oracle of the ocean, delivering prophecies to his observant and reverent followers. Also, no one ever expected Sam to open his mouth.

Shane laughed. 'Nari Bay? Always dead. You gonna go for a paddle, buddy? Get your pool pony out?'

'There's gonna be a northerly wind and a north-east current,' Sam said. 'High tide, 7 am. It'll blow out here, but I looked on the map and Nari will be sheltered, but you'll have the current building just off the point there. Should be good waves.' Sam took a swig of his drink.

Silence.

'Who are you? The fuckin' weatherman?' Shane asked.

'Something like that.'

Minty looked from Shane to Sam and back again. Someone let out a large belch, punctuating the silence.

Ruby pushed her tongue into her cheek watching Sam. 'Should listen to him, Booner. You might learn something.'

Shane flicked her the finger.

'Nari it is,' Minty said.

Shane looked like he was going to be sick. 'You're kidding.'

'Nah, Sam's smart, brah. He's knows about this shit. I'm going to Nari. You should come.'

Walking back to the house, Minty and Ruby were up ahead and Shane sidled up to Sam, just like Sam knew he would.

'I don't give a shit if you're our cousin. You're a fucking kook.' He seemed to be holding his head up higher than usual, trying to accentuate the little bit of height he had over Sam. 'You better be right about tomorrow, kook. 'Cause if we drive all that way and it's mush ...'

'What?'

'I'll have your balls. That's what. You little shit.'

'I'm really scared.'

'You should be. Minty's treating you like you're a lost dog. You might be living in my house, but don't go pissing on my turf. You're not welcome here.'

Shane walked off, turning his head to spit back in Sam's direction.

15

Minty shook him awake, grinning. The room was still in darkness.

'You coming, Sammy? Nari Bay? This is your call, man, you gotta come see if she delivers.' Minty's ropey shape seemed to fill the room as he jiggled his weight side to side, unable to keep still. 'I've got another board for you. Just don't smash it up, ay.'

Sam rubbed his face up and down with his palms, trying to get some feeling in it. 'What's the wind doing?'

'Dunno, blowing.'

'Which way?'

'Ummm.' Minty jogged out of the room and Sam heard the back door whine. Minty returned. 'North.'

'And the point's a wash-out?'

'Yeah. It's crap. Already had a look. You reckon Nari?'

'Yep.' Sam looked at his watch. 4.50 am. 'Tide'll start to turn in half an hour.'

Minty whooped and Lorraine yelled down the hall for him to shut up.

*

Shane was already in the van, a glower on his face that he'd specially prepared for Sam. He leaned out the window and thumped the door.

'You better be right, kook. Fuckin' early for mush.'

Minty handed Sam a packet of Doritos. 'Breakfast. Go by Ruby's, ay,' he said. Shane nodded.

She wedged her board and a wetsuit into the back of the van and sat on the floor with Sam between the shelves of electrician's gear. 'So, this is your call, is it?' she said.

'Yeah.'

'I don't wanna spend all day driving around for a break. Like, just go down the road to Myrtle. It'll be little but there'll be waves.'

'It's worth the drive.'

'It better be.'

'Oath,' said Shane.

'Are you good for it?'

'He's good for it,' said Minty.

They drove along the highway. On the left, when the grassy hills dipped, they saw snatches of the sunrise over the ocean. Shane yelled over the sound of the wind whipping through the cab. He talked to Minty about technique and picking his moment, patience and rhythm. He sounded like a particularly bogan choreographer.

'You can take any of 'em,' Shane yelled. 'You got something none of them have: style, like. You gotta chill, but. You tense up. When you're not thinking about it, it happens, every time. You're a waterman. It's natural. You gotta capitalise on that, brah. You gotta build on it. You got the balls, brah. You can take it.'

'All about the balls, isn't it, Shane?' said Ruby.

'Yeah, it is. That's why he's goin' all the way and you're working in a bakery.'

'Fuck you.'

'Right back at you, sweetheart.'

'If you're relying on someone's mythical balls to win the World Title, you got a problem.'

'I got a problem with you, that's 'bout it.'

'Shhhh, shhhh,' Minty made a pressing down motion with his hands. 'We're all friends here, yeah? We're goin' for a surf. It's all good.'

'I'm saying,' said Shane. 'That you put your mind to it, you can go all the way.'

'I don't know, brah. I just hate it when people are watching. It's like you got everyone on the beach making perfect decisions about which wave I should take or shouldn't take. It's alright for them, they're not out there under the pressure, you know? It stops being about the waves. It's something else … You know, Laird Hamilton caught a forty-five footer at Waimea last month? That's fourteen metres. Picture that, brah. That's what it's about, you know.'

'Tow-in, but.'

'Still. Anyone can do some fancy shit on a six-foot wave. There's nothing to lose. But that … That's the real thing. I never even seen a wave that big in the flesh, to *ride it*. Brah, it would be like climbing Everest.'

'Who's Laird Hamilton?' Sam asked.

Shane glanced into the back with a look of disgust. 'Only the best big-wave surfer in the world, dickwad. That guy has balls of steel.'

'Or,' offered Ruby. 'He's another jock who can't stop talking about his balls. You're all so obsessed with one another's balls, you should—'

'You can get out of the van if you want,' said Shane.

'So you can all make out?'

Shane swung the steering wheel and the van skidded onto gravel. 'Stuff this. Out!'

'Shane, brah,' Minty tried to placate him. 'She's just tryin' to get a rise out of you.'

'I'd have to be Laird Hamilton to get a rise out of him.'

'You bitch.'

'Ruby. Not helping. Shut up, yeah? Shane, you can't leave her on the side of the road, brah. You'll have to leave me too. Come on, we gotta hustle.'

Shane said something under his breath and accelerated back on to the highway. 'Your problem, Mint, is you're Mr Nice Guy. You're everyone's buddy, everyone's friend. You gotta go out there to kill.'

'I just wanna have a good time.'

'Well, you gotta work out whether you're there to have a good time or there to win.' He poked a finger toward Minty's forehead. 'What's in there? Before a comp? You gotta get psyched. I want you zoned, Minty. You win a big comp like Cronulla, you got an open door to the national titles. You place there and you're on the World Qualifying Circuit.

You get paid by Rip Curl, Quiksilver, whoever, to compete. They pay your way if you're good enough. You're good enough. You just gotta get your head straight and show 'em when it counts.'

Minty looked out the window, not answering. Shane pointed a thumb back to where Ruby was. 'She's a bitch but she won everything she entered 'cause she doesn't give a stuff about anything else or what anyone thinks.'

'Wow. That sounds like a compliment, Shane.'

'You competed with girls. If I competed with girls I'd win too.'

'That's bullshit and you know it.'

They drove for another half hour in silence. Then Shane turned off the highway and they snaked through treeless flat streets lined with fibro cottages. The water opened out in front of them and Shane pulled into a dirt car park. The sun was up and the sky was clear milky blue. Waves rolled like corduroy across the sparkling bay.

'Whoo! We gotta break. You paid it, Sammy,' Minty shouted. He swung out of the van and stepped into his wetsuit. Shane didn't congratulate Sam or acknowledge him. He stretched, burped loudly and got out of the van.

'You got lucky, weather boy. You should be cheering,' said Ruby.

'This is my cheering face.'

It was worth the drive and the early start. Out beyond the break the early sun splashed golden light on the turquoise water and out there, on the waves, Sam forgot himself. Forgot everything.

Shane had to work in the afternoon, so he dropped them at the chicken shop where they sprawled in the plastic chairs on the footpath. Ruby picked over the last of the chips and turned her huge dark eyes to Minty. 'So, you gonna, like, start training for Cronulla? Shane's got it all sorted. All mapped out nice and clear. All you gotta do is turn up and be a show pony.' She nudged him with her elbow and there was something intimate in it: something shared, a closeness between people that only comes with time, something Sam didn't have anymore, and the envy of it ground into him.

Minty downed his chocolate milk. 'You're all on me about competing and that, but you should do it if you're so keen. Get a sweet sponsorship deal. Wouldn't have to work.' There was no weight in Minty's words. It was all jest and Ruby played it.

'Sponsorship from who? *Sports Illustrated*?'

'Yeah. Do a bikini spread.'

'Oh yeah! That's a really good idea, Minty! Why didn't I think'a that?'

He laughed and she smiled, cocked her shoulder like a pin-up model and raised her middle finger at him with a wink.

'Aw look, it's your buddy!' Minty said. Ruby looked in the direction Minty was pointing and let out a long groan and put her forehead on the table. Sam looked to see an old woman pushing her trolley toward the chicken shop.

'She still at you, Rube?' asked Minty.

Ruby didn't raise her head but groaned in answer. The woman came to a slow halt in front of them. She was small but there was something big and ceremonious about the way she stopped, like a locomotive gradually slowing. Despite the heat she was coated in layers of clothing, all different colours like the flaking layers of paint on an old house. Like a story. She fixed her bright eyes on Ruby.

'Ruby Jean! There she is.'

Ruby looked up and took a deep breath. 'Can you stop?'

The woman cackled, tilting her head back. 'Who are you, Ruby Jean? I tell you who you are.' She leaned toward Ruby's ear and whispered. 'You a Murri girl.'

Ruby stretched her jaws wide and yawned, as if trying to let out her frustration without being aggressive.

'How's it goin'?' Minty asked. 'I'm Minty, this is Sam. You know Ruby.'

'Aw yes. Ruby Jean. There she is,' wheezed the woman. 'Ruby Jean … waddya say? Whitters … Winters … Whit—'

'Whitterson.'

The woman pursed her lips. 'Nope. No, that's not your name.'

'That's my name.' Ruby's voice was blunt.

'What you doing with these gubbahs?" The woman wheezed again and licked her lips. She lowered herself into a chair beside Ruby. Minty covered his mouth and looked away to muffle his laughter. Ruby rolled her eyes.

'I know you. I know a woman, years back. Toomelah. Murri woman. Mirror picture of you! You're her girl.'

'You know Ruby's birth mum?' Minty asked. He pushed the hot chips toward the woman and she took one. Ruby glared at him.

'Know her gran, she would be. I'm Aunty Violet.'

Ruby stood up. Minty grabbed her hand and tugged her to sit back down, but she pulled away. The woman just laughed. 'You got fire in the belly. Yeah. You Murri girl.' She winked at Sam. 'She real deadly this one.'

Sam looked at Ruby and saw her turn away. He couldn't tell but it almost looked as if her lip was trembling. She straightened her spine and walked away into the shop. Minty looked at the old woman and put his hands up in a what-can-you-do sort of way.

'Tried to teach her some manners,' said Minty. 'Not workin'.'

The woman just rattled with laughter and shook her head. She stood up and shuffled over to her trolley. 'You tell Ruby Jean to come see me when she's ready. Have a yarn.'

'No worries. See you!' Minty said. The woman waved to him.

When she was gone Minty stood and yelled into the shop. 'All clear!'

Ruby stuck her head out the door, craning to look up the road.

'She's gone, Rube.'

'Bloody hell.' Ruby slumped in a chair and lit a cigarette. 'Don't encourage her.'

'You should talk to her,' Minty said.

'No.'

'She reckons she knows your grandma! That's cool, brah.'

'Seriously? You're an idiot, Minty. Do you have any idea the mess that will bring with it? I got all the adopted shit and now I gotta load all this black … stuff on top of it.'

'You can't say "black",' Sam said.

'I farkin' can because I am black.'

Minty pointed a finger at her. 'See!'

'Not now. Got too much goin' on.'

'You don't want to know who you really are 'cause you're too busy?' Minty pressed.

Sam didn't say anything. He knew it wasn't because Ruby was busy.

'I'm not talking about this.'

Minty leaned his elbows on the table and looked at her. 'Rube,' he said softly. 'Just talk to her. It'd be cool to meet your real mum.'

'Cool? Are you that fucking dense? You know what people round here call that Violet woman? "That Abo." What do you think they're gonna call me? And you reckon I'm gonna keep my job here when I'm "that Abo chick, that black bitch"?'

Minty recoiled at her words. 'Don't … Rube.' He put a hand on her shoulder and she shrugged him away.

'Like you care.'

'Rube.'

'Piss off!' She stood up and the plastic chair clattered to the ground behind her. Sam felt his throat tighten. He knew exactly what it was to have a line thrown into the past and have it drag you under. Ruby's pain was visible on her face and it was like a mirror of his own. Her expression articulated something in him he couldn't find the words for. He wanted to shrink away, casually take leave without anyone noticing. There was no chance of that happening.

'My *mum,*' Ruby pointed a finger in what Sam guessed was the direction of her house, 'doesn't even think I should stay in school and she's the only one who knows for sure what I am.'

'I think you—'

'I don't care what you think. Save it for Maddie Clark, Minty,' Ruby muttered.

Minty sucked in his breath.

'Oh, did I hurt your feelings? Go let Maddie help you feel better.' She took her board from where it leaned against the window of the shop and walked away without looking back.

Minty sat staring into the middle distance with a dazed and stung expression.

Sam cleared his throat. 'You gonna go after her?'

'She doesn't want me to follow her.'

'You should go after her.'

Minty looked at Sam. 'I should?'

'Duh.'

'Okay, okay.' Minty scrambled to his feet and jogged off after Ruby. Sam watched as he caught up to her. Minty took the board from Ruby and she crossed her arms, looking away but listening as he lowered his head and talked to her. They seemed to argue for a while but afterwards Minty turned and gave Sam a wave and then he and Ruby began walking in the direction of the Booners' house.

16

Lorraine served up sausages, mash and a side of macaroni cheese for dinner in front of the television. Ruby was there, a ceasefire between her and Minty seemingly in place. They watched *Sale of the Century* while they ate and Lorraine made each one of them put a tea towel over their laps so they didn't get food on their clothes. It was her version of setting the table.

'You get a good surf in today?'

Minty nodded with enthusiasm. 'Sammy picked it. Down Nari Bay. He's got a gift.'

Shane grunted.

'There you go,' said Lorraine. 'Things alright at home, Ruby?'

Ruby shrugged and sipped her can of cola.

'You gettin' on with your mum?'

'For now. See how long that lasts.'

'School starts tomorra.'

'Yeah.'

'What's she say about you stayin' on to get the HSC?'

'Oh, you know: why bother going to school if you can get a job? That's her mantra.'

'I got one of Minty's old school shirts for you, Sam,' said Lorraine. 'We'll go up tomorrow. Get you enrolled.'

Sam didn't respond. Ruby raised her eyebrow at him with a smirk.

'When I win the World Title, I'll employ you as my weatherman,' Minty said. 'You can tell me where the breaks are. We'll get choppered in.'

There was a knock at the door and Lorraine made a face. 'Who the hell is that?'

Minty and Shane didn't respond, their eyes turned back to the television. Lorraine kicked Shane in the ankle.

'I'm watching this!'

'I don't care, get the door.'

Shane got up and lumbered over to the front door. He opened it and stood gawping for a few moments.

'Well? Who is it?'

A voice sounded through the flyscreen. 'Hello, love.'

Lorraine got to her feet, went over and peered out into the darkness. She wiped her mouth with the back of her hand and glanced over at them in front of the TV. 'Stay there,' she ordered, going outside. She shut the front door behind her.

Minty stopped chewing and looked at Shane, who was still standing and staring at the closed door.

'What?' asked Minty.

'It was Nana.'

Minty put his bowl down and jumped up. He pushed the venetian blinds on the kitchen window up and looked out.

'Your nana's here?' asked Ruby. 'Thought she was dead.'

'She is to Mum,' Shane said. He looked to Sam. 'You know she was down here?'

'No, well, yeah. She showed up at the point the other day.'

'And you didn't tell Mum?' Shane was red in the face. 'Why the eff not?'

'I dunno. Didn't know she'd turn up here.'

'What she say?' Minty asked.

'Not much. Pop was an arsehole and that's why she took off. That and she was stressed about ...' Sam glanced at Shane, 'about your dad. She was worried all the time and she couldn't take it.'

'She said that about Pop?'

'Yeah. Dunno. Maybe she's senile.'

'I'm goin' out there,' said Minty.

'Nah, brah. Stay in here,' said Shane. He scratched his chin and watched out the window. Lorraine's voice screeched through the fibro walls. 'Mum's crankin'.'

The front door was yanked open and Lorraine came storming in, slamming the door behind her. She crossed the kitchen. 'What you all looking at?' She pulled a pack of cigarettes out of the cupboard above the stove and shook one into her palm, hands trembling. 'Where's me lighter? Where's me bloody lighter, Shane?'

'I don't know!'

She scrambled around through the drawer and pulled out a little packet of matches.

'Not inside, Mum,' said Minty.

'Oh for eff's sake! It's my bloody house! Stop tellin' me what to do! Christ alive.'

'What'd Nana want?'

Lorraine sucked on the cigarette and pushed the window above the sink open. 'Why don't you ask 'im,' she jerked a thumb in Sam's direction. 'He's the flavour of the bloody month, isn't he?'

'Mum,' Mint said.

'Don't *Mum* me. Don't hear a word from her for years, then Rachel dies and all of a sudden she's Mother-effin-Teresa.' Lorraine spoke as if her sister's death had been a stunt to get attention. '*What can I do?*' Lorraine mimicked a whiny voice that sounded nothing like Nana. 'I'll tell her what she can do, she can f—'

'Is she still out there?'

Lorraine spun around and thrust a pointed finger at Minty. 'Don't you! Don't you go out there.'

'I already spoke to her at the funeral.'

'Oh, that is the limit, that is. What she say? It was all my fault, was it? Wouldn't take youse away from your dad.'

Sam was still on the couch. He watched Lorraine spit and screech as she poured a glass of whisky. There was knocking at the door.

'There's someone at the door,' said Minty. Ruby hid her laughter behind her hand.

'Oh, no shit, Sherlock! Who do you think it might be? Geez. You numbskull.' Lorraine wrenched the front door open. 'Eff off, woman!' she spat through the screen. Sam saw that tears were trickling down her cheeks. Nana's voice was low and calm, like she was performing a hostage negotiation.

'Lorraine, I'm asking for you to have the courage just to let me speak.'

'COURAGE! WHAT DO YOU KNOW ABOUT EFFING COURAGE?'

'Hear me out, love.'

'Don't you "love" me.'

'Hi, Nana,' said Minty.

'Hello, darlin'. Lorraine? Are you drinking?'

'Am I drinking?! Of course I'm effing drinking!'

'Alright. I can see you're upset.' Lorraine opened her mouth to speak but Nana talked over the top of her. 'I'm in the caravan park. When you're ready and you're sober—'

'You just can't resist, can you? Any chance to tear a strip off me. You'll never change. *I*, I do the right thing, the respectable thing and marry a working bloke and start a family and *I've* done the wrong thing, haven't I? But Rachel? *Oh poor Rachel, oh Rachel works so hard, she's really making a go of it.*' Lorraine clenched her jaw and shook her head. 'Don't get me started on bloody Rachel. And then YOU! You piss off to Morocco or Timbuktu or some bloody place and I've got to pick up the pieces.' Lorraine gave a sour laugh. 'Who do you think was looking after Dad? *Her*, I bet. Well it wasn't her, it was me, thank you very bloody much.'

Sam watched her and felt the heat pull and coil in his chest.

'And now! Oh look at that! Who's the one left holding the bloody baby?' Lorraine pointed to Sam and Minty snorted a laugh.

'He's not really a baby, Mum.'

Ruby let out a laugh.

'It's an expression, numbnuts!'

'Lorraine, I'm staying in the caravan park. Number nine. You come and talk to me when you're ready.'

'I was ready seventeen bloody years ago, but you didn't say a word then, did you!'

'Number nine. Goodnight, boys.'

'See ya, Nana!' called Minty.

17

When Sam woke at dawn he got up and pulled on his wetsuit as usual, took his board from where it leaned on the wall and headed out to wax it. Lorraine was waiting for him in the kitchen. She had a mug of tea in her hand, a cigarette between her lips and her game face on. She was primed for battle.

'Oi, no surfing. You gotta get down to the school at 8.30.' She pointed across the kitchen to where an ironing board was set up. 'I got Minty's old uniform for you. Even bloody ironed it. Like you'd notice.'

Sam set the tail of the board on the floor between his feet. He told himself he wasn't hiding behind it.

'Aunty Lorraine ...'

'C'mon. Get in the shower. And wash your bloody hair while you're in there.'

'I'm not going.'

'What d'you mean you're not going. Of course you are.'

'There's no point.'

'No point to a bloody education! Rachel'll be turning in her grave. Get in the shower.'

'No. I'll get a job.'

She watched him as if deciding whether she was qualified to argue with him about the importance of staying in school.

'Your mum would want you to go. I know she would.'

'Well, she's gone.'

'That's not her effing fault.'

Sam wasn't sure if he believed her. 'I'm not going. I'll get a job.'

She pressed her lips into a firm line. 'Yeah, you will if you're not gonna go to school.'

Sam couldn't make it down to the beach.

He lay on the camp bed with his eyes closed. He cranked the volume on his headphones and tried to get the breath to stay in his lungs, but his chest was squeezed like a vice and if he opened his eyes the world leaned in too far and he felt dizzy. He needed to make it stop but the best he could do was shroud himself in the black behind his eyes and the noise in his ears. Shane was right. Minty liked Sam, but Minty liked everyone. Sam wasn't wanted. He wasn't needed. Lorraine had problems enough without some orphan kid turning up on her doorstep. Maybe he did have a dad out there somewhere. But whoever his dad was, he didn't give a shit about Sam. He'd never even tried to contact Sam. He had read that Jeff Buckley had grown up not knowing who his father was. Then when he was in his twenties he discovered his dad was the famous musician Tim Buckley. Sam didn't know who Tim Buckley was, but according to the article Sam had read, he was important. Sam wondered if his own father was a famous musician and how that information would change his life. Which famous musician would he be? Knowing his luck he would probably turn out to be John Farnham.

He was better off not knowing.

The first time Sam heard Jeff Buckley and took notice of the music he had been in his room at home alone. He was supposed to be studying physics. The radio was on Triple J and he had his finger hovering over the record button, waiting to catch Rage Against the Machine or Beck or Dinosaur Jr. A hook and line in the steady stream of sound. The best thing he had caught recently was an acoustic live recording of 'Drive' by REM. You could buy singles and they usually had B sides, but ten bucks was a lot to pay for six or seven minutes of music. CD stores were unreliable in what they stocked, too. You could always get mainstream singles, less so rare recordings. The cheapest and easiest way to get singles was to tape them off the radio. Sam had a stack of tapes on rotation, the best ones marked so they wouldn't be taped over, the others good to go. Always something ready to go in the tape deck.

He was waiting that night, poised, when sharp, delicate notes sounded. Reedy, thrumming, unlike the stuff he usually recorded. The space between the notes was loaded. Negative space. Then the drums kicked in and searing vocals. Sam hit record and the tape began to whir. 'Grace'. And he had the feeling that he was hearing something important. Something with resonance.

People who had seen Jeff Buckley on stage said that he had

a rare presence, a magnetic aura that drew every eye to him, tuned every ear to his breath. He made himself so vulnerable in his lyrics, but it somehow translated into power. He could stand in front of a crowd, hundreds, thousands of people, lay everything bare and be respected for it.

How did he do that?

Jeff made Sam think of one of those Renaissance guys in leggings, cross-legged playing the lute or something. But then with something more: a raw, tortured, seething undercurrent. Like the guy with the lute played a song, recited a few sonnets and then stabbed someone in the neck. Jeff Buckley sang that he wasn't afraid to die. Sam wondered if *he* was afraid to die.

Swimming bright and colourful,
'till away they dash.

The knowledge that he wasn't shuddered into his chest.

He had listened to that first recording over and over; it started twenty seconds into the track. Finally he got the thirty bucks for the album. His mum heard it for the first time and proclaimed that she was going to have Jeff Buckley's babies. Sam really wished she hadn't said that out loud. Girls loved Jeff. They'd probably still love him if he did snap, put down his guitar and punch someone in the head. They'd probably love him more.

Gretchen probably loved him. She was the sort of girl who thought a lot about the world. She wasn't mainstream. Sam had decided this because she was sporty but she wore a 'Zero' T-shirt. Surely she would be into Jeff Buckley. He should have said something about music. They could have talked about it. But it seemed that whenever she was in close proximity everything in his head was erased – like a magnet and a floppy disk. What if the Smashing Pumpkins was the only good band Gretchen listened to? What if she listened to Celine Dion as well? That would be an interesting combination, though. No one was perfect.

No, she was probably perfect.

Minty and his mates would think Sam was pathetic because she really wasn't even super hot, not in an obvious way like the girls Minty was into. She was more subtle. More classy than hot. They wouldn't get that.

Sam had heard enough talk out on the water to know that if you didn't sleep with any girl you had the opportunity to, you were a loser. Case closed. His own virginity felt like a shameful disease, more so since he'd moved to the coast. There was zero chance of him admitting he was a virgin, even to Minty. Sam knew that when it did happen, it wouldn't be with someone like Gretchen. He would never be able to play it right around her. Speaking to the girl was probably a prerequisite and he'd barely managed that much when he'd had the opportunity. And now he was officially a high school dropout, diminishing his chances with her even more.

Shane sat in the line-up and talked about women like they were livestock. Things he said about girls he'd been with made Sam's stomach turn. Minty wouldn't join in exactly, but he'd laugh. He'd call Shane a dirty bastard as if it were endearing to reduce girls you'd been with to bits of meat. Shane didn't seem to care whether Ruby was in earshot or not. In fact, Sam felt that he amped it up when Ruby was out there. If she cared, she didn't show it. Or she'd make some remark about Shane having to look for his dick if he wanted to find it, which would make his whole head flame red, like steam was going to shoot out of his ears, like he might take a swing at her if she was in reach. She never was.

It must have been mid morning when Minty walked in and tugged the earbud out of Sam's ear. 'We're goin' south. Get your board.'

'We' meant he and Shane. Brothers. They didn't need Sam there. He just shook his head and plugged the earbud back in.

In the afternoon, when Sam knew school would be finished, he wandered up the hill to Jono's place. Mrs O'Brien had laid out an epic spread of afternoon tea for her flock of boys and she welcomed Sam into the chaos. Jono said she liked Sam because he looked like Jesus. Sam loved being in the house with the noise and stuff everywhere, the yelling and laughing. Jono's mum looked like she needed a long nap, but Sam found it comforting to be there: a sense that the world was well and truly still spinning and would continue to do so whether Sam felt like shit or not.

Later, in front of *GoldenEye*, Sam shot people and half listened to Jono pretending to be a music historian.

'Look. I'm not saying they're bad, yeah? I'm just saying

that the thing with Stone Temple Pilots is they aren't part of that original movement. They aren't pure-bloods as far as the grunge scene goes.' Jono was lying in front of the screen, propped on his elbows with the console in his hands and his eyes fixed on the game. Sam wasn't aware that he had even begun a discussion about the authenticity or otherwise of Stone Temple Pilots. That detail didn't seem to bother Jono. Sam re-loaded his gun and shot two guys in the back of the head, clearing the way for Jono to kick down the door.

'Nice. I mean, they hit pay-dirt with one solid song. It's a good song, sure. But I'm not sure they deserve to be talked about on the same level as the Pumpkins or Sonic Youth or even Soundgarden.'

'I didn't know anyone was talking about them. I didn't know we were.'

'Oh yeah. They do. But it's people who like to think they are so edgy that they are ahead of the wave, like. I just don't think that if you are having a serious discussion about the scene over the last ten years, you should consider them. They're just pretending they're not totally mainstream. I mean, I think Mellon Collie has changed the tack a bit, of where things are heading. And then the other side of it is the stuff that's coming out of the UK. Tricky, for instance. Portishead—'

'Who?'

'Oh man. Sam. How can you be into music and not into Portishead?' He barely stopped to draw breath. 'And I don't think there's a huge disconnect between them and something like Nine Inch Nails, even. My question is, what have Stone

Temple Pilots actually contributed to the evolution of the sound ...'

Sam was pretty sure that most of what Jono said was bullshit.

'Did I tell you about the thing for *Drum* magazine? Sam?'

Sam tuned back in. 'What?'

'Yeah, *Drum*. You know, the street press? I'm writing an article for them. I'm going to send it in, see if they publish it.'

'Really?'

'Yeah. I want to start reviewing gigs too. I mean, I have to wait until I'm eighteen so I can actually see them. You ask Minty about that Tumbleweed gig?'

'Yeah. He's up for it.'

'Cool. I think music journalism could be something that really works for me. UTS have this communications/ journalism course too. I'm gonna shoot for it. The entry score's heaps high. But I reckon I can do it. And you know, this World Wide Web thing is going to change everything. Like journalism and everything.'

'You think?'

'Yeah. People are gonna have it in their homes, man. It's gonna change everything.'

'I gotta find a job.'

'You can work at Jewel! Got a resume? I'll hand it in. There's nothing going at the moment, but people chuck it in all the time. Something might come up.'

'I'll think about it.'

There was the padding sound of feet coming down the stairs. Sam expected to see some of Jono's brothers in the doorway. He didn't even look up until he heard the female voice.

'Good afternoon, Jono!' Stassi was holding a six-litre tub of ice-cream and a VHS tape. 'We come bearing gifts!'

Gretchen was beside her. Curls everywhere. She avoided Sam's gaze. Stassi looked beyond Jono and her face fell when she saw Sam.

'Oh. You're here.'

He ignored her and focused on the game. Stassi and Gretchen sat on the carpet, in the space between Jono and Sam: Stassi next to Jono, Gretchen next to Sam. He could smell her hair or moisturiser or something. Vanilla. She hadn't looked at him and he didn't look at her. He hadn't seen her since the party on the weekend – when he had ignored her like a massive tool.

Stassi took the console from Jono's hands and handed him the tape. Jono glanced at Sam. 'Forgot to tell you, there's people coming over and we're watching *Pulp Fiction*.'

Stassi gave Sam a cheesy fake smile. 'Jono's Movie Monday. It's an institution.'

'An institution of three people?' Sam intended it to sound like a joke but he got the tone wrong.

'Feel free to leave,' said Stassi.

'Thanks for the heads-up, Jono,' Sam said.

The tape started and Jono opened the ice-cream, passing it and the spoon along the line. Stassi handed it to Gretchen and, despite keeping his eyes on the screen, Sam was acutely aware of her every movement as she moved the spoonful of ice-cream to her lips and, no doubt, her tongue. He wanted to touch her; the space between her body and his was charged with tension only heightened by the fact that neither of them would look at the other. The opening scenes played out, and Gretchen passed the ice-cream to him. His fingers brushed hers. He took a scoop of ice-cream and handed the tub back to her and their fingers touched again. Still they didn't glance at each other. Instead of folding her arms again she left them loose at her sides, her elbow millimetres from his. He moved his arm ever so slightly so it touched hers. She didn't move away. He moved closer, his heart pounding, so his skin was touching her smooth, cool forearm. She didn't move or look at him. The two of them sat for the entire time like that until the movie finished – with Sam barely able to recall anything about it. Stassi jumped up, flicked the lights on and the spell – that he was connected, that he had someone – was broken.

AUTUMN

18

Sam had borrowed a collared shirt from Minty's wardrobe. He didn't have a tie; his mum would have told him to wear one. But it seemed pretty dumb to wear a tie to a supermarket job interview. The manager's name was Garth and he was in his twenties with acne and an old-man's haircut. He carried a clipboard and led Sam into a stockroom out the back of the supermarket. He turned a milk crate over and indicated to Sam to sit down. Sam sat.

'So, why would you like to join the team, Sam?'

'I'm really passionate about customer service and I like working as part of a team.'

Garth wrote his answer on the clipboard.

'And what are your strengths?'

'I'm good with people. I'm punctual. I'm reliable.'

'What are your weaknesses?'

'I'm a perfectionist. I put a lot of pressure on myself to do well, you know? I'm also a workaholic. I just love … working.'

'Sure. Do you have any previous work experience?'

'I worked in a video store in Sydney for a bit.'

'And can they provide a reference for you?'

'It's um, actually closed down now, so …'

'Okay. Who are your references?'

'Um, my aunty. And my cousin, Minty Booner. You know Minty?'

'No.'

'He's a professional surfer. You would have seen him around.'

'I don't like the beach.'

'Oh.'

'Now, I'm going to give you this form to fill out. You'll notice a declaration down the bottom: it asks if you have a criminal record or have ever received a police caution. I would like to remind you that it is a legal document and we will be checking.'

'Sure.'

'I'll leave you to fill it out. You can leave it on the desk there, Sam. Thanks for coming in and we'll be in touch.'

'No worries.'

Garth handed Sam the clipboard and left the storeroom.

Sam stared at the page.

The room had become very small and very hot.

He stood up, put the clipboard on the desk and left.

Outside the afternoon air smothered him and the black static choked his brain. He stood on the footpath and watched the cars. People – mums with strollers, old ladies, kids in school uniform – walked around him like he was a stick caught in a stream. In the weeks since school had started he'd managed to chip away at the hours – the long stretches of time when he should have been in class – listening to music, making notes about the swell forecast, trying to surf, skating and sleeping. When the manager from Jewel had rung and asked him to come in for an interview, he'd felt like maybe it would all fall into place and he would go from a bludging, jobless dropout, to a legit person with an income and options. In the brief instances when he'd seen Gretchen he'd been able to have a chat with her and he felt he was working his way up to something. Now he felt on the edge of panic. Sydney, the trouble he'd been in with the cops and the caution he'd got, he'd thought it was behind him. But it wasn't. Now he couldn't catch his breath, as if he was sprinting instead of standing still.

He couldn't move toward the place he was supposed to be next. He didn't know where to be next. The beach seemed a long, long way away. Everywhere seemed a long way away. How long could you stand there in one spot, not moving, before someone noticed or said something or asked you to move? He was thinking about that when he heard his name being called. He looked up the road toward the chicken shop and saw Minty and his mates sprawled in the white plastic chairs on the footpath – somewhere he could be.

Soon he was among them, slotted in with his shirt untucked, sleeves rolled up. He copped the ribbing for leaving the waves to go to a job interview. He laughed in the right places. Someone had liquor in a drink bottle, who knows what. Sam took it when it was offered. He took the joint too, when it came around. He sat back and waited for the fuzz to dull and the feeling that he might spew to go away.

Ruby was in the shop and came out occasionally, but it was near evening and people were coming in for orders. The manager came out and told them to move on if they weren't buying more food, so they migrated down the road to the big square of dead grass that passed as a park. Someone went to the bottle-o and came back with bourbon. The guys talked about every girl that walked past. Whether they'd do her with the lights on or off, that kind of thing. It was sickening and Sam didn't join in. That made him better than them, didn't it? Minty didn't contribute, but he didn't challenge them either. Was it enough to just not participate? The right thing, the strong thing, would be to tell them to shut up and that they were sick low-life. Sam didn't need his mum to tell him that. They wouldn't keep him around if they knew he thought he was better than them. If Sam was better than them, he wasn't one of them. And if he wasn't one of them he really was alone, not one of the pack. The first to get taken down.

And then.

Gretchen started walking up the hill toward the park. Her seeing him like this was not part of the sketchy fantasy that he pretended was a plan.

Sam couldn't breathe. He felt sick. He was going to stand up and walk away, but it was too late. If he moved now she would see him. She'd have proof that he was a loser with bong-rat mates who ditched school and got high in the park. It would confirm that he was not the kind of guy she should go anywhere near. Sam tried to sink into the ground, praying for invisibility. It started. Gretchen got a seven. Shane said she looked like a princess and the sniggers passed through the group. It was decided she would be an eight with her clothes off. Heat pooled in Sam's chest. He tried to breathe. He felt the tension of the fury climbing up his spine, through his shoulders. His revulsion at Shane's words was volcanic. In his mind it drew the picture of the corridor at his old school in Sydney, the words said about his mother. He heard his mum's words as well, afterwards in the police station, her lip trembling. *You cannot lash out whenever someone says something you don't like!*

Gretchen came within earshot and Shane gave her a loud wolf whistle. Sam turned away, hiding behind his hair like a cowering dog. Maybe she wouldn't see him.

Shane whistled again and Sam could see the grimace on her face, the quickening of her step as she walked along the footpath next to the park.

'Hey baby, come here!' Shane yelled. Gretchen stopped walking and Sam could see her shoulders and back move as she took a deep breath. She turned and faced the group, he could see the fear hidden in her scowl.

'Piss off,' she said firmly.

There were hoots and jeers. 'I think she likes you, Shane!' someone laughed.

She raised her middle finger at them and as she did her eyes found Sam.

He felt his whole face colour and burn, his pulse thudding in his temples. The seconds that he had to establish himself as the person he wanted her to see were over. Gretchen put her head down and kept walking. She was out of sight by the time he got to his feet. He was a scrappy mess because of the drink but he was cleaner than Shane and tackled him to the dirt. Thumping him around the sides of his big, stupid fat head. Shane was all bulk and muscle, but he didn't have the fury powering him like Sam. Someone grabbed Sam by the collar. Minty. He pulled Sam up, spun him around and hissed to him through clenched teeth.

'Farkin' let go, Sam. That's my brother. He's family. He's your family.'

'He's an arsehole.'

'Chill.'

He shook from Minty's grip and pulled away. Minty wiped his mouth with the back of his wrist. 'Go home, Sam. You get into a fight and Mum'll kick you out. Don't doubt it.'

19

Two weeks passed and Sam didn't see Gretchen. He spent a lot of time in the water with Minty, just the two of them now Ruby was at school. He didn't go back to Jono's for Movie Monday and he never went near the concourse or the pool – the only places he knew he was likely to run into her. When he thought of what Gretchen had seen that afternoon, the humiliation and shame burned through him. Most days Shane was working and only surfed early mornings or late afternoon. He rarely even looked at Sam, in the water or at home, and when he did acknowlege his existence it was with a narrow-eyed glare.

The Tumbleweed gig was a small glint of hope on his horizon. He told himself he would have a good time. The bouncer didn't give Sam, Jono or Ruby a second look. He saw Minty and ushered them to the front of the queue, grasped Minty's hand in the usual greeting and waived the cover charge. Despite the sign next to him stating that shoes must be worn, he didn't care that Minty was barefoot. He opened the door for them and they ventured into the darkness. The bass was up and the room thrummed with heat and sound and cigarette smoke. Minty was greeted with the usual howls and backslaps. The place was male-dominated, everyone in boardies and thongs. Sam noticed how Ruby seemed to steel herself against the tide of testosterone, shoulders back, chin up, a confident walk and a piss-off look directed at any guy who looked her over. The chaotic buzz of the support band drowned out any comfortable conversation and people shouted to each other over the top of it. Everyone stood around straight-backed, arms folded across their chest – the same stance reserved for watching the water – only now they bobbed their chins ever so slightly in time with the music. Beer appeared from somewhere; Minty didn't pay for it, Sam was certain of that much. He rarely ever even had cash on him. Sam waited for his eyes to adjust to the darkness and scanned the faces in the crowd.

Gretchen was there.

He wasn't expecting to see her at all, but there she was with another girl Sam didn't recognise, leaning her back against the wall up the back of the room. Her hair was tied in little knots all over her head, like Björk. She was wearing baggy cargo pants and a tight black T-shirt over some kind of black fishnet sleeves. Her fingernails were painted black and she had make-up on. She looked way older than she was and stuck out against all the beach blondes. Jono was talking to him about the band. Sam wasn't listening. Gretchen held a tall glass and rolled the straw between her thumb and forefinger as she watched the stage.

The support band finished and left the stage. Jono was verbally analysing the influence of San Francisco Bay thrash metal when Gretchen clocked Sam. He wasn't expecting it. He wasn't expecting her. He wasn't sure he had remembered to put on deodorant. He regretted his choice of old shorts, old T-shirt and sneakers. At least it was a Jeff Buckley T-shirt. Although there was a hole in the underarm and he couldn't remember whether it was the left or the right. He would have to remember to keep his arms down, not that he was the kind to do any overt gesticulating. His chest lurched and he looked away. He glanced back in time to see her making a face at him – a pissed-off, 'stuff-you' face.

Jono was still talking.

'I gotta go for a second,' Sam said. He put his beer down on the sticky bar table and squared his shoulders. He walked straight up to her.

'What do you want?' she scoffed at him, but he could tell she was nervous. At that moment, he would have chosen Jeff Buckley to play over the sound system. 'Lover, You Should've Come Over'. Instead, it seemed the DJ was in a more humorous mood and it was the Spice Girls. As if whoever programmed the music was completely ignorant of the type of crowd who would be there. He couldn't breathe. He looked right at her. 'Can I talk to you?'

'I'm good thanks. How are you? This is my cousin, Sarah. Sarah, this is Sam. He hangs out with stupid misogynistic dickheads who think it's cool to harass women.'

He didn't know Gretchen well enough to guess, but if he did he would guess she wasn't drinking lemonade.

'Can I talk to you?'

'What? No. I'm here with my cousin, we're going to perve on Jon Toogood from Shihad, even though he's actually quite short.'

'I don't mind a short man,' said the cousin.

Gretchen made a point of looking up at Sam. He could see her steeling herself. 'Neither do I.'

It wasn't going well.

'Can I buy you a drink?'

'Why? I have one. Why are you glaring at me while you ask me that?'

The song changed. Beck, 'Loser'. The most powerful endorsement for being a loser ever. Sam let out a huff of exasperation.

She widened her eyes. 'Don't get shitty with me, punk.' The cousin cracked up. 'You invite me to a party where you ignore me, you do this tricky arm-touching thing at Jono's Movie Monday, then whenever I see you, you barely say anything.'

'But I said stuff.'

'*Then* I see you with your stupid chauvinist, half-wit loser buddies and you sit there while they objectify me and you act like you don't even know me. Now you frown at me and get pissed off when I don't want you to buy me a drink. Gee, am I being a naggy girl? Sorry for my high standards.'

They stood staring at each other. The band walked onstage and the crowd cheered. He inhaled. He took a step toward her and she looked up at him with a scowl.

'Fine. Sorry.' He turned and walked away.

'He is sexy, but,' said the cousin.

*

'How'd it go, Romeo?' Ruby ribbed him with her mocking smile. Sam ignored her and skolled the rest of his beer. He didn't hear any of the music. He stood with the others, looking in the direction of the stage, but he didn't listen to a single sound. All his senses were attuned to her standing across the room as he dissected every single interaction he had ever had with her, every word. He never realised how closely you could watch someone without looking directly at them. He glanced over at her a few times to see if she was looking back at him but she never was.

When the gig was done the lights came up and the crowd surged toward the exits. Sam, Jono, Ruby and Minty joined the tide of bodies and Sam lost sight of Gretchen. Outside, misty, salty rain was falling, sweet and fresh after the crammed heat of the bar. People gathered in loose clumps in the pools of streetlight, full of the buzzy residue of the music. Shane had turned up at some point. He was going on about someone who had said something about Minty and was therefore a whiny bitch. Sam rolled his eyes.

'You got a problem, kook?'

'Nah, man. Please, carry on.'

Minty looked back and forth between the two of them and groaned. 'Brah. We're havin' a good time 'ere. Good music. Good time. Chill.'

'I'll chill out when this kook pisses off to where he came from.'

'Yeah!' Ruby widened her eyes in mock glee. 'Let's have a pissing contest!'

'Go hang with some girls then, Ruby.' Shane hissed at her.

'Brah, come on. Leave her. And Sam's family. He's alright.'

'You think everyone's alright, Mint. I see him and I see a kook. Look at him. Who are you, man? You wearing make-up like Marilyn Manson? You are, you little kook.'

'I'm not. But thanks for the compliment.'

'What the eff is this?' Shane shoved a finger at Sam's T-shirt. 'Look at you and your homo music.'

A few others turned to look.

Jono opened his mouth but the only sound that came out was a weak, 'Hey!'

The tension in Sam built and built until he could feel every muscle and sinew in his body pulled taut. Sam pulled his right arm back and punched Shane across the jaw, picturing the exact moment Shane had said the things about Gretchen on that afternoon in the park. Shane stumbled back, missing a beat, taking a moment to catch up to what was happening. Sam hit him again in the stomach and everything fizzing in his head dissipated. Shane lunged back at him but Sam was quicker. He was stronger thanks to his weight sessions with Minty. He pounded him again, collecting blood on his knuckles. It was a mess of sweat and grit, blood and beer breath, grabbing and shoving, messy punching. He was moving but inside something had stopped, the endless cascade of snapshots, the horrible rotting grey feeling that leached the colour out of everything. While he was fighting with Shane he was seeing in colour. He was quick. He was good at this and he knew everyone was surprised, including Ruby, and he loved that. The pain from each blow he took was washed away by adrenaline. It was like dancing – fighting;

it was intimate, you were in tune with another human. It was sort of beautiful, like that; everything finely focused on the movement and the breath.

Whirring, Sam's peripheral vision caught a familiar figure, Gretchen. He lost focus long enough for Shane to grab him in a headlock and pound his cheek and jaw. Sam's vision went blurry and then he was on the cold, wet asphalt. Minty pulled Shane away and Sam rolled onto his back, feeling the water soak through his clothes. It was like he could feel the ground reverberating beneath him, the scuff and crunch of gravel. He wished Shane was still there to kick him in the head and put him out of his misery. He found the reserves to lift his head and look around for Gretchen, but she was already gone. Jono crouched down next to Sam, his expression aghast.

'Sam? Are you alright? Holy shit!'

'I'm fine.' He got to his feet and shrugged Jono away.

Sam didn't go back to the house. If Lorraine saw him in the morning he was pretty sure she would make good on her promise to kick him out. She seemed like the kind of person who meant what she said. It was something he liked about her, but now was a bit inconvenient. He wandered along the side of the road toward the beach feeling like he was trying to get his footing on a ship's deck. It was a pleasant sort of unsteady, like you get after a roller-coaster ride. Sam tilted his head back and let the rain fall on his face, let it wash the blood and salt and sweat. He looked up at the sky and watched the clouds swirling toward the sea, catching glimpses of the stars between them. Could she see him? It was easy to understand why for thousands of years, people thought the dead were up there somewhere. There was certainly enough space for them all.

She wouldn't like what she saw.

Sam followed the clouds and headed to the water. Down at the beach the sand looked like the powdery surface of the moon, lit stark by white spotlights. The waves were a haze of sound folding and enveloping him. He walked past the pool, its unbroken surface glittery and shimmering, and padded down the ramp to the sand. The rain had stopped. He let his body fall onto the soft cold sand. He lay on his back, looked for her up in the stars and waited for sleep to claim him.

When he opened his eyes the sky was soaked in pale morning light, floss-pink clouds with gilded edges. His left arm tingled with pins and needles and he was cold all over. Sitting up he saw the clock above the surf club: 6 am. Sand was in his ears and on his neck, the creases of his eyelids. Behind him, on the concourse, joggers in fluoro singlets ran along with poodles and labradors attached. Visors and water bottles. They gave him the occasional dismissive, disapproving glance. Another binge-drinking teen with no self-respect, probably on the dole.

Soon enough.

He got to his feet and trudged up the ramp. The rhythmic slosh slosh sound of freestyle came from the pool. There were three swimmers: two guys and one girl. Gretchen. Sam sat on the concrete steps next to the pool and watched her. She swam for another half an hour, back and forth, back and forth. And then she stopped at the end of the lane and pulled her goggles off. She closed her eyes and sank under the water, bobbing up again and sweeping water from her hair. Her skin was like milk, hair swirling and inky in the water. She saw him and didn't smile. Then she stretched and vaulted out of the water onto the pool deck. She tilted her head side to side, working the water out of her ears, and picked up a towel. She wrapped it around her waist and approached, stopping a couple of feet in front of him. No words. Water trickled down her legs, curling around her ankles and pooling on the ground beneath her. She stood perfectly still and looked at him and it took every ounce of courage he had in him to look back. He had no idea what she saw, but it wasn't so horrifying or monstrous that she walked off. Instead, she sat down on the step next to him.

'Are you a tool? 'Cause you seem like one sometimes.'

Sam sniffed. 'I try not to be. Sometimes it doesn't work.'

She pulled her hair over her shoulder and twisted it, wringing out the water. 'I know Minty's a really old friend of Jono's, but I don't get why he still hangs out with him. And I know he's your cousin and you ... Jono likes you and you seem like a good guy, but Minty and them.' She shook her head. 'I wouldn't trust them as far as I could throw them.'

'Fair enough.'

'Did you get beat up last night?'

'What? No. I didn't get beat up. I was in a fight.'

'You do that much?'

'Not anymore,' Sam said.

'Take up boxing or something. They have refs. It's safer.'

'Not really interested in safety.'

'Whoa. Tough guy, huh? So impressive.'

'I didn't say I was a tough guy. I said I wasn't interested in safety.'

'Same thing.'

'I disagree.'

'My friend, Stassi, says I should stay away from you.'

It was crushing to hear it. 'Whatever,' he muttered.

'Okay.' She stood up. 'I'm done. I tried having a conversation like a normal person, but you don't seem interested. So I'm out.' She turned to walk away.

'Gretchen.' It felt good just saying her name. She stopped and looked back at him. Sam stood up and walked over to her. 'Shane's a tool. I ... I'm really sorry about the thing in the park. I had a job interview beforehand and it was a disaster and I felt like crap and they were there and it was somewhere I could be ... I don't think it's okay to do that to girls. So we're clear.'

She stood looking up at him, not moving. He stepped closer to her so that there were centimetres between them. She didn't move away.

'Do you like music?' he asked.

'Yes. I like music.'

'What music do you like?'

'Smashing Pumpkins. Radiohead. Jeff Buckley.'

'Same.'

Neither of them spoke. He watched her breathing, beads of water trickling down her neck, pooling in the hollows of her clavicle.

'Is this you making conversation?' she asked.

'Yes.'

She laughed.

He took her face in his hands and kissed her.

20

Sam couldn't even feel the bruising on his face and the ache in his skull had vanished. The world was dripping with technicolour, a glowing, sun-flared filter that made everything meaningful and sweet. It was stronger than any high he'd ever felt. An intoxicating swirl throughout his body that made him feel capable of anything.

He kissed her and she kissed him back, her arms around his neck, his hands on her waist. Her lips were soft, salty and sweet and he breathed her breath and it was like the rest of the universe dissolved. Her skin was cool against his and her wet hair stupidly erotic.

When they came up for breath and untangled, that luminous expression returned to her face.

'Not so much a talking man? I think I understand now.'

It was the first time anyone had ever called him a man. It did strange things to him. He kissed her again. After a bit she pulled away.

'I still like talking,' she said.

He reached to touch her face and she stepped back.

'I'm going home for a cold shower.'

'Can I come?'

'No. See you.' He watched as she walked away, anchoring the towel around her waist. She looked back at him once to see him staring after her and gave him a grin.

'Wait.' He jogged after her. 'We live on the same street.'

'Do we? What number are you?'

'I'm further up than you.'

They walked together. He was aware that he probably stank, but maybe it just added to the whole manly thing he apparently had going on now.

Up the hill, when they turned onto their street, she stopped. 'This is me.'

He looked up at the house, built up to look over the water, timber and glass and random angles. An architectural oddity in the area, usually reserved for weekenders from Sydney.

'What's your phone number?' he asked

'Do you have some paper?'

'No.'

'Come inside and I'll write it down for you.'

'It's okay, tell me and I'll remember it.'

She told him and he recited it over and over.

'See you.'

She unlatched the gate and disappeared behind the tall timber fence.

Lorraine was out on the porch before he hit the front steps.

'Where the hell have you been?' Her face was grey and

drawn, eyes bruised with fatigue. It occurred to him that she might have waited up for him.

'Oh, you know, just the beach.'

'No, I don't know. What happened to your face? Were you in another fight? 'Cause, God help me, if you were.'

'Nah. Shane beat me up because he doesn't like the music I listen to.'

She folded her arms and assessed him. 'Is that right?'

'Yeah. Bit rich from someone who loves John Farnham.'

She fought a smile and held up one finger. 'One more strike and you're out, mate. You got it?'

'Got it.'

'You look happy with yourself. What you been up to? Wait. I don't want to know.' She turned and went into the house. 'Just use a condom, yeah? I don't want to be Great-Aunty Lorraine just yet.'

Sam ducked past her and retreated to his room.

At dusk he got up and had a shower. He went into the kitchen and picked up the phone. He dialled Gretchen's number and stretched the phone cord so it reached all the way back to his room. He hoped it would be Gretchen who answered, but it was a woman. He took a deep breath.

'Hi, can I speak to Gretchen, please?'

'Sure. Who shall I say is calling?'

'Sam.'

'Okay, Sam, just a minute.' There was a muffled sound and then Gretchen's voice.

'Hi?'

'Hi.'

'Hi,' she laughed.

'What are you doing?'

'Just reading. Listening to music. Mainly listening to music.' Her words tumbled out. 'I find it hard to read at the same time. Sometimes I can do it. If I know the music really well, then I don't get distracted as much. Can you listen to music while you read?'

'Depends on the music. What are you listening to?'

'Tori Amos. *Under the Pink.*'

'Cool. I like her.'

'You've heard of Tori Amos?'

'Yeah. I've heard of most things. Not Portishead though, so apparently I don't know anything at all.'

'Ohhhh, you don't. Don't get me started. Tori makes me want to learn the piano and dye my hair red.'

'You have nice hair.'

'I have crazy-person hair. It's like a clown wig.'

'No, I like it.'

'What are you doing?'

'The same really, listening to music.'

'What did you think of last night? I mean the bit when the band played, not the bit when you got punched in the head.'

'Honestly, I wasn't listening. I couldn't tell you a single song they played. I was too, um, distracted.' He felt his heart thump when he said it.

'Same. So, do you have your own room there?'

'Sort of.'

'How do you sort of have a room?'

'It's kind of a … I don't know. It's weird.'

'Are you whispering?'

'Yeah. I don't really have a bedroom door.'

'Because you only sort of have a room?'

'Exactly.'

Silence. They both rushed to say something at the same time.

'You go,' said Sam.

'Oh. I was just going to ask what you usually do … besides go to gigs you don't listen to and get in fights with your family members.'

'Ha. Dunno, just hang out. I've applied for a bunch of jobs, but nothing's come through yet. Sometimes I skate with Jono. Sometimes I try and surf. I'm not very good at it.'

'No?'

'No. It's amazing I don't drown.'

She laughed. 'Hey, I have to go. Dinner.'

'Sure. Same. See you.'

'Bye.'

Sam went out to the kitchen to hang up the phone. Lorraine was asleep on the couch. He stuck his head in Minty's room, but there was no sign of him. Sam opened the fridge. It was empty except for cans of rum and cola. He took his mum's keycard from where it was hidden in his room and put it in his pocket.

He wasn't sure if her account was still open or if Lorraine had closed it. He put the card in, punched in the PIN and watched the screen. When the machine asked him how much he wanted to withdraw he felt relief flush through him. He opted for five hundred, the maximum, and was folding the notes into his pocket when the familiar whir of wheels sounded on the road behind him. Jono stepped off the board and flicked it up with the toe of his sneaker.

'How's it goin', Sam?'

'Good. You?'

'Okay. You alright, like, after last night? Sorry, I'm not really the guy you want in that sort of … situation.'

'Nah. It's cool.'

'Cool. What are you doing?'

'Lorraine isn't that reliable with meals. Gotta get something to eat.'

'Come to mine,' Jono flicked his forehead to the side, motioning up the hill. 'Mum's doin' lasagne.' He held up a plastic shopping bag. 'Forgot the mince.'

'Nah, it's okay.'

'Dude, you should come. There's heaps of us, another one's no different.'

'You sure?'

'Yeah. Mum loves you. Says you've got nice manners. C'mon.'

Jono's dining room was full of light and noise and movement. His brothers sat along two old church pews either side of a long table. Although not many of them were actually sitting. From what Sam could tell, there were two sets of twins, which explained why Sam didn't know who he had met and who he hadn't. Throughout the meal there was always at least one argument going on somewhere around the table while a picture of a haloed Jesus with a glowing exterior heart gazed down upon the squabble and laughter. Jono's youngest brother was only about four and he kept on looking back at Sam as if he was playing 'one of these things is not like the others'. Jono's mum smiled beatifically at Sam and offered him food like he was a street urchin in one of his mum's Dickens novels. After dinner she served them little bowls of vanilla ice-cream with sprinkles on top. Sam felt the vague outline of a sensation he hadn't experienced for what seemed like years: happiness. It didn't even flit away as soon as he noticed it.

When Sam was approaching Lorraine's he saw Nana standing on the grass. If Lorraine knew Nana was there she didn't do her the courtesy of leaving on the porch light. Sam could only make out her face by the dull kitchen light seeping through the venetians.

'Allo love,' said Nana. 'Hope you've got a good excuse, she's got a bee in her bonnet.'

'What are you doing here?'

'You always out this late?'

Sam shrugged. He wanted to make a wisecrack at her, something to do with her having no right to ask questions about his behaviour. He didn't.

''Cause I know Rachel and I know how she gets when she's in a tizz about something.'

'Lorraine.'

'Beg yours?'

'You know Lorraine. Mum's dead.'

'Lorraine. You know what I mean.'

'She know you're here?'

'Yes, love. She knows.'

'So I'm the consolation prize?' Sam asked. 'Like, you stuffed it with your own kids so you're left with me?'

'No. She's not a kid. She doesn't need me.'

'And I do now? Like, as opposed to seven years ago? Two-and-a-half months ago?'

She regarded him for a moment and didn't answer the question. 'Will I see you tomorrow afternoon?'

'What's tomorrow afternoon?'

'Going out for a swim with Michael.'

He laughed before he could catch it.

'You think it's funny, do you, mister? Watch out or I'll wear me bikini.'

She was back with those words. The flickering, sharp laughing woman who raised his mother and made scones.

'We'll go blind.'

'Mind your manners, young man.' She was smiling his mother's smile and he felt the gut-lurching pull toward her.

'What is it with this family and water?' he asked.

'Buggered if I know, love. I just like being out there. There's nothing like it. You know, in the thirty-four years I was with your grandfather he never once walked on a beach or swam in the sea? I thought I would dry up completely.'

'Lucky he's gone, hey?'

'Love, I didn't mean ... Will you come out with us

tomorrow? Going to swim point to point. Michael thinks he can beat me, but I doubt it.'

'No. I've got something on.'

'What's her name?'

'How do you know it's a girl?'

'Written all over your face, love. Well, goodnight then. Hooroo.'

'Night, Nana.'

Sam closed the door behind him only to face Lorraine nursing a can of rum and cola on the couch.

'Where the hell have you been?' she asked.

'Out. At a friend's.'

'Look buddy, let's get it straight. I was willin' to cut you some slack 'cause you've lost Rachel and I know it looks all loose and free and easy with Michael and Shane and me, very alternative or whatever, but I always know where they are. Minty as least. You can't just disappear until eleven at night and not tell me where you are. Pick up the bloody phone, for Christ's sake.'

'I don't know the number.'

'What?!' her voice grew high and screechy. 'How can you be livin' here for nearly three months and not know the bloody phone number?'

'I mean, I got it written down somewhere. I just, you know, didn't have it on me.'

'43 67 98. Repeat it.'

He did.

'Again … Again … Again. Jeezus in heaven.' She looked up at the ceiling. 'If she knew! She'd kill me if you were out and I didn't know where you were.'

'You know Nana's out there?'

'Yes. She's me bloody stalker, she is. What a happy little picture we are.' She slogged back the rest of the can and got to her feet. 'I'm gonna go to bed. Call me next time.' Lorraine paused when she got to the bedroom doorway. 'And for your information, that's the only one I've had tonight. Smoked a butt-load of fags, but only had one drink. Just in case she was telling you I need AA.'

'Sure. Yep.'

'I thought you'd taken off. Call next time.'

'Yep. Sorry.'

21

Sam always went surfing with Minty and Ruby on Sunday morning. It was his favourite time to go, Shane was never there because he was always hungover from the night before. Sam got up and found Minty out on the front lawn waxing his board and whistling. A little further down the road, Maddie Clark was walking away in tiny shorts and Minty's T-shirt, pulling her bleached hair into a ponytail.

'Sammy!' Every time he saw Sam he still had that look of pleased surprise, like overnight he had forgotten Sam lived at his house. 'How's it goin', brah?'

'Good.'

'Good? You're never good, man, you're always alright.'

'I'm good.'

Minty's grin grew wider, a Cheshire glare of white teeth against a golden face.

'Have a good night? I had a good night.'

Sam took his board from where it was leaning against the wall and they started up the road toward the beach.

'You look good, brah, not as white. Not as weedy either.'

It was true, he felt different. He felt strong.

'Thanks.'

'It's working for you.'

Up on the headland they passed Gretchen's house and Sam looked up to the balcony. She was there, one ankle up on the balcony rail, stretching in her running shorts and faded 'Zero' T-shirt. Minty followed Sam's gaze.

'Bugger me. Never seen that before.'

'Never seen *her* before, Mint.'

'Whatever, brah. Damn.'

She looked down, saw them and smiled.

'Hey, Sam.'

'Hey. You been for a run?'

'Yeah.'

'How far?'

She screwed up her face in thought. 'Fourteen ks.'

'Shit.'

She shrugged. 'I like it.'

'I can tell.'

Minty was looking at him with his eyebrows raised.

'Mint, this is Gretchen. I know her—'

Minty leaned on his board, reaching an arm up to the nose and accentuating every muscle in his torso. He fixed Gretchen in his stare and unleashed the smile. 'How's it goin'?'

'Good thanks.'

'How come I've never seen you before?'

'You've seen me before.'

'Nah. I'd remember you.'

'I don't usually hang out in a bikini, so probably not.'
Sam could tell she was proud of her dig at Minty. He hoped
Gretchen picked up on the vibe that he thought his cousin
was ridiculous.

'I'll see you,' Sam said. 'You home later? Like, lunch?'

'Yep. Should be.'

'I'll come by.'

They walked away, Minty turning so he was watching her
and walking backwards.

'Put it away, man.'

He laughed. 'That her? Shit. Let me know when you're
finished.'

It was the first time he had ever felt anything other than
affection for his cousin.

'Don't say that.'

'What? I mean she's hot.'

'Well, don't say it like that.'

'Whoa. Okaaaay. Touchy, ay? I get it. Whatever I said, I'm
sorry, brah.'

'Sure.'

Ruby was already in the water when they got to the drop-off.
The swell was what Sam would call big and Minty would
call small. The waves were consistent and regular enough for
Sam to catch a few and even have time to attempt to stand up.
Minty and everyone else called this a pop-up, but every time
Sam tried to use surfer language the words felt clumsy and false
in his mouth, like he was only reinforcing his outsider status.

That said, he was getting better at reading the water, understanding where the rips were and that they were a surfer's friend, used to get out to the line-up as efficiently as possible. He was also better at timing his take-off with a wave and predicting the regularity of the sets. It was something Minty did innately, as naturally as walking or breathing. After three hours in the water he, Minty and Ruby climbed the slope back up to the headland and sat on the bluff overlooking the water.

'You're doing good, brah,' said Minty.

'Yeah. Right.'

'No, serious, serious. I see you, brah. You just got to balance yourself more even on the rails. Feel the water under you, brah. Move with it.'

'I don't know how to do that.'

Minty laughed but didn't offer any insight.

'You're full of shit, Mint,' said Ruby.

'Maybe, Rube, but we'll see who goes all the way.'

'Oh, I'll go all the way Mint, just not with you.'

'Both of you, *shut up*. Seriously,' said Sam.

'You seen Sammy's girlfriend?'

'And don't go anywhere near Gretchen.'

'Ha. Sure thing.'

'I'm serious.'

'I know it.'

'Whoa. Who's Gretchen?' asked Ruby. 'Gretchen Luke? That rich girl? She's in my English class.'

Sam bit his lip and tried to concentrate on not blushing, as if it was possible to stop it.

'What the hell is a chick like that doin' with you?'

'She's a classy lady, that one,' said Minty. 'She got an eyesight problem or somethin'?'

'Thanks a lot.'

'You better get a job, buddy, if you wanna keep her around.'

'Whatever. You can talk.'

'Yeah, I can 'cause I'm gonna win the World Title. Won't need a job.' He said it jokingly, but there was a new resolve in Minty's eyes and Sam wondered if this time he really meant it.

22

Sam showered, found some clean clothes and headed off up the street toward Gretchen's house. When he got to the gate he wasn't sure if he was supposed to knock, or go in, find the front door and then knock. He didn't really want to meet either of her parents but he couldn't taste her on his lips anymore.

He needed to.

The gate was unlocked so he opened it and went in. The front yard had little white pebbles instead of grass, with big stepping stones for a path. Lush green plants lined the path: aloe vera, birds of paradise, maidenhair ferns. He still remembered every plant name Pop had taught him. Big double doors with stained glass greeted him on the veranda, surrounded by clay pots of all different sizes and shapes. He pressed the doorbell and contemplated bolting. But then it opened and a tall, graceful woman looked out at him. She had dreadlocks and a cheesecloth scarf wound around her head. No make-up, big pale eyes like Gretchen's. She smiled in a way you wouldn't expect of someone who had found a stranger on their front doorstep.

'Hello.'

'Hi.'

'Are you a friend of Gretchen's?'

'Yes.'

'Lovely.' She opened the door wider. 'Please, come in.' He wondered if she was high. No one should be this serene.

He stepped inside to a small foyer area with more clay pots and a flight of steep timber stairs, the scent of lime and coconut in the air. The woman led him up to a big open space with lounges and a kitchen with huge glass doors looking out over the ocean. There was music playing, something he hadn't heard since his mother was alive. Sixties folky stuff, Joni Mitchell.

'Gretch,' she called up the hallway. 'There's someone here for you! Can I get you something?' she asked Sam. 'I've just made a pot of raspberry leaf tea. Or I have sparkling water if you'd prefer?'

'Um, no I'm okay.'

'I'm Christa, by the way.'

'Hi. I'm Sam.'

'Lovely to meet you, Sam.'

'Thanks. Same.'

Gretchen emerged from the hallway. She looked surprised to see him standing in her kitchen.

'Hi Sam.'

'Hi.'

Christa opened the sliding doors and slipped out onto the balcony, closing them behind her.

'Did she say anything weird? She can be weird. Try not to pay attention to what she says. Try not to connect her to me.'

'She seems nice. I mean she said something about raspberry leaves, but other than that …'

'Yep. There it is. That's the weird bit.' Gretchen bit her lower lip and they both stood there in her kitchen without talking. Her cheeks were flushing pink, accentuating the freckles across her nose.

They both started to speak at the same time. She laughed, more as a way to fill the space than anything else.

'Want to go somewhere?' she blurted.

Sam followed her across the grass on top of the headland, near the car park and the track down to the rocks. She sat down on the grass and flopped onto to her back, looking up at the sky. Sam did the same. For the first time in his life, lying on the grass looking at the sky seemed a worthwhile way to spend a few hours. He lay next to her, close but not quite touching. She didn't say anything and he felt a crushing pressure to make conversation.

'Was that your mum?'

Gretchen turned her face to him. 'Yes. For better or worse.'

'She has dreadlocks.' Talking about her mum wasn't great, but it was a start.

'She's a poet.'

'A poet?'

'Yep. She makes pottery too. She's a potting poet.'

'Didn't know you could make a living from poetry.'

'Pottery on the other hand …'

'You can make a fortune out of that stuff.' Sam was proud of himself for making a joke. He hoped it didn't show.

'Exactly. No. You can't make money from poetry. Unless you win a bunch of prizes. She's won some. She teaches at the university as well.'

'Cool.'

'Don't go thinking she's cool. She's not cool. Dad works there too. He's a psychiatrist and he teaches. He's not cool either.'

'Is he going to analyse me if he meets me?'

'Only if you're interesting.'

'Am I interesting?'

'Well. You're mysterious. That helps.'

'Mysterious?'

'Well … no one knows anything about you except for the fact that you're Minty Booner's cousin. Something I am willing to overlook.'

He propped himself up on one elbow and leaned over her, placing his other hand on the grass by her shoulder so he was above her.

Her curls were a swirling halo around her face and as she smiled a dimple formed in her chin.

He kissed her, letting his body fall gently onto hers. She grasped his neck and shoulder and he had to move his knee up beside her hip to take his weight and free up one hand, which slid up her back, under her shirt. Just touching the back of her bra unleashed hot sparks in his chest. He curled his tongue around hers and she made a little noise which he interpreted as approval. She caressed the back of his neck and put her fingers through his hair, then she pulled away from him with an expression he couldn't read because he didn't know her well enough yet.

He rolled over onto the grass beside her.

'Do you feel better now?' she asked. 'I feel better now. Less tense. I was tense before. Now less so. I get tense a lot.'

Sam laughed.

'I talk when I get nervous.'

'I noticed. Are you nervous now?'

'No comment.'

'Sure.'

Sam could hear the waves crashing on the beach. Seagulls swirled around in the sky above them.

'I really hope one of them doesn't poo on me,' she said. 'I'm nervous about that.'

'Same, now you mention it.'

'So, what do your parents do, Sam?'

'You sound like you're interviewing me for a job.'

'Give me a break. I'm under a lot of stress at the moment.'

'Nothing. I don't have any. I don't know my dad and my mum died,' Sam closed his eyes and counted back, 'three months ago.'

She left it way too long to say something.

'I'm sorry,' she whispered.

'It's okay. You didn't kill her.'

'Someone killed her!?'

'No, just … It's not your fault. Don't say you're sorry.'

'That's really recent.'

'Yeah it is. It's why I moved down here, it's why I moved in with Minty. He … I know … I know what he seems like, but he's good to me … he's the only one.' Sam was learning that it was easy to talk to someone when you were lying on your back on the grass looking at the sky instead of each other.

'Can you ask me about something else?' he said.

'Um … What's your favourite song?'

'One song?'

'Yep. One.'

'"Mojo Pin", Jeff Buckley,' he answered.

'Nice.'

'You?'

'"1979", Smashing Pumpkins. At the moment anyway. I change it all the time. I mean, there are so many songs in the world. Millions.'

'Millions.'

'What's your favourite song that's really embarrassing and you would never tell anyone?' she asked.

'I'm not telling you.'

'Aha! You know exactly what I'm talking about. You have one! You like a really embarrassing song! You're not cool at all! Ahhh, wait until this gets out. It's all over for you. Come on. What is it?'

He turned his head and saw her smiling up at the sky. 'No.'

'Tell me!'

'"I Want to Know What Love Is". Aghhh. I can't believe I told you that.'

She cracked up. 'By Foreigner?' She made fists and sang the chorus into the sky.

'So you know it then.'

'Yeah, I do and it's terrible.'

'No it's not. It's romantic.'

'I can't believe you just said that.'

'You know it's true. So what's yours?'

'"Turn Back Time", Cher.'

'I don't see what's embarrassing about that.'

'Exactly. And I'm not embarrassed by the song, I'm more embarrassed on Cher's behalf for the outfit that goes with the song.'

'The seat-belt harness thingy?'

'That's the one.'

'I really don't know what you mean.'

'You can tell a lot about a person from their secret favourite song. It's also fun to guess what someone's secret song is. It's something I am particularly good at.'

'Oh yeah? Did you pick mine?'

'No. I honestly thought you were going to say "In the Air Tonight" by Phil Collins. I thought there was a high probability you played air drums to that song. I still think that.'

'I'm not going to confirm or deny playing air drums to Phil Collins.'

'Hillary Clinton, for instance: I think her secret song is "Lady in Red".'

'She does wear a lot of red.'

'Yep. John Howard, his favourite is "Fernando" by Abba.'

'You've thought a lot about this.'

'I have. I think he sings it to Janette and she secretly hates it, but can't bear to tell him. The Queen: her favourite is "Wannabe" by the Spice Girls, but she also loves Abba, "Waterloo". She appreciates the historical context.'

Sam laughed.

'Any other insights?'

'Well, I also think a good way to gauge someone's true self is to play "What Would You Rather?" with them.'

'What would you rather?'

'What would you rather: making out with John Howard or the Queen?'

'Oh man.'

'You have to choose. It's like you are Princess Leia and Darth Vader is going to destroy your planet before your very eyes if you don't answer.'

'I'm Princess Leia? Is that part of the game?'

'Not usually, but let's roll with it.'

'I thought you hated sci-fi?'

'I make an exception for *Star Wars*. Two words: Han Solo. But you are trying to distract me! You're avoiding this! I need an answer, your planet is going to die, ahhhhhhhhh!'

'Oh man. Um. The Queen. I guess. I mean, she was a babe back in the day. I've never said that out loud before.'

'I know! And she has a great bosom. Excellent choice.'

Sam couldn't answer. He was laughing too much.

He kissed Gretchen goodbye on the street outside her house, pulling her close to him, smelling her skin and her hair. As he walked back to the Booners' he saw the spindly frame of Nana in the veranda light again, swiping mozzies off her skinny brown arms.

'Oh.'

'Allo love.'

'Hi.'

'Come up to the van? I've made a casserole. Lorraine said you're good to come if you'd like. She even opened the door when she spoke to me.'

'What sort of casserole?'

'Typical male! Beef and mushroom.'

It was too tempting after weeks of barbecue chook and takeaway.

'Alright.'

'C'mon.'

Moths flickered at the streetlights as Nana led the way back up past Gretchen's house and along the headland to the caravan park. People were sitting outside their vans, smoking and drinking. She said hello to every one of them like they were old friends and she'd been there for years. To a few of them she announced that Sam was her grandson. Sam waved and she beamed at him. Her van was a tiny tin can, white with an orange stripe belting its middle and faded sixties-style floral curtains in the little window, which was barely bigger than a porthole. The canvas annex was almost bigger than the actual van. A line hung from the light pole to the side of the annex, two bright bikinis hanging out to dry. Two folding canvas chairs sat out on the grass and she motioned to them.

'There y'are. You have a seat and I'll get you some dinner. Want a lemonade?'

'Thank you.'

She ducked through the door into the annex. Sam sat

down and looked up at the stars in the clear velvety sky. She came out and handed him a steaming plate. 'You right with it on your lap?'

'Yeah. Thanks.'

She returned with a can of Kmart-brand lemonade and an old Nutella jar with Bugs Bunny on the side.

'You're not eating?' he asked.

'Already eaten.'

'Oh.'

'Go on, two, four, six, eight.'

It was rich and creamy, the meat falling apart on his fork. It was weird to cook a casserole when the weather wasn't too cold, but it tasted so good he didn't care. He tried to remember the last time he had eaten one of her meals and couldn't. He only had fragments of snapshots: Christmas ham, apple pie, jelly and ice-cream with custard.

She smiled as she watched him eat. 'I miss cooking for you boys. That Lorraine, I don't know how she keeps you all fed, although from the look of you, she doesn't. I tried to teach her, but she wouldn't have it. Your mum was slightly better. Not much.'

'No one cooks like you, Nana.'

'Ah. That's my boy.'

'You go swimming with Minty?'

'I did.'

'How long you been swimming?'

'Well. Let's see. I started swimming in the ocean when I was in Italy. Got a job as a cleaner in a hotel. They liked me because I could talk to the Pommy customers. Those Italians know how to cook a meal, but it's better for you, you know. Lots of vegetables, never eaten so many vegetables. I was happy, didn't need so many sweets to cheer me up. Started swimming and walking and the weight slowly dropped off. Now you can't keep me out of the water. Up north at Port they have a swim club and I go every day and do laps and ocean swims. That's the ticket.'

He ate the casserole and downed the lemonade as if he hadn't eaten for months. He hadn't felt so hungry since his mum died.

'Michael been teaching you how to surf?'

'A bit.'

'You stand up yet?'

'Yeah.'

'You good at it?'

'Not as good as him.'

'So who's your sweetheart?'

'Pardon?'

'Your girlfriend.'

'How do you know if I've got a girlfriend?'

'You're a handsome devil. You have a sweetheart. Who is she?'

'No one.'

'Well, she'll be thrilled to hear that.'

'Just a girl I know from round here.'

'Nice girl?'

'Yeah. Lives up in that big house on the headland.'

Nana raised her eyebrows. 'Does she now? You're like your mother, you know.'

'What do you mean?'

'Lofty ambitions. You aim high. Not a bad thing. You keeping up with your studies.'

'School? I'm not going.'

'What d'you mean you're not going?!' she squawked like Lorraine.

'I can't … I just don't see the point.'

'You gonna get a trade? Do an apprenticeship?'

'Yeah. Maybe. Dunno.'

Her silence told him what she thought of that.

'Do you remember how Pop used to build us the little jumps for our skateboards?' he asked her.

'Of course.'

'He wasn't all, you know, uptight, no fun.'

She turned her head and looked out over the caravan park. A kid rode past on a bicycle.

'Do you want some dessert?' she asked brightly.

'Sure. Thanks.'

'You're welcome.' She stood up and took his plate without meeting his eye, disappearing into the caravan. Sam sat in the fold-out chair and listened to the cockatoos screeching like dragons overhead. Nana returned and handed him a plastic bowl of fruit salad and green jelly. When he was little jelly seemed like the most delicious thing on the planet: all those dinners at Nana and Pop's. She always gave them dessert in her good bowls, glass ones with pictures of gold bunches of grapes around the rim, like she trusted her grandsons to be careful and never break them. He'd felt so safe there, like nothing in the world would ever go wrong.

'Nana.'

'Yes, love?'

'Do you know …' His mouth went dry and he forced the jelly on his tongue down. 'Do you know who my dad is?'

Her face changed. She put her dessert on the camp table, untouched. 'You don't wanna go there, love.'

'Yeah, I do. I want to know.'

'He wasn't a good man.'

'That's the way it is in our family, isn't it? No good men?'

'Nonsense. You'll be a good man.'

Sam felt his lip wobble. 'Who was he?'

'I'm not doing this, love. I promised your mum. I promised both of them.'

'You promised him as well?'

'No. That's not …'

'Who did you promise?'

She gripped the arms of the picnic chair, her pink fingernails gleaming in the fluoro light. 'There are things you're better off not knowing, love.'

'You don't get to decide that.' He felt it uncoiling in his gut. He clenched his fists on his knees to stop the shaking.

'Look,' her tone was the same as when they were kids and she was telling them the rules in her house. The walls were up. 'I've got nothing to tell you. He wasn't worth wasting your breath on. This ends now.'

'Nana …'

'No. Enough.'

He couldn't speak. He stood up and walked away from her, on auto pilot back to the Booners'.

23

Minty drove Sam in the Datsun up to Gretchen's house. Sam knocked on her door and saw her shape skipping down the stairs through the glass. She opened the door, hair out, short lacy dress, converse sneakers and red lipstick. She looked amazing.

'Good evening.' She beamed at him.

'Hey, I got us a ride.' He stood aside to let her walk in front of him. He opened the garden gate for her and Minty revved the engine of the Datsun, holding up a devil's salute with his tongue out. 'Ignore him.' Sam opened up the back passenger door for her and she got in. He slid in next to her and took her hand.

Minty slammed the car into reverse and shot backwards out onto the street before accelerating in a screech of rubber. 'Bye, Mum!' he yelled out the window.

'Thanks for that,' said Sam.

'Where you lovers going?'

'I heard there's a Chinese restaurant on King Street. Do you like Chinese?' he asked Gretchen.

'They deep-fry things, don't they? I never get to eat deep-fried things.'

Minty drove them as if he was performing a time trial. When they arrived and got out of the car, Gretchen looked a couple of shades paler than she normally was.

'Sorry about that.' He squeezed her hand.

'We're getting the train back, aren't we?'

'Yep.'

The restaurant was crowded and noisy, a whole lot of tables and chairs crammed into a small space, most of which was taken up by a giant fish tank in the middle of the room. Everything – walls, tablecloths, napkins – was apricot coloured. They were rushed to a small table in a corner, the waitress taking their order without writing anything down. Then they sat in silence and waited for the food to come. Sam was overthinking everything and couldn't decide on a single thing to say so he pretended to be studying the wallpaper.

'I overshare when I'm nervous,' Gretchen blurted. 'Sorry in advance. I'm probably going to give you a detailed account of the last time I shaved or something. It was recently, by the way. Coastal living really has its drawbacks.' She scrunched her eyes shut and her cheeks flushed pink, showing up her freckles. 'See, there I go. That's the last thing I'm going to say. I'm not going to speak the entire time we're here. I'm just going to mime everything. Like charades.'

'No, please, tell me more.'

She pressed her lips shut, shaking her head and trying not to laugh.

'What's the most embarrassing thing you've ever said?'

'Um, weren't you just listening?'

'No, there's gotta be worse than that.'

'Um, let me think, there's so very much to choose from. At my old school, in Sydney, we used to get heaps of exchange students. I'm really, really bad at geography, like, appalling. And this one time I was talking to a Swiss exchange student and I asked where he lived and he said Zurich and I asked if that was close to Stockholm.'

'That's bad, but it's not terrible.'

'I'm not telling you the terrible one.'

'Yes you are, look at you. You're dying to tell me.'

'No really, you will have zero respect for me afterwards.'

'Tell me.'

'I was talking to this other guy and I asked him where he was from and he said Montreal and I said "Cool. What part of America is that?"'

'You did not.'

'I did.' She was laughing so much she had to wipe tears away. 'It was his accent! Now, if someone's talking about anything at all geography related I don't say a word.' She made a zipping gesture across her lips. 'Even if I know all about the place, I'll be about to open my mouth and say something like, I don't know, "I'd love to go to Spain, especially Barcelona," and I'll be all like *do not say that, Gretchen. Barcelona isn't in Spain.* Even though I know it is.'

'Have you ever been overseas?'

'Yeah. The US, Asia, Europe a bit. We lived in France for six months a few years ago.'

'Wow.'

'It was pretty cool. You?'

'Um …' He unfolded and refolded his napkin. There was Bali with his mum. It had been the best holiday he'd ever had.

'You know, a bit. Here and there. Never for long. You lived in France? Whereabouts?' As if he knew France at all.

'Loire Valley, a few hours out of Paris. I mean we did Paris as well, of course.'

'Sure.'

'We lived in a little village. It was the quintessential French village: cobbled streets, a chateau, a bakery with amazing croissants …'

Sam nodded wondering how she managed to use the word 'quintessential' in a conversation and not seem like a total wanker. She was so warm, so unassuming despite all the talk about European holidays. When he spoke she leaned in, weighing everything he said as if he was intelligent and important. Plus she had a heart-shaped birthmark on her clavicle and it made him want to touch her skin.

'We stayed in this restored monastery that was like five hundred years old. Our neighbour, she was thirty or something, we could see directly into her backyard and she would spend all day in a T-shirt and lacy underwear painting and smoking. So French. It was hilarious. It was obvious we could see her and she just didn't care.'

'Maybe she did, maybe that's why she wore lacy underwear.'

Gretchen laughed and nodded. 'That's it! You're onto her.'

'Do you speak French?'

'Juste un petit peu.'

'I don't, so you're going to have to translate that.'

'Just a little.'

'Yeah, right. More than me.'

'I did go to school there, so … I'm not as good as I used to be, though.'

'Sure.'

'Really, I'm not. Like France is cool, but it's not everything Australians think it is.'

'I don't believe you.'

'I'm serious. Before I went I just assumed everyone there was really stylish, but there are French bogans.'

'French bogans?'

'Absolutely. They wear tracksuits made out of that parachute material stuff, with like these gross Adidas slide things on their feet. And the bogan French women have mullets.'

'Yeah?'

'Definitely.'

'The one who lived next door?'

'No, she was hot. She had a pixie kind of haircut. She didn't shave her underarms, though.'

'Ew.'

Gretchen laughed. 'I don't know, there was something cool about her … she didn't care. Maybe if you have a face like she did you can get away with it.'

'You have a pretty good face. Do you shave your underarms?'

She laughed loudly. 'What would you rather: have your whole head waxed, or your armpits and pubic hairs waxed at the same time?'

'Um. Head definitely. You?'

'Arms and pubes! I'm a woman! We have to do that crap all the time.'

'What would you rather,' he asked. 'Have a purple cloud come out of your butt every time you fart *and* it hangs around for twenty minutes, or have all your thoughts displayed for everyone to see for three hours a day?'

'The purple fart. Because I think that would become a novelty, you know, like I could go on breakfast television. I would become a minor celebrity. I could do it at parties, people would love that.'

'I did not expect you to say that.'

'What would you rather: your life partner be the most beautiful woman in the world but really into *Star Trek*, like *really* into it – only wears *Star Trek* T-shirts, has a whole house full of *Star Trek* merchandise – or have a great personality, like your best friend, but covered in blue fur, all over. This is the person you are spending your whole life with. And you're completely monogamous.'

'Fur?'

'Like cat fur. All over.'

'Do they moult in the summer?'

'That's your concern?'

'Well, would it get all over the furniture?'

'You're worried about your furniture? You have to have sex with this person!'

'There's a lot to weigh up, here. And I feel I'm going to be judged ...'

'Are you kidding?' she laughed. 'Take the *Star Trek* fan!'

'I don't want to be superficial.'

'No way. I take the fan. You're not going to care about the *Star Trek* merch when this person is naked.'

'I think you're a very shallow person.'

The food arrived and Gretchen used chopsticks like a pro. She tried to teach him but he couldn't do it properly.

'It's been twenty minutes and I still haven't got any food in my mouth,' he laughed. 'Is this your scheme to make sure you get all the food? Or are you hinting that my bum is getting too big?'

'That's it. Definitely. You need to lose weight.'

'Good to know.'

They shared fried ice-cream for dessert and he decided that it was a success as far as dates go. He paid the bill with his mum's keycard, opened the door for her and they stepped out into the night. He slipped off his jacket and put it over her shoulders. 'You look cold.'

'Whoa. You're good at this. Should I be worried?'

He grinned and took her hand. They walked along the road toward the train station. At the ticket office he pulled out his wallet and asked for two tickets. The teller pointed to a sign. 'Track work,' he grunted. 'There's a bus in forty-five minutes.'

'For real?'

'Afraid so.'

Sam shook forty cents out of his wallet and went to the pay phone. He dialled the house number, not really expecting anybody to answer. He was right. He hung the phone up and the coins cluttered down. It was embarrassing that he didn't have a car.

'Let's walk,' she suggested.

'Walk?'

'Yeah, it's about forty-five minutes along the coast. There's a path most of the way.'

'You're happy to walk?'

'Of course,' she tugged on his hand. 'Come on.'

So they walked and she told him stories about embarrassing things she'd said in French.

'Do you want to go back to France?'

'Yes. I want to do a semester of uni over there.'

'You've got it all planned.'

She shrugged. 'I want to go to Sydney Uni. Live in a college up there. I've been waiting to do that for so long, it would be so cool. What about you?'

'Don't know.'

'What do you want to do?'

'Not be on the dole. Other than that ...' He shrugged. 'Nothing really seems important anymore, you know. I had plans before. Mum had a little fund, saving up for uni fees. I could have stayed living at home, it was close to Sydney Uni. Now, it's all gone to shit, hasn't it?'

'Don't you have access to that money? Didn't your mum leave you something?'

'My aunt controls it all. She said Mum was in debt so all her assets have been sucked into that. There's nothing left for me.'

'That doesn't sound right.'

'Well, that's the way it is. I dunno. Minty's going to go to Hawaii. Maybe I'll go with him.'

'What would you do in Hawaii?'

'Surf.'

'But that's not *you*. That's not really what you're into.'

'How do you know?'

'I just do, I can tell.'

'Based on my secret favourite song?'

'I know what you should do! You should be a sound engineer.'

'Yeah, as if that's going to happen.'

'Dude, your attitude sucks.'

He stopped walking and swung round in front of her. He tried to speak gently. 'Can we talk about something else? I'm over talking about it.'

She looked hurt. 'Sure. Whatever.'

They walked in silence and he felt the heavy tension between them. He hated it. He reached over and took her hand in his, pulled her closer to him.

They were near the beach now, the roar of the waves amplified in the quiet of the night. Misty salt hung in the air.

'Wanna go for a paddle?' she asked.

'Absolutely.'

They took off their shoes and walked across the cold sand to the water. It was pitch dark and for a while they giggled and stumbled until their eyes adjusted to the darkness.

He kicked water at her and she squealed, ducking away. He chased her and caught her around the waist. The knowledge that she would do better than him crept up and stunned him. He would be a sweet memory for her – that surfer guy she had a fling with before she moved on to someone more serious. The feeling dug away at his insides. He took her face in his hands and kissed her, pulling her hips close to him so their bodies were pressed together, moulded into each other. His hands were in her hair and she held onto his neck; they staggered backwards up out of the water to the dry sand. He pulled her down onto the sand, she on top of him. He rolled her over, his mouth over hers, her tongue everywhere in his. He ran a hand up her thigh, under her skirt and she didn't stop him. He pulled her dress up and over her head so she was there in her sneakers and underwear. She pulled at his shirt, taking it off him. Her skin was so warm against his: skin and sand and salt on his tongue. She tilted her head back and he kissed her smooth neck.

Suddenly she stilled and spoke into his ear, 'Not here. Stop.'

He pulled away and tried to get his breath.

'I can't. I've … I've never done this, it's going to be messy. I can't here. And I don't have a condom.'

'I do.'

'Not here.'

'Okay. You're going to have to put your dress on. I need a minute. Sorry.'

'It's okay.'

She reached over and pulled her dress from the sand, standing up to shake the sand off it. She handed him his shirt and he pulled it over his head.

He held her hand and they walked back up the sand to the path. He put his jacket over her shoulders and when they got to her house she started to take it off to give back to him.

'Hang on to it. It's cold.'

She kissed him and let herself into the house. He watched her go up the stairs and liked the thought of her in his clothes.

24

Over the next two weeks Sam learned things about Gretchen. He learned that she used to be scared of swimming, but was asthmatic and swimming was supposed to help, so her parents made her do it and she discovered that she loved it. She also loved running, but she didn't play team sports because her co-ordination was crap. Now she was training for her first triathlon with her dad. He was a long-distance runner. Sam knew that she hated horror movies and had a low tolerance for any sort of fear in general; roller coasters were out of the question. She played the violin. She had knocked her front tooth out when she was twelve, the result of a misjudged backflip into a pool. Her front left tooth was false and she wanted the dentist to fix the gap when they put it in, but her parents wouldn't allow it. She was allergic to tomatoes. She didn't like chewy caramel that got stuck in your teeth. Her mum made her learn Keats's poems in primary school during a brief stint of homeschooling. 'Before she realised it was hell spending all day everyday with her own kids,' Gretchen laughed. Her brother was four years younger and his name was Roan. He was nerdy. She didn't usually cry in books or movies except for *Bridge to Terabithia* which brought her undone every time she read it. Her favourite artist was Mark Rothko and he liked that she was the sort of girl who had a favourite artist he'd never heard of.

Sam was aware that if someone asked her what she knew about him she would struggle to produce an extensive list.

Now they were lying on the grass on the headland and he was trying to explain the plot to *The Usual Suspects* without giving away the ending. He concluded that she would just have to watch it.

'Maybe I will. Maybe tomorrow after dinner. What are you doing for dinner tomorrow?'

'Nice segue.'

'I know, right? I should be on the radio.'

'I'd listen to you.'

'Thank you. I was just, I mean, do you ... My parents kind of want to have you over. They're those sort of parents. It's unfortunate, but I can't seem to change them. Will you come have dinner tomorrow? You don't have to stay ages. You don't have to come at all. I understand if you don't want to come. I wouldn't have dinner with them at all except they are my parents. Don't worry about it, forget I said anything ...'

'Sure.'

'Really?'

'I have to have dinner with you? Sounds alright to me.'

'Dinner with me and my family. My pretentious, annoying family. You do realise they're going to be there, right?'

'I'll cope.'

'I wasn't expecting that. I wasn't expecting that at all. I'm stunned. I'm in shock. I can't speak.'

'That's a first. Don't worry, I can handle parents. They're a novelty 'cause I don't have any of my own.'

She was quiet and he could tell she didn't know what to say.

'Plus, mums love me.'

She laughed. 'I bet.'

Minty lent him another shirt. Sam tried it on in Minty's room, in front of his mirror. He wondered if he should shave; the stubble and the shaggy hair made him look like some kind of unkempt wolf man. Her parents wouldn't want her with a wolf man. He went into the bathroom and Minty followed him, leaning on the doorframe, flicking through a surf magazine.

'Gonna be good tomorrow, Mint. Southerly wind. Groundswell and that cyclone from up north.'

'Yeah? You're good to have around, brah ... Dinner, ay?'

'Yeah.'

'With her olds?'

'Yep.'

Minty grinned and shook his head. 'I've never met any girl's parents. She's got you on the leash, brah.'

'As if. Just because I'm going to meet her mum and dad?'

'Oath. She's got you by the balls.'

'Because I actually talk to her?'

'Ha. Brah, you don't talk to anyone.'

'I talk to her.'

'About what?'

'Dunno. Stuff.'

'Yeah, well you go to dinner with her olds, you're practically engaged to her.'

Sam finished shaving and didn't answer him.

Christa opened the front door, just like the first time he had visited. Her smile was warm and she took Sam by the shoulders and kissed his cheek.

'Welcome, Sam. So glad you could make it.'

He followed her up the stairs into the living room. The sliding doors to the deck were open and the curtains billowed in the sea breeze. The house was like something out of a magazine. He could see a man leaning on the railing with a glass of red wine, looking out at the water.

'Hey, Sam.' Gretchen was sitting cross-legged on the calfskin rug playing scrabble with a kid who Sam guessed to be her brother.

'Roan, this is Sam.'

Roan beamed at him.

'Hey man.'

'Do you have a skateboard?'

'Yeah.'

'Did you bring it?'

'Um ...'

'Roan,' Gretchen said. 'Sam's here for dinner. Not a

skating demo.' She stood up and stretched. Her pants were a loose, semi-sheer fabric and they hung from her hips. She was curvy, straight-backed and toned, like a dancer or an Olympic diver. She padded across the living room and stood on her tiptoes to kiss him on his cheek. He could smell the vanilla conditioner she used in her hair.

'Is this the famous Sam?' The man came in off the balcony and offered his hand to Sam. He was short and bearded, with glasses, and he looked exactly the way Sam expected a psychiatrist to look. He didn't treat Sam as if Sam was imagining the bits of Gretchen that were under her clothes.

'I'm Marcus. Pleased to meet you.'

'Hi.'

'Can we get you a drink, Sam? Water, juice, wine?'

Christa was floating around in the kitchen, checking pots and stirring things. 'I have a lovely bottle of red open,' she said, as if it was nothing to be offering underage visitors alcohol.

'Ah, um. Just water, please.'

'Marcus and I are vegetarian, so if you were hoping for a steak, I'm afraid we're going to disappoint you. I have a spiced cauliflower dhal and a coconut eggplant curry.'

'That sounds amazing, thanks,' said Sam, accepting a glass of water from Marcus.

'You're most welcome.'

'Come! Sit down!' said Marcus. 'I must interrogate you!'

'He's joking,' said Gretchen. 'I'm pretty sure he's joking.'

Sam sat on the couch and Gretchen sat next to him. Marcus took his wineglass to one of the leather batwing chairs that looked more like art sculptures than things you would actually sit on. Sam tried to figure out what his mother would have made of these people with their designer furniture and exotic food. They were kind. She would have paid them that.

'Gretchen tells us you are new to the area, from Sydney?'

'Yeah. Enmore.'

'And how does our little enclave compare to city living?'

'The views are better.'

Marcus laughed a generous laugh and sipped his wine. Christa came into the room and selected an LP from the shelf. She lifted the needle of the record player and put it on. It was some sort of soul music, authentic-sounding. Sam figured that if he could make it through the evening without saying something stupid he would be okay. The unexpected thing was that he liked being there in the house with Gretchen's family. They were relaxed in a natural way, not like uptight people pretending they were easygoing. They asked him questions and seemed to genuinely value his opinions. The conversation over dinner moved between politics to Australia's preoccupation with sport to the reasons someone might choose to climb Everest. The kinds of things his mum used to talk to him about. Sam didn't so much participate as sit and let it wash over him – the tranquillity of a family who had never known real fear. The only time he felt uncomfortable was when Christa asked him if he kept in touch with his friends from Sydney.

'Yeah, you never talk about Sydney people,' Gretchen said.

Sam put down his fork. 'Not much to say. I moved. They're doing their thing. I'm doing mine.'

'It's like you are an alien with no past dropped into Earth,' said Gretchen.

'Well … that's because that's the situation exactly.'

They laughed but kept looking at him like they needed more of an explanation. Like they had established an intimacy with him by feeding him lentils and offering him wine and they were his newfound confidants. Even Roan was leaning in like he was expecting more clues.

'I dunno, I wanted to start fresh. Like, I'm not gonna call them and talk on the phone. And I'm not the letter-writing type, so …' he trailed off and they laughed, seemingly satisfied. Christa got up and served rosewater pannacotta in little handmade dishes and Sam pretended it was something he had heard of before.

After dinner they slipped out the front gate and he held her waist and kissed her, her arms around his neck.

'Was that okay? I feel it might have been okay,' she asked.

'Yeah, I like kissing you.'

'You know what I mean.'

'I'd like to eat a steak, but other than that, fine. Do they always offer your friends wine?'

'No. It means they like you.'

'Why do they like me?'

'They can tell you're a good person.'

Gretchen's words took him back to the apartment in Enmore. The spaghetti in the bowls. He held Gretchen's soft hands and tried to anchor himself in the present moment, tried to ignore the way his breath shortened and the sick hollow feeling that threatened to open up inside of him.

'I should go,' he said.

'I'll walk back to your house with you.'

He shook his head. 'No, I don't want you walking back alone.'

'It's, like, three hundred metres.'

'No.' He kissed her lips. She kept hold of his hand as he pulled away.

'Sam?'

'Yes, Gretchen?' He wanted to kiss her again.

'What happened to your mum? Was she sick, or ... ? It's okay. Sorry. You don't have to talk about it ... I just. I want to know about you. Sorry.'

'It's okay. She,' Sam paused, 'yeah, she was sick. Cancer.'

'Oh. I'm sorry.'

'I'll call you tomorrow.'

25

He opened his eyes and Minty was in his face, the morning light still weak, the house silent.

'It's up, man! C'mon.' He threw a wetsuit on the bed.

Sam stretched and rolled over. 'I'll come down later.'

'No way!'

Sam opened one eye. Minty's reaction was as if he'd said something deeply offensive.

'You don't understand, Sammy. This is it. I can feel it. I have this sense, when it's goin' to be crankin', I just know. Intuition, like. You have to come down, I'm not lettin' you stay here. Ay, how was your date? Where is she, under the bed?'

'Shut up.' Sam got up and fumbled his way into the wettie. It was impossible to say no to Minty.

The sun was just beginning to peek over the horizon. Seven cars were in the car park, more than usual for that time of the morning. A few guys waxed their boards on the grass; they whistled at Minty and he waved but didn't stop, already at a jog by the time he hit the gravel of the car park. Sam followed him down the winding goat track through the saltbush and snake grass. It was steep, but each of Minty's steps was quick and assured. Sam tried to keep up. The tide was out, leaving the rocky platform exposed. Usually it was windy out on the point, but this morning the fresh autumn air was still. Waves built just south of the furthest outcrop of rocks and rolled, perfectly coiled, north, around the headland all the way into the beach, almost a kilometre behind them. Other surfers began to trickle down the headland. Sam hung back and watched Minty skip across the rocks, taking a direct line to the easternmost point, the most formidable spot to jump in, but the quickest way to the biggest waves. He would take his place first in the line-up and Sam was fairly sure no one would come along who could usurp him. A wave came in and broke over the rocks at his feet; Minty chose his moment and vaulted out, riding the foam as it sucked out to the ocean, sliding under the next rush of water that threatened to throw him back on the rocks.

It wasn't until Minty had paddled out that Sam got a sense of the scale of the waves. The other surfers tracked this way and that across the rocks, tentative in their choice. Most picked the easiest spot to enter, where the water was deepest. Sam's heart was in his throat as the soles of his feet left the rock and the cold water splashed his face. He hadn't felt this uneasy before. The ocean had become his solace, but not now. He wondered what he was doing wrong. He clawed across the water, buffeting the face of each wave, trying to block out the churn in his guts. People were streaming down the embankment now, scattering and throwing themselves at the water. Offering themselves. Sam lay on his board and watched the sets rolling in. It was quieter than you would think out on the water, the sound of the waves more like television static turned down in the background. It didn't match up with the picture and Sam realised it was because the waves were so good, they weren't collapsing on themselves and crashing onto the rock, they were rolling fast and perfectly smooth, like cresting and curling liquid glass.

It looked like most of the other people out were decent enough surfers until you saw Minty get a wave. Others pumped and jerked the board around, hanging onto the wave for as long as it would allow them. Minty danced the board into the curl, swivelling calligraphy lines across the face. He switched directions and flicked the board off the crest of the wave like a skater in a half-pipe, landing the jump in whitewater, where you expected it to swallow him, but he sailed out upright. He did it again and again. It was absurd what he could do.

A few times Minty rode a wave toward Sam and left it, gifting it to him. Sam almost wished he wouldn't, he felt the preciousness of every wave, he had to use it well otherwise Minty would have sacrificed it to him for nothing. No one was more reviled than the person who took a wave and wasted it. Before, whenever Sam had caught a ride and managed to stand, he'd felt the brutal tranquillity of the rest of the world falling away, the present honed into sharp focus. But now he was wobbly, his reflexes jarring. During one ride he felt as if he was going too fast, bailing over the side of the board and tumbling under the water, panic coursing through his limbs. He came up, grabbing onto the board, trying to orientate himself and saw Ruby jogging down the grass track of the headland. She padded across the rocks to the eastern point without hesitation, vaulted into the water and paddled into the line-up next to Minty. A big one rolled in and Minty motioned that it was hers. She paddled onto it, springing to her feet in a quick, assured movement, pushing her weight through her back foot, driving the board across the wave then crouching down, slowing as the barrel curled over her. She rode it out until it died, when she dived off the board and bobbed up a few metres from Sam. She flashed a smile toward him and he was surprised that she'd even noticed him there.

'Well, that was worth ditching work for.' She hoisted herself out of the water and straddled the board. 'How's it goin', lover boy? I saw you get caned. What happened?'

'Dunno. You skipped out on work?'

She didn't answer, just looked out at the horizon, sniffed and swiped water from her eyes.

'Don't lose your job.'

'As if.'

'How's things?' Sam asked.

'You know: work, school.'

'Didn't see you round last weekend. You haven't been in?'

'Yeah, I have, just not here.'

'Where?'

'Down south.'

'Why?'

She didn't answer straightaway, her eyes were on the line-up. 'Guy I know, he goes down there. He's a bit older, different crew.'

'Minty know about him?'

She flashed him a look. 'Why would Minty care?'

He didn't try and answer. They both sat on their boards, with the water rolling underneath them, and watched as Minty caught a spectacular wave. He did a jump off the step and swivelled the board.

'He's been practising?'

'Yeah, I guess.'

She nodded, watching Minty in silence. Sam expected her to paddle away but she didn't. He sensed her wanting to say something.

'You alright?' he asked.

'Had a fight with me mum.'

'Oh.'

'Asked her about my birth mum, about what that woman – Aunty Violet – said. The Indigenous stuff.'

'What she say?'

'She went off her nut.'

'Know what that's like. I asked my nana who my dad is and she clammed up.'

'What's wrong with these olds, you reckon? What are they all so friggin' afraid of?'

'Dunno. The truth must be a scary thing.'

'Guess so.' She slipped onto her stomach and paddled back out into the line-up, leaving Sam bobbing over the waves.

*

It was hot in the sun and his mouth was dry with thirst and nerves. The swell seemed to be getting bigger. If he wasn't afraid to die, why was he scared? He wondered if others could see it in his face, if Ruby could see it. Was he tolerated out here because of pity or because he was Minty's cousin? Which was worse. *What would you rather?* He realised that he had been drifting further out the back and around the point without noticing it. He was in the channel that was pulling out directly to where Minty was, where the waves were biggest. He realised too late that if he kept drifting, the only way to get back in would be to catch a wave.

Minty clocked him and beamed, raising his eyebrows. He thought Sam had made a conscious decision to take this on. Minty's pride in him was evident, strong enough to steal Minty's focus from the water. The swell out here was edging on four metres. As a wave built and rolled toward Sam – no one on it – he felt like he was going to puke over the side of the board. He could sense eyes on him, Minty's and the others'. There was no choice. If he didn't take it, it would be obvious he'd lost his nerve and he was shitting himself – he was a coward. Sam turned the nose of the board toward the beach and paddled, faster and faster; the wave picked him up. He waited for the stillness to come, the rest of the world to drop away, but it didn't. He was trembling. Wobbly, he popped up. The water was moving too fast, it was all happening too quickly, the board was pointing down the wave, when it should have been parallel to it. His position was all wrong and he was four metres in the air. Time didn't slow until the nose of the board caught the face of the wave and he was flipped, spearing into the water head first, whitewater all around, his body like helpless refuse, discarded by the ocean. His feet were somewhere over his head and he couldn't quite account for all his limbs and what they were doing. Then a force like a shattering brick wall coming down on him, pushing him into an ocean floor that felt as hard and unforgiving as stone. The Leviathan had him. There was no breath. He couldn't even remember his last breath. He wanted to inhale, his lungs telling him to breathe the water. *What would you rather: death by drowning or a crushed spine?* Somewhere there was light; he surged toward it and in a blissful moment his head broke through the water's surface. He gasped and swallowed air. He was sorting the water from the sky when another wave came down on him and he was under, flipping, tumbling, with barely enough time to register what had happened. He was down there again, in the dark, chaotic vault, flipped and flung and useless. His eyes found the bright white bubbles, he followed them and then he felt something grip onto his upper arm. He was hauled out of the water and onto a board, gasping like a stunned fish.

'You're right. You're up, you're right.'

On the beach Shane slapped Sam on the back. His nasal passages were scoured with salt. He sneezed and it felt like someone dragging a thick rope up this throat and through his nose. His stomach convulsed and he spewed onto the sand. 'Took on some water. You're right.' Shane sat him on the sand, stood over him with his arms folded. 'Happens to the best of us.'

'Why'd you pull me out?'

'Not gonna sit back and watch you drown.'

'Thank you.'

'Whatever.' Shane picked up his board and jogged back into the water.

When he was gone Sam let the tears roll down his cheeks.

26

Minty unzipped his wettie and rolled it down to his waist. Sam copied him. They sat together on the beach for a bit, the hot lick of the sun beating on their backs. After a while Ruby came in. She grinned at Sam. 'You got caned, lover boy.'

'Epic, ay!' said Minty. 'It is pumping out there. El Niño! This guy totally predicted it would be epic, ay. He's a genie.'

'That's not the word you're looking for, Mint,' she said.

'Whatever, Ruby Jean.' The three of them started the walk up the beach. Minty turned around so he was walking backwards, facing them, doing little backward skips. 'This is it, this is what I'm talkin' about. The ocean, you respect her and she will provide.'

'You're full of shit,' said Ruby.

'Nah, you know it. It's the vibe. It's the El Niño vibe. Ay, you got any food?'

Ruby looked disgusted. 'No. I'm not your friggin' mother.'

'But sometimes you have food. I'm starving, Rube.'

'Boohoo. You got money?'

'I'll pay you back.'

Ruby narrowed her eyes and shook her head. 'You owe me so much money, Minty.'

'I know, but—'

'You need to learn to live like a normal person who pays for shit.'

'I'm sorry, Ruby Jean.'

She shoved him on his shoulder and Minty put his arm around her.

'Gunna come watch me in the Open?'

'I'm not coming to watch you like some bimbo. You never want anyone there anyway.'

'This is gonna be different. I need you, Rube. You gotta come. You come and I'll take you to Hawaii.'

They leaned their boards against the window of the chicken shop. All the tables were taken, so Ruby stood in front of a group of younger guys and told them to move. They did. The queue to order was out the door, but Ruby went behind the counter with a nod to the owner and served herself, opening the till and putting her money in. She bought five dollars' worth of hot chips and scallops, dumped the fat package down on the table in front of Minty and popped open a Coke.

'Any burgers?' Minty asked.

Ruby ignored him and unwrapped the chips. Sam could feel the salt in his ears and on his eyelids; his skin was sticky with it. His whole body ached. The skin on his face felt slapped raw and he realised it was from hitting the water.

'So did you and Shane kiss and make up?' Ruby asked Sam. 'I don't see him here, so I'm guessing not. Why you guys hate each other so much, anyway? I mean, I hate Shane. But still.'

Sam shrugged. 'Dunno. He's never liked me.'

'Nah, Shane's alright,' said Minty. 'He's just all about family. The unit.'

'Sam's family!'

'Yeah, but … I dunno.' Minty struggled to find the words. 'It's deep, ay. He's seen a lot, old Shane. He's like an RSPCA dog or something. Misunderstood.'

Ruby watched Minty with a look of amusement. 'An RSPCA dog, Mint?'

'Yeah. He's tough, but you just gotta scratch his belly right.'

'Ew, Mint!' Ruby pegged a chip at him. 'I'm not scratchin' his belly.'

Minty took a bite from a potato scallop and wiggled his eyebrows at her.

'Argh. Piss off.' She turned back to Sam. 'Why did you go at him that night anyway? He hurt your feelings?'

Sam didn't answer her. He peeled the edge of his drink label, keeping his eyes down.

'Are you like Captain America or somethin'? Fighting injustice. Getting the bad guys.'

'That's it exactly.' He hoped his sarcasm would warn her off but it didn't.

'You get in fights up in Sydney?'

'I just … You want another drink, Mint?'

'Yeah. Fanta.'

Ruby scrunched up her nose at him. 'Fanta?'

Sam left them and went into the heat of the chicken shop. He opened the fridge door and stood there, letting the cool air bathe his face, trying to control his breath. The shopkeeper yelled at him to choose before he opened the door. Muttering an apology, Sam pulled two bottles at random from the shelf and paid the shopkeeper. By the time he came back out the conversation had moved on and it was Minty asking the questions.

'So, just over a month until Cronulla, Ruby Jean. Still time to enter.' Minty put a chip in his mouth and pointed at Ruby.

'Don't call me that.'

'Twenty-five thousand prize money.'

'For the men. Girls get fifteen. It's crap.'

'It's better than nothing.'

'I'm not entering.'

'You snooze, you lose.'

She squinted at Minty. 'That's not even the right saying. Are you that dense?'

'Not where it counts, baby.' Minty shoved chips into his mouth and reached for the drink Sam had put on the table. 'Apple juice? What the fark, Sam?'

'Sorry man … no Fanta left.'

'So choose a Coke, brah. Apple juice?' He frowned and skolled the bottle anyway. 'I'm goin' back out. Comin'?'

'Soon.'

Ruby and Minty picked up their boards and Sam watched them walk off down the street together. The wind turned cold but Sam sat on the plastic seat unable to move.

The police hadn't charged him. He told himself that if he was a really bad person, they would have pressed charges.

Instead they had sat him down in a small room with his mother and spoken to him with grave seriousness, calling him 'son'. They told him that if they had decided to charge him he would most likely go to juvenile detention. Game over, they'd said. Maybe they were lying. Maybe they weren't.

If it hadn't have happened, if he'd never got in the fight in the first place, he wouldn't have been home on New Year's Eve. He would have been out, there would have been no one there with her when she'd collapsed.

As if it made any difference.

When Gretchen found out what he'd done, who he was, it would be over, he knew that much.

Sam didn't go back in. Instead, he sat on the headland and watched Minty and Ruby. The wind began to change and the tide was retreating. The water was sucking back off the rocks and rearing up ferocious and hungry, like a tantruming kid, chucking surfers into the air, breaking perilously close to the rocks. By late afternoon, most people had left the water and now stood on the bluff watching those brave or stupid enough to stay in: a handful of older, more experienced guys, Minty and Ruby. The pack on the headland whooped and whistled with every wave that was caught, and laughed and cawed at each wipeout. Sam listened but didn't join in. Any guy that got a wave was 'heavy' and 'charging'. Anytime it was Ruby there was bemused silence or murmured scepticism. Sam knew that as long as Minty and Shane were there Ruby would stay in. Someone drove a car across the grass and turned the stereo up, boot open. Grinspoon boomed across the headland and drowned out the sound of the waves. Sam kept his eyes on Ruby and Minty, holding his breath every time they were wiped out. It wasn't until dusk had fallen that Minty, Ruby and Shane eventually straggled up from the rocks, dripping and elated, ready to relive every moment with beer and an audience.

The music was turned up, a bonfire lit and people were dancing and jumping on each other, whooping, screaming. A car did laps on the grass while guys took turns surfing on the roof. Minty handed Sam a drink, clinked his bottle and sat on the grass. 'Sammy! You were charging this morning!'

'Wouldn't use the word charging. Drowning maybe.'

'Brah! You're getting it, ay. Lot of these guys, they don't respect the water, but you've come here and it's like you're open and that. Everyone gets wiped out, s'part of the game. Brah, that's the heaviest I ever seen it here. Faaaark.' Minty laughed and shook his head. 'But it's like that, ay. You just know you gotta put it all on the line, sometimes. Otherwise? You're just pissin' around.'

'I'm cool with just pissing around from now on.'

'Yeah, 'cause you got ...' Minty paused, searching for the word. 'Scope. You got other shit goin' on and that. For me, this is my life. It's all about the next wave. I don't do drugs no more, but I'm a junkie, ay. It's always about the next hit. That's the way it is for all us guys out here. And I think that's real beautiful. Sounds soft, but that's it for me: it's beautiful to live like this.'

'I don't think Ruby sees it that way.'

Minty took a swig of his drink, a mellow sadness seemed to come over him.

'It's a farkin' waste, that is. She's got it, brah. So much potential. She's got a gift. She's got the guts, she's got the attitude, she's got everything. She could make it all the farkin' way, but she's just gonna waste it.'

'I think she's got a lot going on with her family.'

'Maybe, maybe. But it's a shame is all. She could have it. Ay, where's your chick, man? You should get her over here.'

'Don't know if this is her scene.'

Minty looked confused, like he didn't understand how sitting around in a park drinking and endlessly talking about waves wasn't everyone's idea of a good time. 'Nah, go get her.' He nudged Sam. 'You done it yet?'

Sam didn't answer.

Minty gaped at him. 'No way! Come *on*! It's been weeks, brah? What is she doin' to you? She's playin' you, Sammy.'

'You're a relationship expert?'

'I get laid, man, and it makes me very happy.'

'You screw Maddie Clark while you shut your eyes and pretend she's Ruby.'

Minty leaned back from the impact. 'Whoa! What the hell, brah?'

'Sorry,' Sam muttered. 'I just ... you know, if you like Ruby you should just ...'

'Should what? Tell her so she can tell me to piss off? As if. And as if I'd ever meet her crazy standards.'

'I don't know if not screwing around all the time is a crazy standard.'

'So I should just be alone 'cause that would impress Ruby?'

'It might show her you're serious.'

'Serious? About what? Stuff that, brah. I'm just livin' life.'

'You're a good guy, Mint. Stop pretending you're a dickhead.'

Minty didn't say anything for a few moments. He folded his arms over his knees and looked away. 'It makes you weak, you know. Start gettin' attached to someone, lose your nerve in the water. It's not good, brah. Think you know what I'm talkin' about.'

'I'm just saying that time runs out,' Sam said. 'It does. I've seen it. If you don't do something about Ruby, you'll regret it for the rest of your life.'

'Yeah, time runs out. If you don't root that girl soon, your dick's gonna fall off. I know that much,' he laughed. 'You always been deep, brah. I get it. But the only thing I'm ever gonna regret is not gettin' the biggest wave out there.'

'Sure.'

They sat in silence, watching as a bunch of guys tried to set the slippery dip on fire.

'They know plastic doesn't burn?' Sam asked.

'Probably not.'

Sam was well and truly smashed by midnight but not so much that he didn't know it was time to go home if they were going to make Lorraine's curfew. He staggered across the road with Minty, pausing out the front of Gretchen's house where he gazed up at the windows and wondered if he could figure out which was hers and if he would have the balls to climb through it.

27

Sam spent the following morning in the water with Minty. When the wind blew out the swell in the afternoon he went back to the house to read *Rolling Stone* and listen to music. He put Jeff Buckley on and, when he closed his eyes, he could see Gretchen's face. He was waiting in the flames, just like Jeff said. He was going to be burned up and destroyed if he remained there. But he had no choice, it was more powerful than him. 'So Real' came on and it wasn't about a nightmare anymore. He'd never understood why Jeff sang that he loved a girl but he was afraid to. Now he got it. Every time Sam had ever liked a girl up until that point felt like a simulation. This was real.

It was just a matter of time before she discovered he was nobody, a weak idiot. The track changed and Jeff sang that love was like being defenceless, stripped bare.

At four-thirty the house phone rang and Lorraine stuck her head through the curtain into Sam's room.

'Oi, there's a girl on the phone for you.'

'A girl?'

'Yeah.' She stretched the cord over to the camp bed and handed it to him.

'Hello?'

'Hi. It's Gretchen.'

'Hi.'

'What you doing?'

'Not much. Listening to Jeff Buckley, again.'

'You know, this is probably going to come as a rude shock, prepare yourself – but I think you are actually a nerd.'

'Really?'

'Yep. It's masked because you are nerdy about cool things, and you've got the whole surfer thing and the cool hair and everything, but your level of nerd-dom about Jeff Buckley is, like, off the scale.'

'I'm ruined if this comes out. It's over for me around here.'

'Yep, it is. Say he toured here again, how long would you sleep out for tickets?'

'Like at the ticket place?'

'Yep. With your sleeping bag, how many nights would you sleep out in line for tickets: one night? Two?'

'As long as it took. A week, I don't care.'

'What if it was raining?'

'Yeah, it would be worth it.'

'Someone would see you though, they would recognise you and say, "Hang on, I thought Sam was cool, yet here he is sleeping out for a week for concert tickets, that makes him a nerd!"'

'I could just wear a disguise.'

'You could get a blond wig and some temporary tattoos and pretend to be Minty.'

'That's pretty much my life strategy at the moment anyway.'

She laughed at his joke, but Sam didn't join her.

'Well, that's confirmed. You are a nerd.'

'Thank you.'

'Um, so …'

'Yeah?'

'Do you want to come over tomorrow afternoon? Mum has to take Roan to an appointment in Sydney.'

'Are you saying your house will be empty?'

'Yes. We could hang out and stuff.'

'And stuff?'

'And stuff.'

On Monday Sam was out of the water in time to have a shower and change before meeting Gretchen outside the school. He held her hand as they walked back to hers. He didn't talk much. She chatted a lot and he could tell that she was nervous too. She opened the front gate and led him inside, through the front door and up the stairs into the silent house. She put her bag down at the top of the steps.

'Do you want a drink or something? Water? Tea? Juice? Whisky?'

'Ha. Juice.'

She took a heavy glass from a high cupboard and he saw the pale skin of her stomach where her shirt rode up as she reached. He saw the smooth curve of her hipbone above her waistband. She filled the glass with orange juice from a carton in the fridge. It was the expensive stuff, fresh and pithy. She didn't seem to even think about watering it down.

'Ice?'

'Sure.'

She pressed a button on the front of the stainless steel fridge and ice cubes clinked into the glass. He took the glass from her and his fingertips brushed hers. She made one for herself. They stood in the kitchen, looking out at the water in silence. It was as if they'd never met before.

'Want to see my room?' she said eventually.

'Yeah.'

He followed her up the hallway watching the gentle sashay of her hips and the curve of her bum. She reached to flick a light on and he noticed how beautiful her wrists were. Something in him slipped and he couldn't take it anymore. He could smell her hair, the whole house smelled of her. He reached forward – bolder and more self-assured than he'd ever done anything in his life – and placed a hand on her waist, turning her so she was facing him. He pushed her back against the open door and kissed her. He told himself that he knew how to do this. Her skin was smooth and warm under his hands. She tilted her head back and he kissed her neck. She pulled his shirt up and over his head, pulling away to look at him. He thought she was going to stop it, but she didn't, instead pulling him back toward her. He was grateful for every weight session he'd done with Minty. He caressed her stomach under her shirt and let his hand go up to the lace of her bra. She pulled her shirt off and her hands went to his belt buckle; he helped her undo it and kicked off his shorts.

She giggled and shimmied out of her skirt. Her undies were bright green with polka dots and she unhooked her bra from behind while she was kissing him. There was nothing like the warm feeling of her bare skin against his, the closest he'd ever felt to another human being. He thought of asking her if she was sure about this but he didn't want to in case she said she wasn't. He half walked her, half lifted her backwards onto the bed. Taking her weight in his arms and lowering her down, pulling back to look at her face, her neck. He saw it then, flashing before his eyes: the clearest snapshot of his mother's eyes rolling back in her head, the whites of her eyes and her body dropping in front of him. Him catching her. It was so real he let go of Gretchen. She was confused. Of course. Her mouth was still open from his kiss and it took her a moment to open her eyes and register the fact that she was almost naked in front of him and he had stopped kissing her. She sat up, looking around as if waking up from a dream. She pulled the sheets up over her torso, under her armpits.

'What?' she laughed, nervous and unsure.

He turned away from her and picked up his shirt and shorts from the floor. He couldn't speak, his hands trembled and he dropped the shirt, picked it up again as he left the room. He pulled it over his head. She didn't call after him; there was nothing but dead, stunned silence from the bedroom. Sam lurched down the hallway and stumbled down the stairs to the front door.

*

He came home to a mercifully empty house. There was no space he could be, nothing of his own. He wanted to run and run until he threw up, smash something, put a fist through the wall, anything. He could feel his mother's judgement. *I did not raise you to undress a girl and leave her alone in her room without a goodbye or an explanation.* His breath thudded in and out of him violently, heart thundering. He paced the three-metre width of his room and wondered what a coward did in his position and if it was the same thing he was doing now. His thoughts swung around in his skull. Would this happen every time he held a girl? Was he doomed to forever see his mother's dead face when he was getting it on with someone?

A knock on the door. Sharp. Now was not a good time to be having a cup of tea or a milkshake with Nana. He went to the door and tried to think of a plausible excuse to get rid of her: he was sick, vomiting. It wasn't far off the truth. He turned the handle and found Gretchen. She had pulled on a pair of jeans and her old 'Zero' T-shirt; her hair was a crazy frizzy cloud. He expected she might yell or hit him or lash out in some way. But she was quiet, questioning him with her pale eyes. It was worse than if she was angry.

'What's going on?' Her voice was so soft he hardly heard her.

'I'm sorry.'

'Give me a reason.'

'I'm sorry … I'm not a good guy.'

'I think you're a good guy.'

'I'm not.'

'What is this? Are you breaking up with me?'

'No … I don't know.'

She nodded. He was expecting her to tell him where to go and to storm out. To end it for him. She waited. But he didn't know what to say. There was nothing. *I was kissing you and I thought of my dead mother?* The more she knew about him, the worse he was getting. Like she was chipping away trying to get clarity from him, only underneath he was dust that crumbled to nothing. He wanted to open his mouth and tell her everything, everything that was in his head, everything that cleaved his chest open and bore through him. The black star that sucked his world in.

She waited while he tried to find the place to begin. But surely if she knew him, *really* knew him, she wouldn't want him anyway.

'Is this it? Over?' she asked.

He couldn't answer her.

'Can't even give me that much?' She turned away and walked off across the dying lawn with her hands in her pockets, head down and her hair falling down her back. She paused and turned back to face him. 'You know, you got me. I thought you were different from every other stupid, surfie numbskull, but you're not. You're just like them. Have a nice life.'

She was right, he'd been leading her on, pretending he was something he clearly wasn't.

Sam tried to tell himself he'd done the right thing. It was better this way, to end it before it went too far and she had to make the inevitable decision to drop him for someone better. He stood in the kitchen for how long? He didn't know. An age. Then he opened the cupboard above the fridge and pulled out Lorraine's bottle of whisky. He didn't bother with a glass.

28

Half the bottle down and he took his skateboard, tearing up the road. The trees bent in strange lines and the sky warped. The numbness that crept through his limbs was exquisite; a warmth enveloped his scalp. The sky was darkening and the streetlights were a bright dot-to-dot above. At the shops he skidded out across the road and cars blasted their horns. He shouted at them like a dog barking, crazed in the wind. He clipped a guy coming out of the TAB and stumbled forward, his board skidding into the gutter. 'Farrk!'

'Watch it!' He was bald, wore a trucker singlet, had tatts on his knuckles, but not so big that there'd be no contest. Sam laughed, not believing his luck. 'Piss off, arsehole!' Sam yelled and he watched as the guy's whole face blazed red as if on cue. There was power in it, the way you could say a couple of words and have someone react, explode before your eyes. You could control them, even if only so very briefly. You could ride the wave straight into the rocks. The big guy hurled Sam backwards into the wall and Sam swung at him. He landed the punch on the guy's cheek and was struck in the stomach.

They went at it swinging and pushing and Sam revelled in the realisation that he was better than this guy. If he wasn't pissed he could have beaten him. But if he wasn't drunk he wouldn't be here. Sam was finishing off the thought when he lost his footing and the guy kneed him in the crotch. He doubled over and fell on the ground. The guy booted him in the ribs and Sam shielded his face with his forearms.

'Hey! Get off him!' It was a voice Sam knew but couldn't place. 'Get off him! Help! Someone!' Sam was curious. He looked up to see the trucker guy turn around and punch Jono in the face, sending him to the asphalt. Sam scrambled, trying to get to his feet. There was squealing, shrieking and Sam saw two of Jono's young brothers wide-eyed with terror, clutching their skateboards, knee and elbow pads strapped on, helmets with Ninja Turtles stickers.

A TAB worker stepped in then, pulling Sam back by the collar as he tried to lunge at the attacker. The trucker took off, running a crooked path along the street. Sam was released with a shove. People stood back watching. Others slowed but kept walking, all with expressions of disapproval.

Blood dripping from his nose, Sam went to Jono. He was out cold.

Sam started to cry, sniffling, shuddering with sobs. He rolled Jono onto his side, yelling his name. He started to scream, shut his eyes tight and smacked his palms into his head. It was like Sydney all over again.

Jono opened one eye, the other swollen shut; he moaned and drew his knees up to his chest. He looked up at Sam. 'Are you alright?'

'Jono. I thought you were dead. Fark.'

Sam helped him sit up. Someone else was with them now: Ruby in her chicken-shop apron, a bunch of ice blocks wrapped in a tea towel.

'You fucking idiot,' she spat at Sam and pushed him back. She crouched down and put the ice on Jono's eye.

'He was being attacked, like fully attacked,' Jono said.

'He wasn't attacked.' She looked back over her shoulder at Sam. 'You think I didn't see you? Fucking idiot.'

'I'm sorry.' He used his T-shirt to mop the snot and blood from his face. Jono's brothers stood in silence, watching their brother on the ground.

She straightened up and pushed Sam away. 'Fuck off. Just go. You fucking muppet.' Ruby looked at the two kids, her face soft. 'He's alright. Just copped a fist to the head.' The smallest one burst into tears. Ruby glared at Sam. 'I swear, if you don't get the hell away I'm gonna punch you myself.'

Sam stumbled backwards. 'I'm sorry.'

She ignored him. Sam looked around and saw people in shop doorways looking at him with disgust and fear, like he was rabid vermin. He backed away, turned and picked up his skateboard.

The house was still empty. The bottle of whisky half full on the counter. Sam staggered in and grabbed at it, knocking it off the table. It rolled across the lino floor. He scrambled for it. Unscrewed the cap and chugged it down like water.

He woke up under the shower, propped up against the tile wall, cold water soaking into his clothes. Minty was standing over him. Sam came around spluttering and panicked, like a fish slapping on a hook. Minty crouched down in front of him, shaking him by the shoulders.

'Sammy? Sam? You right, brah? You're right.'

Sam turned his head and vomited onto the tiles. His head spun and he had to steady himself with one hand on the floor.

Minty laughed. 'There you go, buddy. You're good, brah. Farkin' hell, Mum's Jack Daniel's. She's ballistic! Didn't even save me any.'

Sam registered that the light was on and there was darkness outside the window.

'What time is it?' he asked.

Minty shrugged. 'Dunno. Seven? How long you been out, brah? An hour? More? What happened? You bin fightin'?'

Sam nodded. Minty stuck his head out of the bathroom door and yelled: 'He's right!'

Lorraine pounded up the hallway and pushed into the small bathroom. She leaned over him and hissed her words.

'Get up. Get dressed and get out.'

'Naaaah, Mum, come *on*! Go easy on him.'

'No. Get your things, get out of my house.'

'Mum,' Minty pleaded.

'Out. You were warned. God knows I've done my best, but this is the limit. You think this is a joke? Who you gonna hit next? Your girlfriend? Get the hell out of my house.'

Sam, dripping wet, found his feet and held the wall for support. He made it out of the bathroom; Minty was after him and shoved a backpack into his hands, a Rip Curl one with the tags still attached.

'Here. I'll help ya.'

He emptied Sam's drawers into the backpack. Shoved his Discman and CDs in the top and zipped it up. Sam stood and watched, swaying on the spot, woozy and sand-mouthed. Minty took Sam's arm and put it around his own shoulder, propping him up like they were comrades at Fromelles. Lorraine stood in the kitchen, hands on her hips, and watched Minty drag Sam out the door and down the steps. She slammed the door shut after them.

'Hehe. She's pissed, brah.'

'Can tell,' Sam slurred.

'I'll take ya to Nana's. Get in.' Minty opened the car door and pushed Sam in. He reversed the car out onto the street. Minty looked worried. Sam had never seen him worried.

'What's goin on, brah?'

'I did something dumb.' Sam laughed. 'I did a lot of things dumb.'

'Nah. You'll be right, brah.'

'Will Lorraine let me back?'

'Don't know. She's stubborn as, when she makes a decision.'

'I got a mate beat up.'

'Fark. What happened?'

'I started a fight, he tried to help me and he copped it.'

Minty raised his eyebrows.

'Am I a bad person, Minty?'

Minty scoffed. 'Nah. You're better than most.'

'You don't know me.'

Minty shrugged. 'What's there to know?' He pulled the car up in front of Nana's. Minty got out and rapped on the annex door. She came out and Sam watched them talking, then she walked over to the car, bent over and looked through the window at him.

'Well, well. What do we have here?'

She only had one bed, so she went to a neighbour and borrowed an inflatable pool li-lo which she told him to set up in the annex. The li-lo was deflated and there was no foot pump. She handed it to him.

'You'll have to blow that up. I haven't got enough breath.'

He stood there trying to blow air into the thing but soon he was dizzy and nauseous. He put the limp mattress on the floor and collapsed onto it, feeling the hard concrete under his hips and shoulders. Moments later he was asleep.

She woke him up at seven and handed him a bowl of rice bubbles.

'I feel horrible.'

'You look horrible.' She dropped a folded towel onto the bed. 'Shower block's that way. I'm going out for a bit. I'll see you this afternoon.'

It was cool and drizzling outside and he realised that he didn't have any sweaters or warm clothes. Nana was right, he looked horrible. Like he'd been dragged through the dirt behind a car. Like he'd been beaten up. After he was dressed, he walked up to Lorraine's house and knocked on the door. She opened the door and scowled at him.

'You're not coming back. You can go, thank you very much.'

'I don't have a jumper. It's cold.'

She assessed him through the screen door and made a 'hmpff' sound, vanished and came back holding a hoodie of Minty's. She opened the door and handed it out to him as if he was a dog she didn't want in the house.

'Can I have my tape deck? Pop gave it to me.'

'For Christ's sake.' She went away and returned with the tape deck. She went to close the door and hesitated.

'I've been through hell. I'm not gonna stand around while you turn into something ... You're a good kid. But you're making gawd-awful choices. You don't need me to tell you that. You need to learn that you can't do whatever you feel like when you're pissed off. You need a lesson, buddy.'

She closed the front door.

He lay on the li-lo with his earphones in. Sometime after three he realised he hadn't eaten anything. He got up, took his skateboard and headed for the main street. He was near the bakery when Stassi Miller came thundering toward him, in her school uniform.

'Oi, arsehole.'

He ducked his head and sidestepped her but she blocked his path, almost as tall as he was.

'What have you done?'

'Can you move?'

'No, I can't move.'

He pushed past her.

'Uh-uh!' She caught up to him and grabbed his arm. 'You know what? Gretchen thinks you've got some emotional, brooding Mr Darcy thing going on. Me? I think you're a root rat.'

'A root rat?'

'A root rat and an arsehole in general.'

'Congratulations. Start a club, there's heaps out there who think the same.' He started to walk away.

'Where's Jono?'

Sam stopped.

'Wasn't at school. People are saying he was beaten up because of you. That true?'

He spun round and stepped closer to her. 'I'm an arsehole! You got me!'

'Whoa. Are you threatening me?'

He closed his eyes and took a deep breath. 'I'm asking you to leave me alone.'

'Because for a second there it looked like you wanted to hit me.'

'I don't want to hit anyone. I want to be left alone.'

Stassi made a show of looking at the empty space on either side of him. 'Mission accomplished. Have a nice day.' And she walked off, triumphant, chin in the air.

With a sausage roll in his hand he skated back to the caravan park and formed the realisation that the most inconvenient thing about being kicked out of Lorraine's was that he no longer had access to her liquor cupboard. It's usual for a person to have something in their mind unless they have reached a supreme state of zen. Sam felt pretty close to having nothing in his mind, but he hadn't achieved a state of zen; he was on the opposite end of the spectrum. The only thing in Sam's head was a dark, hanging heaviness. An unnameable shape that blocked any light from coming in, a sensation that made any future inconceivable, a shape that closed off all doors and shoved him into a corner with nowhere to move. Like the faulty instinct to draw breath when you're under the water and you've run out of air. A Buddhist would say it was the desire to breathe that was the problem.

He was locked in, checkmate, do not pass go, do not collect two hundred dollars. It was even worse than after his mother died. At least then there were practical steps to be taken: go with Lorraine, move into her house, start over. Now starting over for the second time was not an option. He knew that much.

He could take a length of rope and find a tree branch, somewhere a stranger would find him. But what if it was a kid who found him? He could walk south around the headland and find somewhere to jump, but he didn't know if there was anywhere high enough. He could get a bus up north to where the hang-gliders took off. But there were always tourists there. He could go at night. He didn't think the buses went at night. And if he landed in the water and just vanished, they would all think he was missing, not dead. And that was worse. He knew it. But who were 'they'? And would they care for more than a couple of weeks?

Who would miss him?

What would he rather: be dead and missed, or alive and alone?

He came to Nana's van. His surfboard was leaning against the door and a wetsuit sat folded on the doorstep. Nana wasn't anywhere to be seen. Sam dropped his bag and picked up the board.

It was almost May and the winter groundswell was building bigger, cleaner, more regular waves. Sam knew the water. He could read it. Some surfers were trying to battle out from the beach. Sam knew better, he ran down the side of the headland and across the rocks to the easternmost point. He didn't think about any of it. He jumped and dived under white water, paddling hard. Ruby was lying on her board; she looked over her shoulder, a death stare prepared for whoever was cutting in on her position. It softened when she saw it was Sam, but only a little.

'Watch it, Captain America. You drop in on me and I'll rip your balls off.'

'I know. Don't worry … Is Jono okay?'

'He'll live. What happened with you yesterday? Have a fight with your girlfriend?'

Sam didn't answer straightaway. After a while, he said, 'You can talk. You told Minty you love 'im yet?'

The glower returned. 'Some of us know what's good for us. That means cutting Minty loose.'

'He know that?'

'He will soon enough.'

'He's your best friend.'

'No. He's a bloody liability is what he is. I stick around him, I'm gunna get sucked right in, forget what I want.'

A big wave rolled toward them, Ruby nodded toward it.

'There y'are, weather boy. Show us what you're made of.'

Sam paddled for it, there was no fear. He didn't think about what it would be like to be held down under it; he didn't think about anything. He met the wave as it crested and popped up onto his feet with more fluidity than he'd ever managed before. He drove the weight of his left leg down like he had seen Minty do, which pushed the board forward, accelerating across the wave. He felt it more strongly than before, the sensation Minty tried so clumsily to describe: a delicate paradox where he was, for a short time, in control of his world while simultaneously being at the mercy of the ocean. Sam sped along with the wave, lifted and weightless, but he was sliding too deep into the bowl, it would cave over him. He managed to swivel the nose upward and climbed a little, too high; he rode it back down and it closed out over him, pushing him deep. In a wash of bubbles and foam, his shoulder clipped the bottom of the reef and he was pinned down. He remembered what Minty had said: close your eyes and pretend to be somewhere else, enjoy the ride. He was spinning and spinning, he was in a club and Jeff Buckley was on stage playing 'Mojo Pin'. Was this his time? Jeff wailed and sang about all the pain he would leave behind. Sam saw Gretchen across the room and she didn't know him but she saw him too and she loved him. He opened his eyes and seeing the glare of sunlight through the water, surged up toward it.

Breaking through the water's surface he gasped for air and the first breath was the sweetest thing. The next wave loomed.

She didn't know him at all.

On the headland they sat in the inky autumn gloaming, warmed by the flickering glow of a bonfire, watching the ocean like they were guarding it. They drank and talked about the waves, Minty's next comp and how sweet life would be when he was world champ. Ruby didn't stick around. She had one beer and wandered away; Minty watching her go like a mournful puppy.

Whatever it was that had changed in Sam, Shane seemed to sense it and he was more tolerant of him. He included him in the conversation; he laughed when Sam cracked a joke. It was as if he'd made peace with Sam being there, like Sam had finally proven his commitment to the water and was now allowed in the fold. Or maybe Shane just felt sorry for him: now he was out of the house he was no longer a threat.

Sam slept in his clothes, huddled down in the cheap sleeping bag Nana had bought him. The ache in his limbs was satisfying rather than uncomfortable. The surf exacerbated the bruising on his ribs from the fight and the wound above his eye felt scraped raw by the salt water. He was sore but cleansed.

29

Sam spent his days in the water because he wanted to, rather than because that's where Minty was. Minty developed a bloodhound's focus on the upcoming comp. It was all he talked about and when Sam, Shane and Minty weren't in the surf, they were doing weights, or watching the videos Shane made of Minty when Lorraine was at work. If the surf was flat they drove for ages listening to tapes, hunting for a break. Shane came with them when he wasn't working. One weekend Sam asked Minty where Ruby was and Minty shrugged. 'Dunno, ay. Haven't seen her for a while.' Sam didn't push it any further.

Nana provided hot meals and talked about things she had seen on her walks, talkback discussions from the radio, football, anything. She didn't ask him a single question about what he was doing with himself, how long he was going to stay with her or if he ever planned to get a job.

Sam never went around to Jono's. He did everything he could to avoid seeing him. If he were to dig deep enough into himself he would have found the knowledge that Jono reminded Sam too much of a person he couldn't be, with a family he couldn't have.

When he walked past Gretchen's house he told himself that he didn't notice if her bedroom light was on.

The approach of winter brought less partying. Minty said summer was the off-season. Winter was the game. On the headland with the wind blustering his hair and water trickling down his salt-licked back, Sam felt it: the satisfaction of a day in the water, the salvation of it, fierce and brutal and constant. The sea rolling, inhaling and exhaling them. Over and over. The crisp air, the salt, the sun and the water. Scalding showers, deep exhausted sleep and dark, early mornings. Sam was fully converted. He grew his hair past his shoulders, stopped shaving and regularly challenged Minty to twenty pull-ups on the monkey bars after a session.

Sam formed the knowledge that people who weren't part of that world didn't understand it. The perception was that surfing was easy because surfers were lazy, degenerate, bludging scum. Outsiders didn't recognise the devotion, the pilgrimage, the sacrifice of everything else: money, security, relationships. Outsiders didn't realise the monasticism of a life in the water. On the headland after a long, cold day surfing it was beautiful in a way that no one says it is between mates: that easy silence, nothing needing to be said and no one really listening anyway. Everyone just watching the water.

The black hole still opened up within him now and again, but he could dodge it for several hours at a time, as long as he didn't let himself think about school, abandoned plans, his mother or Gretchen. As long as he didn't let the snapshots enter his mind: his dead mother, or blood on his knuckles and a figure motionless on the ground.

One evening they walked up to the shops. Minty went inside and ordered hot chips; Sam slumped in a white plastic chair. He saw Jono round the corner by the video shop, skateboard in his hand, trudging up the hill. There was no way of getting out of it. Jono saw him and gave a nod, looking about as keen for a catch-up as Sam was. Sam thought he might keep walking and it looked for a minute like he would.

'How's it goin'?' Sam asked. It was too weird not to say anything.

Jono stopped. 'Long time no see.' There was nothing friendly in his tone. His expression was indifferent.

'How's it goin'?' Sam asked again.

'Fine.'

'What's goin' on?'

Jono looked away. 'Not much. Getting a video.'

Minty came out of the chicken shop. 'Jono! How's it goin, brah?' He grasped Jono's hand in greeting and Jono endured the gesture. 'What's up?'

'You know, nothing.'

'Haven't seen you round.'

'Been busy.'

'Oh sweet. No worries, brah.'

'See you,' Jono began to walk away. Then he stopped and turned to face Sam. 'Hey, just so you know, Gretchen's a friend of mine.' He stopped and shook his head, ran his tongue over his bottom lip. 'Not cool, man. Really not cool.'

Sam wanted to say something, but he couldn't. Blood pounded in his temples. Jono shook his head and stepped onto his board; Sam watched him glide away. Jono's Movie Monday. Snapshots began to elbow their way into Sam's head and he stared at a crack in the concrete pavement, trying to push them out again. He tasted the salt on his lips, felt the aching in his shoulders and tried to use them to anchor himself in the present, where he was okay, where he was a local, where he had a place.

'Whoa!' Minty laughed and opened the chips. 'What the hell, dude? You pissed Jono off. Not easy.'

'Hey, how come Ruby's not around?'

Minty shrugged and didn't answer.

'I just haven't seen her around heaps. And she's not working.' Sam flicked his head to the door of the chicken shop. 'I think she's dating someone.'

Minty's shoulders squared. 'Why? Why would you think that?'

'I just … she's been off the radar. She mentioned someone. She's hot, she wouldn't be on her own.'

'You don't know anything.'

'I'm just saying.'

Minty stood up and brushed off his hands. He started off down the street and Sam followed him.

'Mint. I was just asking.'

Minty stopped and turned around, chin up, inches away from Sam. 'No you weren't. You're looking to get your head punched in. I'm not doin' that for ya.'

'You waste your time with other chicks, someone's gonna get in there.'

'Who? You?'

Sam shrugged. 'Maybe.' He was riding the wave straight into the rocks but he couldn't pull out.

Minty's jaw clenched. His nostrils flared with his breath. 'Shut up. Shut the hell up.'

'You should know.'

Minty grabbed the front of Sam's shirt and shoved him into the side of a concrete bus shelter. Sam didn't fight back. Minty grabbed him by the throat, holding him by the jaw with one hand. He was much stronger than Sam and Sam felt the squeeze of pressure on his larynx. Minty pulled his arm back and curled his lip, ready to smash Sam's face. Sam knew Minty could kill him with one punch. He waited. But Minty exhaled and shoved Sam's face away with his palm. He walked off, leaving Sam crumpled against the bus shelter. Then he stopped and turned around, strode back up to him.

His voice was hoarse. 'You can't make me be that guy. I'm goin' home. Sun's up at six-forty-five. I'll pick you up at six for Nari.'

Sam wandered up to the beach. It was always dark when Gretchen finished her run. He worried about her walking back to her house in the dark. She came to a stop next to the kiosk at 7 pm, the same every evening. He kept his distance, in the shadows up beyond the change rooms. He always made sure he was there, out of view. He followed her as she walked home, waiting until she closed the gate behind her. Was he the type of person he was trying to protect her from?

If he was down on the beach or the concourse he could sense when she was nearby. He would know exactly where she was without looking in her direction. He couldn't look at her or take his eyes off her. The force that drew him to her was unrelenting and he was always on guard and acutely aware of it. Yet he behaved as if he didn't know her and he never had. If it was gutless, he wasn't sure.

He couldn't handle the cheap sleeping bag on the floor of the caravan annex just yet. Instead, he walked to the grass on the headland, where he had lain next to Gretchen. He tried to find the exact spot. He lay down on the dew-damp grass and watched the stars, hugging himself against the cold.

Minty pulled up the Datsun in front of the caravan before dawn. Sam was up. He downed a glass of milk and Minty helped him anchor his board to the roof racks. They skidded out of the van park, heading south toward Nari Bay.

The radio was tuned to a commercial station. Sam leaned forward and turned the dial, listening as the red needle moved over the numbers. He stopped when he hit a Blur song. The announcer began to talk over the end of the song.

'If you've just joined us, we're trying to confirm reports that Jeff Buckley has gone missing and is presumed dead. Reports are saying that Buckley went for a swim in the Mississippi

River last night local time and has not been seen since. We will bring you more information as it comes to hand.'

Sam felt like someone had a chisel and they were tapping the end of it with a hammer, prying open his chest. He felt hot and dizzy and his fingertips hummed with a horrible sensation. He gripped the seat as if in danger of being thrown from the car. He couldn't find his breath.

'Stop the car.'

'What?'

'Pull over,' Sam said. Minty pulled the car off the road, the tires crunching over the gravel. 'Did she just say Jeff Buckley died?'

'Yeah. Can we keep going?'

'No. Turn around.'

'Brah, we're goin for a surf.'

'Please. Take me back to the van.'

'For real?'

'For real,' Sam snapped. Minty held up a hand to placate him and made a U-turn. Sam turned the radio up, but the same information was repeated intermittently. Nothing new.

Back at the van, Nana had already left for her morning swim. Sam slid the door open and sat on his sleeping bag. He switched the radio on and listened. They played 'Mojo Pin' and Sam felt as though he had to somehow hold onto himself to try and stop the plummet. He lay down and felt the silky coolness of the sleeping bag against his wet cheek; he drew his knees to his chest and made himself as small as possible. He was a pebble at the bottom of the sea, the current rolling him over and tossing him, skittering helplessly.

Swimming bright and colourful,
'till away they dash.

The announcer came back on, her voice was quiet and mournful. 'We can confirm that Buckley is missing, presumed dead. A search for his body is underway.' She kept talking but Sam wasn't listening. His mouth was dry. The fabric against his face was wet with tears. He uncurled and stood, holding the walls to steady himself as he edged into the kitchenette. With trembling hands he took a glass and when he raised it to his lips it sloshed and spilled down his front. The door slid open and Nana bustled in through the annex and in to the kitchenette. There was barely room for two people.

'What you doing here? Thought you'd gone for a surf with Michael? What's wrong, love? You're white as a sheet.'

'Nothing. Someone died.' Sam wiped the tears from the corners of his eyes.

'What? Who died, love? Who?'

'No one, just ... a singer, a musician.'

'A mate of yours?'

'No. I just heard on the radio.'

Nana took a jar of peanut butter from the cupboard next to him. 'Oh. You gave me a start. Thought you meant a real person. I remember when Elvis died. Everyone was very upset. Never mind. I'm going to put on the kettle. Do you want a cup of tea?'

Sam turned and left the van without answering her. He walked along the concrete path, beyond the shower block to the beach. He never came this way, never walked on the beach like he had done with Gretchen that night, his jacket on her shoulders. He always took the route along the headland, straight down to the rocks. The wind was blustering, ripping and biting through him. The water was a shifting, churning mess. He sat in the sand and watched the waves. The wind stung his eyes and the sand grazed wherever his skin was exposed: the backs of his hands, his cheeks. He looked up the beach and saw a figure: female, long dark skirt billowing in the wind, curls whipping around her face. He recognised her, how could he not? He didn't give a second thought to walking up to her. Gretchen turned and watched him, arms folded, the sleeves of her knitted jumper pulled down over her fingers. Her eyes were rimmed red and her cheeks were wet. She didn't say anything, turning to look back at the water. He stood next to her and she didn't move. They didn't speak. After a long time she turned and walked away.

WINTER

30

Sam was lying on the li-lo on the concrete floor of the caravan annex. The radio announcer told him that a witness had seen Jeff walk into the river fully clothed; a wave from a passing speedboat had pulled him under the water.

No one had taught Jeff how to handle himself in the water.

The radio was playing an interview with him from a few years before, punctuated with phone calls from bereaved fans. Some were still holding out hope Jeff was fine and was wandering the banks of the Mississippi writing song lyrics. Sam's experience had taught him that the worst possible scenario was usually the true one.

A rapping sound came from the door. 'Sam? It's Lorraine. Need a word.'

He got up and slid open the annex door. Lorraine stood in her tracksuit and thongs, cigarette between her fingers.

'Hey Aunty Lorraine.'

'You coming to the comp tomorrow? Minty needs you. Says he wants us all there.'

'Yeah.'

'We're leaving at six-thirty. Be there if you want a lift. Been in any more fights?'

'No.'

'Minty tells me I should let you move back in. I've got bloody social services on the phone askin' why you ain't bin to school.'

'They ask where I was living?'

'Don't you be smart with me, Samuel. What are you doing with yourself?'

'Been surfing with Minty.'

'Well. He's gonna be world champ. What's your excuse?'

Sam shrugged. 'Dunno.'

Lorraine mimicked him. Unimpressed. 'You're a smart kid. I got bloody Shane.' She pointed over her shoulder with a thumb. 'Thick as two bricks. Can't teach him anything. You, *you*, though. You got a future.' Lorraine looked into the van. 'Where's Nana?'

'Out. She goes dancing on Thursdays.'

'Dancing? Bugger me. That woman.' Lorraine sighed. 'Where's she dancing?'

'Up the club. They do line dancing there.'

Lorraine rolled her eyes. 'Of course they do. I come here to talk to her about the prodigal bloody son: he's at home, she's out bloody dancing. She reckon you should be in school?'

Sam shrugged and Lorraine mimicked him again. 'Geez, between the two of you, it's the bloody mafia, no one saying anything.'

'I think ...'

'Oh yes? What you think?'

'I think she just wants me to stay. So she's, you know, she's laying off me.'

'That what you think I should do?'

'Dunno.'

Lorraine took a drag on her cigarette and exhaled through her nose. Sam remembered how when he was small he and his mum used to call her Puff the Magic Dragon.

'Your mum's apartment has sold and the loan has been covered. There's a bit left, together with her superannuation. I been moving her savings over into an account for you. Put it all in there. It's yours. You're only gonna get it if you get your HSC and sort yourself out.' She pointed a pink fingernail at him. 'I'm not gonna let you piss it away. Got it?'

'It's too late to start year twelve.'

'Then you repeat year eleven. Look at me, Samuel. If you think we're gonna stand around and let you piss away your life and everything your mother taught you, you got another thing comin'. God knows we had our problems, but she was still my sister. I love her despite it all.' Lorraine dropped the cigarette butt and ground it into the dirt with the toe of her thong. 'Go to bed. It's late. I'll see you in the morning.'

He didn't sleep. His mother was too close. He could see every crease on her face, every worry line he'd ever given her.

Before first light Sam left the caravan and walked up to the Booners'. Minty was sitting on the front lawn, beanie pulled down over his ears. Shane was sorting wetsuits and organising the back of the van.

'Hey Mint.'

Minty was nervous, he nodded at Sam without making eye contact.

'You sleep?' Sam asked Minty.

Minty shook his head.

'Where's your Walkman?'

Minty motioned toward the garage. Sam went in and found it on the bench press. He carried it over to Minty.

'It'll help.'

Minty didn't look convinced.

'Think of the cash. Think of Hawaii.'

Shane placed a hand on each of Minty's shoulders. 'This is yours, Minty. Yours. You got this. You're gonna charge.'

Shane nodded toward the boards lying on the grass. 'Load her up.' He whooped and slapped the bonnet of the car.

Lorraine came out as they were loading the gear. She would drive in Minty's Datsun with Sam. When it was time to go she took Minty's face in her hands and pulled his forehead down to meet hers, talking softly to him. The gesture sliced through Sam.

In the car Lorraine was quiet but distracted. She kept fiddling with the radio and darting from lane to lane for no reason Sam could make out.

'Nana coming?' he asked, knowing he probably shouldn't.

Lorraine shot him a furious look. 'No, Nana's not bloody coming. Jesus!'

'I thought she might.'

'Not if I've got anything to do with it.'

'Sure … So … you've got funds put aside for me?'

'If you go to school.'

'Thought you'd pocketed it all.'

'What?'

'I thought you were keeping all the money from Mum.'

'Christ alive! What do you think I am?!'

Sam shrugged. 'I dunno. I saw her balance kept going down.'

'What did she tell you about me? Geez. Well, I never.'

'Nothing. Mum never told me anything about you … about what happened between you and her.'

Lorraine leaned forward over the wheel, pointed her left index finger at Sam as she spoke.

'It wasn't my bloody fault. Everyone always assumes it was my fault.' She shook her head and muttered to herself. 'If only they knew.'

'Knew what?'

'Look, you. All you need to know is I've done the right thing by you and if you go to bloody school, get your HSC and do university like you're supposed to, you'll be right. You'll be set. And if you think I didn't know you were helping yourself to a little spending money, you got another thing coming. I was draining that account to put it in a high interest one for you.'

'Oh. Thanks.'

'You're bloody welcome.'

*

When they made it to the edge of Sydney, Sam directed Lorraine through the back streets and they came to the beach with a car park already half-full. Flags and banners with sponsorship logos flickered in the breeze. A TV broadcast van was setting up. People milled about and pitched positions on the sand. Lorraine pulled the car into a space next to Shane's van and lit a cigarette. Sam got the impression she didn't want to be around him for the moment so he left her and got out of the car.

When Minty opened the door to the van a bunch of surfers he knew whistled to him. He didn't even wave. He put his hands in his pockets, head down, and wandered to the edge of the car park, looking out toward the beach. The other surfers watched him. Some called out to him, but he ignored them.

Shane opened his door and spat on the asphalt. 'That's a start,' he said. 'You can't psych anyone out if you're all buddies.' Shane started unloading the boards and Sam followed Minty down to the beach. The wind whipped their faces.

Minty locked his eyes on the horizon. 'There's a fucking grandstand.'

'Whatever, Mint. Block it out. Look at the swell. What do you see?'

'Northerly current. Shallow sandbar. It's small. Grovelly. Not awesome.' Minty looked over his shoulder where more people were arriving and suiting up.

'Ignore them. Go down the beach.' Sam handed Minty his Walkman and Minty stuck the earphones in. Sam slapped him on the back. As Minty walked away, people tried to talk to him and he ducked around them, head down.

Sam couldn't help but think of Minty as a little kid, tucked into the big bed with the blanket pulled up to his chin, desperate not to go home. The contrast was stark between the eager-eyed daredevil in the water and the small boy who wet the bed and flinched at loud noises.

31

The sponsor's tent was set up with chairs and eskys full of cold drinks. There was a massage table and racks of boards. Lorraine parked herself in a folding chair on the outskirts, her face hidden behind her oversized wrap-around sunglasses, a tattered cowboy hat on her head, strap done up tight beneath her chin so it wouldn't blow away. Family members of the other competitors milled around, but Lorraine didn't attempt to mingle with any of them. She rapped her nails on the arm of the deck chair and watched the water. Shane and Sam carried Minty's boards down from the car, slotting them into place on a rack reserved for him. Shane ran a hand down the smooth edge of a board. 'He should take this one in: light, wide, skim on the surface of a smaller wave. Lot of people won't like these conditions, waves are gutless, shore wind chopping it up. Mint'll use that. He'll go for some air the way these older guys won't. You know Mint. He'd surf in shit creek if that's what was on offer. Where is he?'

Sam nodded toward where Minty sat in the sand further down the beach.

'He's shitting himself,' said Shane.

Sam didn't answer. He didn't want to acknowledge out loud that his invincible cousin was anxious.

'He should be,' Shane said. 'This is the real thing. Go to the rego tent. Get his rashie.'

No one looked at Sam twice when he gave Minty's name. He fitted the scene without trying anymore. He was handed Minty's rashie: lime green with logos and a big number on the back. 'There y'are,' said the steward. 'Minty Booner, boy bloody wonder. Can he live up to the hype?'

Sam just smiled. He was heading back to the tent when he saw the familiar figure of Ruby, up on the dunes, back from the beach, watching with her arms folded. He approached her and she tilted her chin in greeting.

'Didn't know you were gonna be here,' Sam said.

'I'm not.'

'He'd want to know you're here.'

'Don't care what he wants.'

'Then why come?'

'I want to see him win. I want to see the moment his life takes a whole different direction from mine.'

Sam held the rashie in his hands and listened to the fuzzy growl of the waves hitting the sand.

'You could go in the same direction.'

'No thanks.' She looked at Sam, squinting in the glare. 'He's gonna take off, you know that, right? If he gets this.' She laughed in disbelief. 'And I never thought he would, but if he's actually put his head down and worked for it, he'll win. He might get a wildcard to an overseas comp. Boom. Gone. What about you?'

'What about me?'

'You gonna ride on Minty Booner's coat-tails?'

'It'll be fun for a while.'

She raised an eyebrow. 'Oh yeah? You having fun?'

Sam shrugged. 'See ya, Rube.' He left her on the dunes and trudged across the sand to Shane and the sponsor's tent.

'There talk?' Shane asked.

'What?'

'They talkin' about Minty?'

'Oh. Can he live up to the hype? That sort of bullshit.'

Shane folded his arms. 'He can and he will as long as he doesn't let the nerves get to him. He needs to use it.'

Shane explained the system to Sam: three surfers in each heat of the first round. Thirty minutes on the clock, they had to get as many waves as possible and score as high as possible on each wave, the two highest wave scores combining to make a final score. There was a priority order, first gets top priority of waves, anything he passes up is open to the other two. Minty, being the most junior, was not the priority surfer. He would have to take whatever was left over. It was definitely not what he was used to.

Minty's first heat was early: 8.30 am. He was up against Seb Tyler and Xavier Dunn. Seb had priority, was older and well known. He had fans and Minty was definitely the mythologised underdog. Xavier was somewhere between them: on the circuit a few years but not quite established. The three competitors stood between two big flags metres from the shoreline. A horn sounded and they sprinted into the water. Minty took a different line to Seb and Xavier: he headed north, paddling furiously and letting the current drag him up and out. He nosed through the whitewater and Seb had already got a wave before Minty was even in the line-up.

'He's losing time,' Sam said.

Shane shook his head. 'He'll be okay.'

Seb had a long ride. There were cheers and whistles from the beach, but Sam didn't think he'd done anything spectacular: a few turns, that was about it. He finished and bailed into the white wash as Minty sat on his board and waited for a wave. Seb was back out in the line-up by the time anything rideable came around. He took priority and paddled into it. If Minty was stressed, he gave no sign. Xavier took the next wave. Another wave rolled in, small and messy, but Minty paddled for it. He seemed to pull speed out of nowhere and the watching crowd hooted and whistled.

'See,' said Shane. 'He's got speed without bouncing, lower centre of gravity. He can surf behind a breaking wave. No one can do that, not many anyway.'

Sam watched as Minty drove the nose of the board to the crest of the wave and flicked the tail over the back. It looked like he would fade out but he surged through the flat into the next pocket of water.

'He's linkin' the flat sections. Not grabbin' the rail. He can do so much with so little.'

The wave petered out and Minty bellied down onto the board, stepping off it into the shallow foam near the shoreline. Shane whistled. Lorraine, hugging herself, kept her expression neutral.

'You watch,' he said to Sam. 'These other two, they're gonna get frustrated. This isn't what they want. They're too precious. Minty'll take anything and make it shine.'

The rest of the heat went the way Shane predicted. Minty took anything he could and milked it, keeping speed where the other two dropped off.

The siren sounded and Minty caught one last shitty wave in and jogged up the sand between the flags. Sam watched his cousin as people crowded around him, slapping his back, whistling. Minty looked like a startled animal, buffeted by the acclaim. The announcer's voice sounded over the loudspeaker and a hush fell. The scores were read and Sam didn't even hear Minty's before the cheers started. He had won the heat and would progress to the next round. Minty's eyes found Sam and he grinned, although the furrow didn't quite lift from his brow.

The quarter- and semi-finals played out in the same way: Minty eliminated his competitors, big names whose pictures he had stuck to his bedroom walls. Between rounds he sat in a fold-out chair next to Sam and Lorraine, earphones in, his left knee bouncing uncontrollably. He didn't seem to be watching the other surfers or listening to the scores. Sam couldn't tell if he was enjoying himself or not; either way, he ended up in the final.

At the end of the day, when Minty was announced as the winner he didn't seem to quite comprehend it. Shane spoke to him, hands on his shoulders and then Minty dropped to his knees in the sand. It was a few moments before he looked up, his face breaking into his trademark smile. Lorraine was looking around in disbelief, her hands over her mouth, tears streaming down her cheeks.

Sam couldn't account for the empty feeling in his chest. His cousin's life had changed. He should have been happy for him, but if he scraped below all the encouraging words, all the support, all Sam felt was fear.

The day finished around a bonfire at the reserve. Ruby had turned up without letting on once that she had been at the comp. Minty had hugged her tight and now they sat side by side with the firelight on their faces. The big newspapers had been on the phone; Minty was the grommet made good, they wanted to send photographers and journalists. There was talk of a feature article in the Saturday papers. Shane went from coach to press secretary, screening requests because Minty said yes to anybody and anything.

'You go see Nana?' Sam asked.

'Yeah, she wanted to come up for the comp, ay, but Mum did her nut.'

'You didn't need that distraction anyway, brah,' said Shane.

'She said she listened to it on the radio,' Minty said.

'She stoked?'

'Yeah.'

'You just qualified for the national titles, Mint,' said Shane. 'You know that? You could get a wildcard to California ... You're gonna do it. I told you.'

'Twenty-five grand's enough to get to Hawaii.'

'You're not gonna go to Hawaii, Mint. You gotta keep goin'. You could join the World Qualifying Circuit.'

Ruby chewed her lip and listened without comment.

'Shane, brah, chill.'

'I'm serious, Mint.'

'You know the biggest wave I ever got? Five metres. That's nuthin' compared to what's out there.'

'Minty,' said Ruby. 'You know you gotta do this.'

'I don't *have* to do anything. I got a cheque for twenty-five grand. I'll buy you a ticket to Hawaii.'

Ruby shook her head and didn't return Minty's smile.

'Either way,' said Sam. 'You're not gonna be in Archer Point forever.'

'Damn straight.'

At some point in the early hours, sleep took each of them. Sam was last of all. If anyone had the excuse to throw away his life and do nothing but surf and drink, it was Minty. If Sam were to table the hardship of his own life against his cousin's, Minty would come out as the one with the odds stacked against him, the licence to piss it all away. And yet here he was, twenty-five grand richer, the press knocking on his door, the whole world opening up before him. Sam lay on the grass watching the sky and thought of his body, stuck there on the ground, while the earth spun and spun and spun.

*

In the morning they were back in the water, Sam's feet numb with the cold despite the steamer Minty gave him. Across from Sam, along the line-up, Ruby sat straight-backed astride her board. She ribbed Minty gently and he took it the way he always did. You didn't have to know her to see how proud she was of him.

Later they rinsed off up on the concourse, the cold water from the showers warmer than the ocean. Ruby pulled her arms from her wetsuit, Minty watching her.

'Goin' to Toomelah next weekend,' she said. 'Aunty Violet's taking me.'

Minty didn't say anything.

Ruby took a deep breath. 'I had a plan. I was gonna get out of here. I hate it. I mean I love the water, but, it's weird, I just know this isn't my place or whatever. I'm not supposed to be here. I want to go overseas … but now I might be this whole other person.'

'You're still the same person,' Minty said.

She shook her head, 'Nah. That's not how they see it.'

'Who?'

'The blackfellas. I'm one of them. That's how they see it, that's how they see me.'

'How do you see it?' Sam asked.

'I don't know.'

'It must be good to feel like you're really connected to something, to people,' Sam said. 'Anchored like, and you were all along. You just didn't know it.'

Ruby nodded. Minty gripped his board and looked out over the water, his jaw tight.

'You goin' with anyone else?' Minty asked.

'Um … maybe … not sure yet.'

He put his board down and folded his arms. 'I'll come with you.'

'You've got the nationals.'

'I don't care. I want to come.'

'No, you don't. You wanna say that, but you don't wanna give up the nationals.'

'I thought you'd be there with me.'

Sam turned away, walked a few metres up the concourse and pretended to be suddenly very interested in a ship that was out on the horizon. But he couldn't tune out of the conversation.

'I'm not gonna be the girl who waits for you, Minty.'

'I'm not askin' you to do that.'

'Yes, you are. You want me to wait around while you do your comps and mess around with your little groupies. Screw that. I want someone who's gonna wait for *me*. Us? You and me? It's not gonna happen. You and I both know it.'

When he looked back he saw Ruby walking away with her board and Minty watching her go. When she was out of sight Minty picked up his board with both hands and let out a scream, throwing it off the edge of the concourse onto the sand. He turned, pacing with his hands clasped behind his neck. Sam approached him and, as their eyes met, Sam saw the pain on his face, knotted in his forehead.

'Just piss off and leave me alone,' Minty said through clenched teeth.

Sam did as he was told. He walked up the concourse to just beyond the kiosk. He could still see Minty pacing back and forth, staring up at the sky with his hands gripping his hair. Sam felt for his cousin; he loved him like a brother. But he also recognised the repulsive twinge of satisfaction that Minty couldn't get everything he wanted. He pushed the thought aside, put his head down and headed for the caravan.

32

The school was close to the beach, like an uglier, low-budget version of Summer Bay High: boxy brick buildings with tiny windows jammed shut. Students sized Sam up as he walked across the yard. He had gum. He chewed it and squared his shoulders. The office lady looked sceptical when he said he wanted to enrol in year eleven. She made a phone call, talking quietly and keeping her eye on him like she was worried he might try and nick a stapler or something. When she hung up she told him to follow her to the principal's office. It was a cramped, damp-smelling room with a tiny, prison-sized window. The principal lectured him about taking responsibility and stepping up. He used the words 'commitment' and 'ownership' a lot. He made Sam explain what had happened at his last school: the fighting, the suspensions, the incident when the police gave him an official caution. Sam sat in his crumpled clothes and chewed the inside of his cheek, watching a line of tiny black ants march across the peeling paint of the windowsill. He wondered what the point of it all was if you could drop dead at anytime,

anytime at all, no matter if you were the greatest musician of your generation, a world champion surfer or a nurse studying to be a doctor. Life was all just padding people put around the truth: everyone was going to die and they were powerless to stop it. It didn't matter if you were a good person or not. He didn't feel it so much in the ocean; in the ocean it was just him and the water and it barely seemed to matter if you lived or died. On land it was different. Both he and Minty knew it.

After so much time spent in the water, days in the classroom took on a dragging, wasteful feeling. Sam looked out the window and wondered what the swell was doing. Crisp, bright days were the worst. He imagined the swell to be better than he had ever seen it. Each of his teachers gave him a thick folder of notes and told him he had serious work to do. It gave him an excuse to keep to himself, so mostly between classes he sat in the study hall and listened to his Discman. He didn't hang with anyone at school. Jono kept away from him and – despite the occasional glance – Gretchen was still a stranger. Ruby was as friendly as Ruby ever got, but she kept her distance. Every afternoon he went down to the beach and slotted in beside Minty. She never came with him.

Late one afternoon he walked up the headland, board under his arm as the sky was darkening. Seagulls sat huddled down on the grass, their feathers lifting in the cold wind. Gretchen was sitting on the little fence at the car park on the headland. She wore running gear and a grey hoodie, arms wrapped around herself. He couldn't walk past her as if she was a stranger. The pull of her was too much and he finally gave in to it. He dropped his board and sat next to her.

She turned and looked at him. 'What?'

'Nothing ... I just, I saw you and ...'

'Like you've never seen me since ... ?' She didn't fill in the last word, just made a gesture with her hand.

'I'm sorry.'

Gretchen scrunched her eyes shut. 'Don't. Please. I was just having a breather, I'm not waiting for you or anything.'

'But I am sorry.'

She sucked air in between her clenched teeth and turned to face him. 'Do you know how that feels? Like, how repulsive must I be that you would walk away while I'm there fully naked?'

'You're not repulsive. You're beautiful.'

'What then? Please, I'm listening. Any time when you want to explain why I'm not even worth ...' She didn't finish the sentence. The two of them sat and looked out at the horizon. 'It's so dumb. It's been months. I'm not supposed to care ... You were the first person I thought of when I heard he was dead. I hate that. I hate that I think of you at all.'

'Do you think of me?' The cleaving feeling returned to his chest, like his breath was clawing out of his lungs. He'd imagined this moment. He'd imagined their reunion. But the look on her face was one of disgust.

'Yes. Because it wasn't just a fling or whatever. Relationships aren't a recreational thing to me. Not cool, I know.'

'It wasn't like that.'

She didn't say anything. She didn't get up and walk away either. Sam didn't move. They sat next to each other watching the water.

'I can't believe he's dead,' Sam said. 'And there won't be any more music.'

'I'm pretty sure he was the only guy in the world with a good heart.'

Sam had no answer to that.

'I mean, it was bad when Kurt Cobain died, but you didn't feel that the world had lost the last great romantic.'

'I don't know. Singing about being horny is pretty romantic.'

She glared at him, but she was half smiling. Then her face changed and she stood up. 'No, no, no, no. You're not doing this. Don't look at me with your stupid, beautiful face.'

'Gretchen.'

She turned around.

'You're not repulsive … I wasn't … it wasn't you—'

'Oh! Oh nice! HA. Good one. Classic line. Thank you.' She started walking away.

'No. I'm … It's all screwed up. I'm not a good person to be with, Gretchen.'

She stopped and watched him and he could see her deciding whether or not to hear him out. He still wasn't sure what he was going to say if she did.

'I'm … I do dumb things. And I don't set out to hurt people, but … it always ends up that way.'

'Tell me why you walked out and left me there.'

He opened his mouth to make the words but he couldn't shape them in his own head.

287

'I'm listening.' She wasn't walking away.

It was the same moment that he'd had with his mother on the last night. He wanted to tell her why he'd done what he had done because he wanted her to say that she loved him anyway.

'Sam?'

'My mum, when she died …'

Gretchen's eyes were suspicious.

'She … I was … she was teaching me to dance. She didn't have cancer. She wasn't sick. It was sudden. Out of nowhere.' Sam's throat tightened and he blinked back the tears.

Her expression softened.

'She wanted me to … to be a gentleman.' The tears welled and he laughed at how pathetic he must seem. 'It was important to her. She … she turned and I held her arm up.' He closed his eyes and he could see her. He could feel his mother's hand in his own. 'She fell, collapsed like. And I caught her. And her head was kind of back …' He pulled in a ragged breath. He couldn't open his eyes. 'When you and me were … when I lifted you up …' Sam rubbed his face up and down with his hands. 'I saw it, the picture of what she looked like. Do you think in pictures?'

'Yes.'

'I have snapshots. Everything important that has ever happened, that I've done, I have a snapshot. And they're always there. Whether I want them or not. But … I haven't really thought about it. About the fact that she died. Or how. It's just easier not to. But when you and I … I could see it. It's screwed up, Gretchen. Me. I'm screwed up.'

'Oh Sam.' She stood with the wind whipping her hair, searching his face. 'I don't really know you,' she said gently.

Sam swallowed and nodded.

'I need to think.'

Please don't.

'I think it's good you're at school.'

He nodded. 'I don't know which guy I am. Am I the one who goes into the water fully clothed? Or the guy driving the speedboat? I think I used to be one and now I'm the other.'

'I don't know what you mean.'

'I mean that … Minty, Minty would go swimming in a river, wouldn't give it a second thought. It's like he tries to get everything he can out of life … I don't want to be the one who does the damage.'

She didn't say anything.

'He died. It's horrible.'

'Yes,' she said. 'Yes, it is.'

33

Nana made him hot dinners and packed his lunch for school like he was in year seven: two devon sandwiches on white bread, a packet of Smith's chips and an apple. During class time he wondered if he had made the right decision – going back to school. He could just stay on with Nana and surf. But he was sleeping on a li-lo on the floor and his back was killing him. There was no space for him, no space to himself. It was now too cold to eat outside, so the two of them squeezed into the little breakfast nook for meals together. She made sweet and sour hotpot and boiled white rice, just like when he was a kid. It only served to remind him of the way life was back then: meals with Nana and Pop, skateboarding on the driveway, Easter egg hunts in Pop's garden with Minty and Shane. A time when Sam unwittingly believed the illusion that he came from a happy family, a hardworking family of people who loved each other, a Nana who loved his Pop, cousins without bruises under their clothes. A time when ten-year-old Minty wet the bed because he drank too much soft drink at Nana's. Not because he was petrified of going home.

*

After he had been back at school a while she served up dinner and the two of them sat listening to the radio while they ate. Nana listened to 2CH *Easy Eleven Seventies:* dance hall standards interspersed with Cliff Richard and John Denver. She kept her salt and pepper in the same black cat shakers he remembered from when he was a kid. Distorted shapes with elongated necks and big green eyes from a psychedelic dream. He picked one up and turned it in his hand, watching the light on its glossy surface, running his thumb over the cat's familiar, chipped left ear.

'How'd you get these?' he asked.

Nana took a sip of cordial. 'How'd you mean, love? I've always had those.'

'But they were at the house in Punchbowl.'

'Yes.'

'When you left Pop said nothing was taken.'

She winked at him and chewed her food.

'Did you take them?'

'You boys loved them when you were little. You especially. Of course I took them. I told you, he knew I'd left him. I took a small bag with a few things: change of clothes, what have you.'

'You knew about Minty's dad. We needed you.'

She stood and cleared the plates. 'I knew they were going to be alright.'

'How?'

'I just knew.'

'That's bullshit.'

'Please don't swear at me, love. I've copped enough of that in my time.'

'How can I even believe what you say? You're a liar.'

She put her hands on her hips and faced him. 'We're all liars, love. To some degree. We all put on a front. Leaving was the most honest thing I ever did.'

'That's convenient.'

She leaned forward, looking into his face. 'And what about you, young man? Bright young Sammy. Charmer, slay-you-with-a-smile Sam. What were you up to before? You think I didn't have contact with Rachel? Just because you didn't know about it. You think she didn't talk to me when she thought you'd gone off the rails? You'd stopped talking to her. Your marks were dropping. You'd been in fights. Our lovely little Sam, like butter wouldn't melt in his mouth.'

Sam felt the blood rush from his head.

'Next thing, she's gone and you're down here. You're just the way I remembered you: quiet, gentle,' she tapped a finger to her forehead, 'more going on up here than you let on. And I think to myself, surely she must have been exaggerating. Look at him! Lovely kid: got himself a nice young lady, dealing with your mum's death like I don't know what – so well adjusted! And then you roll up here one night with a bloodied nose, all beat up and Lorraine's kicked you out! And I think to myself, a mother *always* knows. Always. So are you going to tell me what was going on in Sydney before you left?'

Sam couldn't say anything. He stood up and moved past her, out through the sliding door of the annex into the dark caravan park. Nana didn't let him go; she followed him.

'Stop, Samuel. Look at me.'

'What do you want me to say?! There was this kid, at school, he was a dickhead. He said stuff about mum, alright? And I lost it. I punched his head in. The cops were called. I got a fuckin' caution and was suspended from school and I screwed my life up. Happy? At least I was *there*. At least I didn't piss off and leave her on her own.' Sam's voice faltered over his words. 'Why did you leave me?'

'Leave you?'

'Everyone was gone. One minute I had Mum and I had you and Pop and Minty and Lorraine, next thing it's just me and Mum. I was the only one she had left … And now she's gone too. And you know who my dad is and you won't tell me. It's like you want me to be all alone.'

'No, darlin'. That's not true.'

'What happened then?! What happened between Mum and Lorraine and you? WHAT?'

'Glen was a bad man.'

'What's that got to do with anything? He's in fuckin' prison.'

'I know, love, I helped put him there. I made sure he was put away. I would have never taken off if he was still around. They needed evidence for a string of hold-ups and I knew where it was.'

'What's that got to do with *me*?'

'It was a mess, love. It still is.'

'What's it got to do with *me*?' he repeated. 'He was a violent arsehole. I get it now. Wasn't Lorraine happy he went away? And why the hell does that stop her and Mum talking?'

Nana watched him without answering. She stood silhouetted in the doorway between the kitchenette and the annex of the van. She seemed to be holding on to the doorframe for support. 'Answer me!'

'Glen … He's not the kind of father you need to know.'

'No. NO. WHAT?'

In those seconds Sam felt as if everything he knew about his life was a trick, a shoddy cardboard theatre set. One little nudge and it all came crashing down.

'How? How could she?'

'Same way Lorraine could, love. Glen was a handsome bugger. He could be as charming as all hell. You and Minty got all the good bits of him. She was young and made a stupid decision the same way we all do.'

Sam staggered backwards, grabbing around for something to hold on to. 'Holy shit.' He laughed again, giddy, dizzy. There seemed to be nothing else to do. 'That's why they left? That's why they moved away?'

'I gave Glen up to the cops. He blamed Lorraine. He told her he'd slept with your mum all those years before. He wanted to hurt her and to destroy her family and it worked.'

'Minty doesn't know, does he?'

'No. I'd like to keep it that way.'

'Shane knows.'

Nana nodded.

34

Out in the line-up, Sam picked his moment. He kept it together until Minty had a wave that took him into shore. It bought Sam ten minutes. He paddled over to Shane, who was sitting astride his board with his eyes on the horizon.

'I know.'

It was all he needed to say. Shane turned to face Sam and his eyes were cold, unreadable. Sam could tell that he'd heard him and he knew exactly what he was talking about.

'How?'

'Nana.'

Shane swore under his breath, his jaw clenched.

'Am I like him, Shane?'

Shane looked him square in the eye. 'Don't start askin' yourself that question. You'll never be able to stop.'

He slid onto his belly and paddled for the next wave.

*

At the caravan, Sam lay on his back with hands clasped behind his head and listened to Jeff sing about how he wasn't afraid to die.

It seemed so unlikely and pathetic that a grown man could be drowned by the wave of a speedboat. Maybe it was the Leviathan that took him.

If he wanted to, Sam could recall every detail of the last night with his mother: the smell of spaghetti bolognaise filling the flat; her open textbooks pushed to the side of the dinner table; the tears in her eyes. He wasn't allowed out. He wasn't allowed anywhere. She wasn't angry. She'd never been angry, not even when she'd had to go with him to the police station. Instead there was a horrible, hurt silence. She'd closed herself off from him and he was so ashamed he hadn't been able to talk to her about what happened.

He was never home on New Year's Eve, yet here he was and suddenly, after a few wines, she was crying.

'What did I do wrong?' she'd asked him.

'Nothing … it wasn't …'

'I must have done something wrong.'

'You didn't.'

She shut her eyes and shook her head, running her thumb and forefinger up and down the stem of the wineglass.

'It's my job to make you ready for the world. You're not ready for the world if you think it's okay to punch someone in the head.'

'He said something about you—'

'He hasn't even met me.'

'I know, but he called you a—'

'I don't care what he said.' Her voice was soft. 'You're supposed to be bigger than that.'

They ate in silence, his mum wiping tears from her cheeks with the back of her hand. There had never been tension between them like there was that night. It was awful, the gulf that had opened up. She felt it too, she was always one step ahead of him.

She wiped her tears and steeled herself. 'I'm gonna teach you to dance,' she said, as if the last ten minutes hadn't happened, as if none of it had happened.

'Mum—'

'Come on. Up,' she said.

'Mum. No.'

'Yeah, come on. It's my job to teach you important stuff and this is important.'

'No, it's not.'

The whole time it was like he'd been the one who had done something wrong. Something terrible. Something that had hurt her and hurt them. But it was nothing compared to the lie she'd told him his entire life. The first Christmas after the Booners had moved away and Nana had gone AWOL, Sam had pined for them. He'd felt the enveloping bleakness, the same fear and uncertainty in the very centre of himself that he felt now. The gaping hole had begun to open up all those years ago, long before the dinner and the dancing and his dead mother on the ground.

It was all because of her.

If his mum hadn't been so thoughtless, so selfish and stupid to sleep with her sister's husband the whole family wouldn't have disintegrated.

If his mum hadn't been so thoughtless, so selfish and stupid, Sam wouldn't exist.

He didn't know what to do with that.

He just needed to talk to her.

Lorraine was at the kitchen table, smoking a cigarette and reading *New Idea*. Sam tapped his knuckles on the screen door and she looked up. Her expression was grim. She never smiled at him and now he knew why.

She opened the door and leaned her hip against it. She looked about five years older than the last time he'd seen her.

'Shane talked to me,' she said. 'You know about Glen.'

Sam felt wobbly. He swallowed. He could feel the sweat on his forehead, despite the fact it was June. 'I've still got a few things here. Clothes and that. I'd also like to take her blanket.' He motioned to the patchwork of knitted squares on the couch. 'I'll say goodbye to Minty. He's still in the water ... First train tomorrow goes at six.'

'Where you going?'

Sam shrugged. 'Dunno. Sydney. Still know people there.'

'Where are you gonna sleep? On the bloody street?'

'Dunno. Maybe. I'll sort something out.'

'I said you could come back here.'

'You don't want me here.'

Lorraine watched him with his mother's eyes and stood aside for him to come in. He went through to the spare room and collected the last of his things.

'You know, I saw her when she was eight weeks pregnant with you.'

Sam turned around. Lorraine was in the doorway. She pinched the bridge of her nose, eyes closed.

'She hadn't been around. I hadn't seen her, which was odd for us, we were always in real close contact. I'd spoken to her on the phone and she just told me she was busy with work. Shane was three, I was six months pregnant with Michael. Bumped into her at the supermarket. She saw me and all the blood drained from her face. I said to her, "Rach, what's wrong!" and she just burst into tears ... She didn't want to tell me she was pregnant, but I guessed. I could just tell.'

Sam dropped his things on the floor and sank onto the camp bed.

'She said she was gonna get a termination. All I could think of was how it was a cousin for my little ones, you know? I told her we'd help her, we all would. She was a bloody mess.' Lorraine sniffed. 'She was always, I dunno ... on her own. No blokes stuck, I don't think any of 'em were good enough. And she was so young: twenty. A kid by today's standards. I told her she could keep it.' She shook her head. 'But it was tearing her apart, I could see it.' Lorraine opened her eyes and looked at Sam. 'I convinced her. And you came along and ... you were the best thing that ever happened to her. Just the sweetest little thing. "Aunty Rain" you used to call me. It was always like I had three boys ...'

Sam blinked back tears.

'She broke my heart, Samuel. I thought of you as my own. I loved you. Glen was off the rails, completely.' She sighed and shook her head like she was trying to get the memory of him out of her head. 'But I always had my family. They kept me strong.' She took a deep breath. 'And then Glen was going to be put away, I was free of him. And he told me. About you. It just …' She couldn't speak anymore. She clasped her hand over her mouth and nose.

Sam sat frozen. His hands gripped the blankets, either side of his knees. His knuckles were white and when he tried to let go he started trembling.

'It takes two to tango, but I know now … it was his bloody fault. All of this is his fault. I shouldn't have ever married him. But he gave me these beautiful boys. It's the strangest bloody thing.'

Sam managed to stand up. He put his things in his bag. On his way out the door he paused and kissed her on the cheek. 'I'm sorry, Aunty Lorraine.'

He didn't look back but he knew she was standing at the door, watching him go.

35

At dusk Sam got up and opened the sliding door of the annex. He pulled a beanie over his ears and began the walk down to the concourse. He would meet Minty as he came out of the surf. He would be direct and he wouldn't let Minty talk him out of his decision.

The hand on his shoulder startled Sam and he swung around to see Shane standing there. His neck was thick like a tree branch and his arms had more muscle on them now than Sam felt he had on his entire body.

'Mum wants you to come back and live at the house.'

Sam didn't know if it was an invitation or a threat. 'I can't do that.'

'Well you farkin' have to, she's a mess.'

'I'm going to Sydney.'

'No, you're not. Letter came for Minty. He doesn't know it yet. He's got a wildcard to California. Gotta be on a plane in two days' time. He needs his head straight. You pissin' off and Mum flippin' out ain't gonna help. He's already lost Ruby.'

A cold wind slashed through the tree branches above them. Icy pinpricks of rain spat on Sam's cheeks.

'You can't talk to him about any of this till he gets back from the US,' Shane said. 'Come back to the house.'

'Maybe.'

'What else are ya gonna do?'

'I dunno.' Sam put his hands in his pockets and kept walking.

'I was always heaps jealous of you. You know that?'

The comment caught Sam mid-step. Shane crossed his arms and tilted his face up to the angry sky. 'You and your mum, like. Didn't know how come I got the sucky family and you didn't. You were always so bloody happy.'

'Not anymore, I guess.'

Shane shrugged and gave a wry smile. 'We're gonna have a dinner for Minty. Celebrate. Mum even wants Nana there. Everyone. One hour. Be there.'

The table was cleared and covered in a faded orange tablecloth. Steam clouded the kitchen windows and outside the salty wind whipped at the headland and scoured the fibro cottages. Lorraine's face was tear streaked. She sat on a chair holding a shandy while Nana moved around the kitchen, chatting to her grandsons as if she had never been away. When she set the casserole dish in the centre of the table Minty leaned in like an excited child.

'Shepherd's pie, Nana?'

'My word, love. Your favourite.' She scooped it onto a plate and handed it to him. Minty could barely sit still. The same restlessness from when they were little was still there. Sam thought that maybe it would never leave him; Minty would always be that kid with the grin, building the jumps higher.

'Who's paying your way?' Nana asked.

'Rip Curl,' said Lorraine. 'They're gonna take care of him.'

'Have to sign a contract telling me exactly where to put their stickers on the board and how many hours a day I have to wear their T-shirts,' said Minty.

Lorraine shook her head with a rueful expression. 'You've never even been on a plane before.'

'How's it feel, brah?' Shane asked.

'Weird. Good but weird.'

'Ah. Well, that's life, isn't it?' Nana squeezed Minty on the shoulder and took her seat next to him. If Sam were to close his eyes and listen he could almost pretend that it was all those years ago and his mum was sitting there with them.

After dinner he went to leave with Nana and head back to the caravan. Lorraine pulled him up on his way out. She pointed through to the camp bed. 'You can sleep here, love. Please.'

'Okay.'

In the days following Minty's departure, Sam alternated his time between school and the water. He gradually moved his belongings back into Lorraine's. As the southern ocean cooled it pushed a stronger groundswell to the south coast and he and Shane were in the surf every afternoon until dark.

If Ruby was in Sam would smile at her, but keep his

distance. He didn't want word getting back to Minty that he was being too friendly with her.

One evening he rinsed his torso under the shower and made his way around beyond the kiosk, out of the wind. He leaned his board against the wall, watching the path that followed the curve of the beach, and waited.

'Are you gonna follow me home again?'

The voice gave him a shock. Behind him Gretchen was standing in the silvery light, hands stuffed into the pocket of her hoodie.

'Hi! I'm ... I just ...' He contemplated walking away. Instead, he took a deep breath and hoped she couldn't hear the thundering beat in his chest. 'What would you rather?'

'I was walking home by myself for ages before you turned up.'

'Sure. Yeah. I know. Sorry.'

'And I never had a problem with anyone lurking around.'

'I don't mean to lurk. I'm a dick. Sorry.'

'Fishing for compliments again.'

She could still make him smile.

'I'm going back now. If you want to walk with me, I won't call the cops.'

Steam rose from their shoulders and hung on their breath, misting into the chill twilight air as they walked. The sky was wide and cloudless, threaded with a fading vanilla light above the weatherbeaten cottages. Sam walked beside Gretchen, the two of them so quiet they could hear each other breathing. At her gate she stopped and turned to him. The hair at her temples and the nape of her neck was damp with sweat and clung to her skin. It took determination to run fourteen kilometres no matter what the weather. And patience.

'Minty's gone to the US?' she said.

'Yeah. Be back in a week or so. Supposed to be, anyway. If he doesn't take off looking for big waves.'

'What about you? Are you sticking around?'

'Um. I don't know. I'll see what happens. Maybe. Yes.' He felt his heart thudding against the walls of his chest and wanted that moment alone with her to stretch on forever. It felt like anything he said would cut it short. She wouldn't look him in the eye and he couldn't tell if she felt the same way he did or if she just thought it was really awkward. The feeling that he wouldn't get this chance again crept through him.

'I still really like you.' He tried not to rush the words. 'More than that. I want you to know. You have to know.'

She looked up at him without saying anything.

'I'm sorry,' he whispered.

It felt like an age, then she reached out and took his hand, lacing his fingers through hers.

'I know you are.'

'Even if you were covered in fur. I'd still choose you.'

'Well, now I just think you're an idiot.'

'Even if you were a crazy *Star Trek* fan?'

'That's better.' She gave him a small smile. Then she took his fingers and kissed them. That moment felt more intimate than any of the others he'd ever had with her. She let his hand go and went through the gate, latching it behind her.

SAM'S MIXTAPE

Beastie Boys 'Get it Together'
Beck 'Loser'
R.E.M 'Drive'
Jeff Buckley 'Grace'
Jane's Addiction 'Jane Says'
Pixies 'Where is My Mind'
Jeff Buckley 'Lover, You Should've Come Over'
Split Enz 'I Got You'
Radiohead 'Creep'
Rage Against the Machine 'Killing in the Name'
Green Day 'Longview'
Foo Fighters 'Alone + Easy Target'
Nirvana 'About a Girl'

ACKNOWLEDGEMENTS

Thanks must go to my draft-readers: Marcella Kelshaw, Nathan Zorn and George Bryan. Special thanks to George, my dad and a grey-belly from way back, who acted as my consultant on all things surf related. Thanks also to Carla Brown for allowing me to borrow from her extensive catalogue of 'What Would You Rather' questions and Lauren McCorquodale for her insights into the Queen's favourite songs.

It would not have been possible for me to write the characters of Ruby or Aunty Violet without the consultation and detailed guidance of Dr Ernie Blackmore of the Woolyungah Indigenous Centre at the University of Wollongong. A lot of the ideas for Ruby's history and her future came from Ernie who embraced her with enthusiasm. Thank you, Ernie, for your generosity and wisdom.

As usual, I must finish with thanks to my super-duper editorial and publishing team: Kristina Schulz, Kristy Bushnell and Jody Lee. Youse guys are ace.

Claire Zorn lives on the south coast of
New South Wales with her husband and
two small children. Her first young adult
novel, *The Sky So Heavy*, was a 2014
Children's Book Council of Australia
Honour Book for Older Readers;
shortlisted in the 2014 Inky Awards;
and shortlisted in the 2013 Aurealis
Awards – Best Young Adult Novel.
Her second young adult novel,
The Protected, was the winner of three
awards: the 2015 Prime Minister's
Literary Awards for Young Adult Fiction;
the 2015 Victorian Premier's Literary
Awards – Young Adult Fiction Prize;
and the 2015 Children's Book Council
of Australia Book of the Year for Older
Readers. It was also shortlisted in the
2015 Inky Awards. *One Would Think the
Deep* is her third novel for young adults.

clairezorn.com
@ClaireZorn

Also available from Raven Books

CONNOR'S BRAIN
by Malcolm Rose

Connor began his second life at the age of fifteen.
He started it with a thirty-mile-an-hour brain.

Connor's first life ended when a virus in his brain stripped
him of almost everything – his memory, language
and a sense of time.

Now Connor lives in a permanent present that he doesn't
understand. The 'new' Connor doesn't recognise or remember
his parents, his brother, his friends – or his girlfriend Hattie.

New-Connor can't remember the old Connor, but there are
people who can. People who have reasons to keep him quiet –
or to hurt him.

Because old-Connor had a dark past.

Now read the first two chapters.

CONNOR'S BRAIN

MALCOLM ROSE

CHAPTER 1

Joy lost her childhood at the age of fourteen.

At the end of the summer term, she was tossed from a moving car like a bag of rubbish. Dazed, dumped and abused, Joy fell into the gutter under the railway bridge. She rolled onto her front, gagged and blacked out. A little blood ran from her forehead into the rainwater, making a pink puddle. The first passer-by hesitated only to take a photo of her on his mobile. The fifth passer-by hesitated, squatted down by her side and then called an ambulance.

Like other girls before her, Joy Patterson had been groomed, introduced to men, seduced by their glamorous lifestyle, fooled into thinking she was loved, passed around, paid with drink and drugs, exploited until she was soiled and spent, and finally discarded on a street in central Leeds.

Stripped of her innocence, she was second-hand, unwanted.

CHAPTER 2

Connor began his second life at the age of fifteen.

There were three people in the room. A man and a woman were holding hands on a sofa in the corner and a younger woman was sitting behind the desk. She was a funny colour. The couple looked sad and the dark woman was smiling in a serious sort of way. Connor could not recall any of them. His eyes were attracted more by the single red-topped volcano that poked out from the clutter on the desk.

The younger woman jumped up with a bright, 'Hello, Connor.' She was shorter than Connor but she seemed much more grown-up. While she ushered him to a seat at the side of her desk, she asked, 'Do you remember me?'

'Erm … '

'I saw you this morning. I'm Ranji Nawaz – the doctor looking after you from now on. You're going home today but, every other day, you'll come and spend some time here with me.'

'Oh.' Connor shuffled round on his seat to get nearer to the volcano.

The doctor leaned towards him and said in a friendly voice, 'Your mum and dad and I have been thinking about what to tell you, how much to tell you. In the end, we decided you should know everything, so I'm going to explain exactly what's happened to you. We think that's best.'

Connor drifted. He put out his hand and touched the velvety top of the volcano. At the same time, he sniffed. 'Volcanoes smell.'

'Volcano. Yes,' Ranji said. 'We call it a *flower*, Connor. It's a nice smell and someone bought it for me because it's my birthday today.'

'Birthday.' Connor nodded uncertainly. He didn't know what she meant.

'If I'm going to tell you all about yourself, it's easiest to show you with pictures.'

She picked up a photograph and held it out so that Connor could see it. He was used to looking at pictures and trying to explain them, but this one was weird. There was no action to describe. He'd seen nothing like it before. It didn't seem to be anything – just a fantastic shape. It was all wrinkly and grey, like a partly deflated kicking ball. Finally losing interest in the volcano, Connor stared at the extraordinary image, in the same way that he would sometimes focus on clouds and find faces, animals and fierce monsters in their fragile forms.

'This,' Ranji said, 'is a normal brain. It's a sort of photograph of what's inside a head.'

'Wow,' Connor replied, suddenly enthusiastic. He stood up, put out his hand and ran his eels across the strange, wonderful picture. Then he clutched his own head. 'I've got hair and funnybone. No bottle. No see inside.'

For a moment, Ranji seemed puzzled. Then she said, 'I've got a special way of taking pictures through hair, skin and bone. I've got a really clever machine that doesn't need a window to see a brain. It can even take a picture of what's inside the brain. Like this.' She picked up a brain scan and showed it to him.

It was even weirder. Marbled grey with splashes of red and black. Even more like clouds. Storm clouds. Open-mouthed, Connor was enthralled.

'When I used the machine on you, Connor, I got a picture of what's inside your brain. Do you want to see?'

Connor nodded eagerly.

'Here it is.' She held it up next to the other picture.

When he gazed at it, Connor felt a warm shiver engulf his whole body. He had never felt anything like that before. Not that he could remember anyway. Awestruck, he placed a reverent eel on the shiny paper and traced the outline of the image, slowly and carefully. 'Mine,' he whispered. The picture enchanted and thrilled him. His hand came to rest by the black hole on one side. His brain was different. The normal one didn't have a hole. 'Mine's best,' he murmured slowly. 'Pretty shape.'

'Let me tell you as best I can what this pattern means.' Ranji took a deep breath. 'That hole means you have part of your brain missing, Connor. Your memory and most of the things you knew have gone, but you can learn quite a bit again. You know yourself you've already learned a lot. You've done really well. Come to the window.' She pointed at it and added, 'What you call a bottle.'

But Connor was still preoccupied with his brain scan. To distract him, Ranji took his hand and walked with him to the view over the city.

'Look down into the street. See? It's packed with cars. How fast do you think the cars are going? Do you know about speed?'

Now captivated by Ranji's hand, Connor exclaimed, 'You've got something on it.' He poked at the hard and shiny surface attached to her soft peel.

Ranji smiled. 'Yes. It's called a ring.'

Connor watched her take off the shiny yellow band and hold it out for him. She let it drop into his palm and he looked at it closely, turning it over and over. 'What's it for?'

'It's ... a decoration really.'

'Decoration.' Connor closed his fist around it.

Behind him, the man who had not uttered a word, said, 'Give it back to Dr Nawaz now, Connor.'

Reluctantly, he held it out to her.

She said, 'Thanks,' and slid it back onto her eel. 'Look out of the window at the cars, Connor.'

They were three floors up from the road and, below them, the street was seething.

Connor muttered, 'Cars?' He had been shown photographs of cars, but he did not recognize them in the street. That was the wrong place for them. They belonged in pictures.

'Yes. They're called cars. People drive them to get from place to place.'

'What place? Where?'

'Some are going to work, some are going home, but do you know what speed they're doing?'

Connor shook his head vacantly. Again, he didn't know what she was talking about.

'They're going very slowly. Thirty miles an hour at most. But you know, people buy cars that'll go over a hundred miles an hour. A lot of those down there are very powerful. They can zoom – very fast – but here in the city they can only do thirty miles an hour.'

'Why?'

'Because of the crowds, because there's a law that says they mustn't go faster. That's the speed limit. So, they can't use all their power.' She walked him back to her desk and held up the scan of the normal brain. 'That's like a hundred-miles-an-hour brain, Connor. It's very powerful, but people with this type of brain don't use all its strength. Like cars that could go at a hundred miles an hour, they still stick to thirty. You, Connor, have a thirty-miles-an-hour brain. It won't go any faster. You have to accept that. But it means it'll work just as well as everyone else's, because they're not going at full speed. You've just got to learn how to use yours as best you can. Because it's a different sort of brain, it'll mean you'll do things in different ways. It'll take a bit of getting used to, but you'll get there.' She smiled at him again. 'What you need now is driving lessons.'

The woman was talking *to* him, not talking about him to the other people in the room as if he wasn't there at all. She spoke clearly, slowly – but not too slowly – and not too loud. She didn't treat him like an idiot. Even so, he could barely understand her words, but the picture ... The picture was different. The picture of a no-zoom brain he could understand. He took it and clutched it against his chest as if it were a teddy bear. Indifferent to Ranji's word explanation, he asked, 'Why is your peel a funny colour?'

The quiet man interrupted. 'Connor, we don't ... '

'It's all right,' Ranji cut in. 'It's because my family originally came from another country, a country where everyone has dark skin.'

Connor turned away from the nice woman who took pretty pictures and looked at the other two. 'Who are you?' he asked innocently.

The man's mouth opened hesitantly. 'We're your parents, Connor. Mum and Dad. You ate lunch with us a little while ago.'

Connor tilted his head to one side and gazed at them with curiosity. The man was big and his knuckles were white. His head peel was shiny with no hair, so he looked like a funnybone man. Strangely, the woman clutched a small piece of white cloth between both hands. She had bare legs, lines round her eyes and her hair was patchy – brown and grey.

'No,' Connor declared simply. 'Don't remember.'